MW00618232

WITCH WAY IS UP

SILVER SISTERS BOOK 3 PARANORMAL WOMEN'S FICTION ROMANCE

JENNIFER L. HART

ELEMENTS UNLEASHED

❀ Created with Vellum

WITCH WAY IS UP

Witch Way Is Up
Hart/ Jennifer L.

1.Women's—Fiction 2. North Carolina—Fiction 3.
Paranormal—Fiction 4. Witches—Fiction 5. Faery—Fiction
6. Humor—Fiction 7. Small Towns—Fiction 8. Home
Renovation—Fiction 9. American Humorous—Fiction
10.Mountain Living —Fiction 11. Midlife— Fiction 12.
Sisters—Fiction I. Title

ISBN: 978-1-951215-96-5

She's single and killing it. Literally.

Siobhan's relationship status is...complicated. Any time she gives in to carnal temptation, her lover ends up dead. Forty, frustrated, and newly empowered as a witch, she and her sisters cast a spell to discover a way to reverse her curse.

Magic Hunter Sebastian never failed to collect a bounty. He was the stuff of legend until he met Siobhan. Now his magic is gone and he and the Silver sisters are the top targets for every supernatural bounty hunter in existence.

Can these two star-crossed lovers finally put the sins of their pasts to rest? Or will destiny crush their hope forever?

Witch Way is Up is the third book in the charming Silver Sisters paranormal women fiction series. If you like magical hijinks, true-to-life characters, and soul mates, don't miss Jennifer L. Hart's enchanting series.

Buy *Witch Way is Up* and summon your sister witches today!

TRIGGER WARNING FOR SENSITIVE READERS

Possible spoilers ahead.

Not every book is for every reader. This is a survivor story. Sexual abuse and rape are parts of life and while I try my best to handle the topic with sensitivity, I know reading about these things can be too upsetting for some readers. I have plenty of other books for you to enjoy so if you need to skip this one, I understand.

Love and light,
  Jennifer L. Hart

WITCH WAY IS UP

SIOBHAN

"Come here, you sneaky little bastard," I cooed to my quarry. "I've got something for you."

A big effing knife with his name on it. Or maybe I'd use my hands. He knew it, too. Didn't matter what anyone else said. This guy was no fool. He understood that I had been pushed past reason and that he was being pursued by a witch ready to commit murder.

Bright green leaves rustled, indicating his position in the bushes behind the library. The sounds of children's laughter, music from the bluegrass band, and the scent of fried dough filled the warm spring air. For a moment, I entertained myself with the delightful thought of wrapping my hands around his neck and squeezing the life out of him right on the town green in front of all of those happy people.

Might ruin the carnival. But it was a tempting thought.

I approached cautiously. More rustling, and then he made a break for it. He was deceptively fast for his build and was halfway across the town green before I'd taken a step.

"Over there!" I shouted to Kal, my brother-in-law, who had also been dispatched to hunt down our target.

Kal turned. Spying the fiend, he took off in hot pursuit. Running wasn't Kal's strong suit. He was built like a professional linebacker gone soft. I caught up to him as our prey dodged between legs and past the various booths.

"Gimli!" Kal wheezed at the dog. The corgi didn't even slow as he disappeared beneath a tent flap.

"Damn it. How does he keep slipping this thing?" Kal held up the bright blue harness that was shy one derpy canine.

I'd read online that Welsh corgis were said to pull chariots for the fae. That would explain a few things about Gimli and his littermate, Grogu. My idiot brother-in-law had adopted the G & G wrecking crew six months earlier. The dogs, like the fae, were tricksy and caused havoc wherever they went.

*S*ix months ago, I would have laughed it off. Six months ago, I didn't know that the fae were real beings, not just made-up stories. Six months felt like a lifetime ago.

Note to self: Never accept anything from the fae. Oops, too late.

We had been chasing the fool creature for the better part of an hour while my sisters, niece, and nephew enjoyed the carnival. It was Maeve's fault. She was the one who had insisted we bring the dogs to the Spring Fling because she couldn't bear the thought of them being crated all day. Because he was a moron in love and could never refuse his wife anything, Kal had agreed.

"Now what?" Still sounding winded, Kal asked as he hesitated outside the tent.

I paused by his side and sucked air into my starving lungs. "Now one of us has to go in there and drag his furry little hide out. I vote it's you since this is all your fault."

No, I didn't sound bitter at all.

Kal shrugged and made to step forward just as the tent flap was tossed back and a middle-aged blonde wearing long flowing black robes and carrying a panting ball of fluff emerged from the depths.

"Gimli." Kal moved forward to take the trembling critter from the woman. "You're a very bad dog."

Gimli licked his face. Kal smiled. I sighed. And so the reign of corgi terror would continue.

"Y'all belong to this guy? What a cutie." The robed blonde wore big, chunky earrings and so many bangles that they clacked together when she reached up to scratch Gimli between the ears.

Her voice sounded familiar, but I couldn't place it. It had happened on more than one occasion since I returned to Eckhart the previous fall. Other than my sisters, I didn't have many friends in town.

"Don't let the looks fool you," I told her. "He's an escape artist and a runner."

The woman laughed. "Same could be said about you, Siobhan Silver."

I blinked at her. She grinned. "You don't remember me at all do you?"

"Not well," I admitted.

"I'm Tully Banks. We had art together in my senior year."

"Right," I said having no memory of the class or her. "How have you been?"

It was just one of those things that you say to people just to be polite. I wasn't really inquiring. Unfortunately, no one had told that to Tully.

She laughed. "You wouldn't believe me if I told you. Why don't you come on in and we can catch up? I'm on my dinner break now, but I have to be back to it in a few."

"I...." I looked helplessly to where Kal was struggling to refit the harness over Gimli's pointy ears.

3

Kal nodded to me. "Have fun. I better get him back. Evie and the kids will be worried. It was good to see you, Tully."

I thought about going with him. I really didn't feel up to a good-old-fashioned Southern inquiry that passed for small talk. I had too many secrets to hide.

But Maeve had Kal. And Alys had Brock. The twins were busy and even Gimli and Grogu had one another. The thought of returning to the blanket as the proverbial fifth wheel was too depressing. Tully's tent was the lesser of two evils.

So, I followed her inside.

The interior was dark, lit only by some battery-powered candles that flickered from strategically placed sconces. There was a small round card table that had been draped with a burgundy bit of velvet. One stool sat on the far side and two metal folding chairs were placed on the other. The tent itself smelled slightly of mildew beneath the overpowering scent of incense and burnt herbs.

Tully picked up a Styrofoam plate that had ended up face down on the ground and laughed. "The little stinker got my whole hamburger. Came tearing in here so fast he scared me and I dropped my plate. He wolfed it down before I knew what was happening."

I'd been about to sit down but hesitated at her comment. "I'm sorry. Let me get you another."

She waved it away. "I'm supposed to be on a high protein, low-fat diet. The critter's keeping me honest. So, what's new?"

I tried to think of something to say as she chucked the plate into a small garbage can behind her stool and then turned to face me. "Oh, you know, same old same old. What have you got going on in here?"

Sibby's survival tactic rule one—the best ways to keep people from prying into your business? Invite them to talk about theirs. People are more interested in themselves than they are in you.

"Madame Tallulah's fortune-telling." Tully waved her hand theatrically then dropped her tone to a conspiratorial whisper. "It's just a side-hustle for now, though I have my eye on a shop in downtown Eckhart for a full-fledged occult store. After I finish my business degree of course."

"You're into the occult?" And here I thought Tully was a good southern church-going sort. "What does your family think about that?"

"It's a relatively new interest. Besides, compared to what my brother does on the weekends, my parents have no room to gripe. And Paul thinks it's kinda hot that he can bed down with a witch." She winked at me.

I had no idea who Paul was and wasn't in the mood to talk about anyone's love life or my own witchy roots. "So, what sort of reading does Madame Tallulah do?"

"Right now, I'm focusing on tarot. Hey, you want me to do a reading for you?"

"No, that's—"

But she had already glommed onto the idea and reached for a small black satin pouch. Out came her deck and a bundle of herbs. She pulled a purple Bic lighter from somewhere and ignited the tiny flame. She held it to the herbs and the smell of burning sage filled the tent. I coughed delicately.

"It cleanses the energy from the last reading," Tully explained.

My Aunt Jess had grown sage in her greenhouse, along with hundreds of other plants. She was a horticulturist. Though I had never been permitted into the greenhouse when she'd been alive, I'd helped her by hanging herbs to dry, or sometimes pouring sugary confections into molds for candy or creating cooking oils infused with rosemary or garlic or hot chilis. As far as I knew, she hadn't burned any of them.

But like me, Aunt Jess had been great at keeping secrets.

Tully put the still smoking sage into a small ceramic dish and then began to shuffle the cards. "Think of a question you would like answered. How, what, and why questions are best."

The words floated into my mind. I hadn't meant to take this reading seriously, but the thought had been plaguing me.

Why does every man I sleep with end up dead?

Tully pointed to a spot on the table between us. "Past." She put down a card in the spot then moved over a few inches. "Present."

It didn't take a carnival psychic to figure out what came next. Though the card that was laid before me made all the hairs rise on my body.

Death.

"Don't freak out," Tully said after a glance at my face. "It isn't literal death being foretold. The death card symbolizes change."

I stared at the black-armored knight riding the pale horse. Change. Did that mean that my lovers would *stop* dying?

"Now this is interesting," Tully tapped the first card. "The knight of wands. When he's upright he represents passion, energy, and forward movement. But when he's like this," she pointed to the upside-down card, and then her brow furrowed as she considered how best to put it.

Though I had never delved too deeply into prognostication, I knew enough about tarot to see that the reversed card represented the opposite of its usual meaning. Instead of passion, my past held frustration. Well, that was spot on.

Sexual frustration, thy true name is Siobhan Silver.

"I guess this could be someone who comes on too strong," Tully finally admitted.

My lips twitched. "That's more polite than how people usually describe me."

She flashed me a grin and I could see the relief in her eyes.

"What about this?" I gestured to the middle card. It depicted three women with long hair holding a silver chalice aloft between them. It reminded me of me and my sisters drinking the empowerment brew that had called magic to us. "That's the present, right?"

She nodded. "The three of cups. Three represents stability in the deck. The three legs of a stool. This particular card symbolizes friendship, growth, and healing."

I looked back at death on his pale horse. "And all that's about to change."

Her brows pulled together and she scooped the cards back up. "How about I do a deeper reading? I normally don't at the carnival but I could use the practice."

She waved the sage bundle across the deck again. Her movements were sharp and I could tell that she was nervous. Why? Had she seen something in the cards that I'd missed? She handed them to me and indicated that I should shuffle. I did, carefully. The cards were longer than a standard playing card deck and shuffling felt a little awkward. "Should I be thinking of a question?"

She shook her head. After a moment, Tully indicated that I should hand them back over.

"This is the Celtic Cross spread. Self, situation, recent past, higher guidance, foundational influences, near future, hopes and fears, external influences, advice to follow and the potential outcome." She spoke each word with the placement of the accompanying card.

"What?" I shouldn't feel alarmed. It was a beautiful spring

day. We were in an old tent on the town green. But something about her reaction had all the small hairs on my body standing on end.

Tully was staring at the cards laid out between us. "It's just, I've never seen a spread with so many major arcana cards."

Our eyes met and she muttered, "This reading is very important."

I stared down at the ten cards she'd carefully laid out. I recognized the three of cups again. What had she said that position meant?

Tully went through the cards one at a time pointing with a bejeweled index finger. "You are the Queen of Cups. But you are crossed by the Magician, reversed. He's confusing you, scattering your focus. You've been struggling to make a decision about something."

Sebastian. I dismissed the thought before it could take root. My decision was made about the lying dark fae who had made me burn. He was bad news. And not just because his job was to suck out my soul and the souls of my sisters. If ever there was a doomed relationship, it was ours.

"This is your recent past. The hermit card and he's reversed. You've been lonely."

"Is anyone not lonely these days?" I tried to make light of it but the tone fell flat.

"The fool is your higher guidance."

"That explains a few things," I grumbled as I looked at the young man that appeared ready to mince off a cliff.

Tully shook her head. "No, this is actually good. The fool represents innocence, maybe naiveté. I think the cards are telling you that you've grown too cynical. You need to listen to your inner self more."

I gritted my teeth. Easier said than done. Inner Sibby made very bad choices.

8

"This came up again." She pointed to the three of cups, "And it is in the foundational influences position. This is an essential card for you. You need friendship to heal from what has come before."

We were only halfway through the reading but I wasn't sure I wanted to finish.

"The eight of wands represents travel."

"Well, you got that right," I murmur.

"But it's near-future travel. Are you going somewhere?"

Yeah, to the council of elders so that my sisters and I could get the magic hunters off our asses for good. Never mind that my witchy cast was a traveler. When I was turned on, I could jump halfway around the world.

The problem was, traveling was getting tiresome. What had excited me at twenty-one bored me at forty-one. Were there any real adventures left worth taking?

But I said none of this to Tully. "It's possible."

She bobbed her head. "Right, so the thing is, you can do a quick course change from this card. This position is in your control. So don't feel like you have to run away again."

She smiled at me. I could tell the reading was freaking her out and she was doing her best to keep the tone upbeat. I tried to force my lips up, but they were pressed so tightly together that I figured the expression was more of a grimace than a smile.

"Hmmm," Tully murmured as she studied the next card. "The Lovers, reversed. Somebody's got a fear of commitment. It's understandable. At our age, most of the men who are still available are damaged, perverted, or both."

Sebastian was definitely damaged. I never found out if he was perverted.

I really wished my brain would get with the program and defrag all thoughts of that dark fae bastard. How could I delude myself into believing he didn't matter when I thought of him every other minute?

"External influences, the King of Wands, reversed. This is…well, normally I would say this is an overbearing father, but yours isn't around, right?"

I'd never known my father. At my nod, she continued, "Yeah, so this is some asshole male authority figure. Someone who behaves in a domineering or controlling manner. Can you think of anyone like that?"

Because his name kept springing to mind I pictured Sebastian. But what she had described….

The dark fae was sneaky as hell, secretive, and manipulative. But he wasn't controlling.

"I really can't."

"Keep an eye out. And now for your advice. The Moon. This is awesome advice. She's telling you to trust your intuition. Follow your gut. For this outcome."

I looked at the last card. "What does that mean?"

Tully frowned at the final card. "This is The World. This represents your journey's end."

"So my journey will be over? Does that mean my travel or…?"

Tully reached for the deck. "Pull another card."

"Why?" But I did as she asked.

And I stared once more at the black knight on the pale horse. Then turned it to face her.

Death was coming.

SIOBHAN

"*I*t's just a stupid carnival psychic," Alys repeated as she poured me a glass of white wine. "Don't let it get to you."

We had returned to Aunt Jess's cottage after Maeve and her family had gone home to do whatever families did after a fun day out.

The sun had dipped below the distant hills, but wouldn't set for another hour or so. I cupped my palms around the stemless glass, though I didn't sip it. Instead, my gaze went to the fire in the small firepit Alys had put in before Christmas. Combined with the comfort of the Adirondack chairs and the view of the lake, this had become our new favorite hangout. "I'm telling you, the energy in that tent was intense. I can't just dismiss what she said."

"Tully is a wacko. She's been running around town since last Halloween telling everyone that she's a witch. I think it's some sort of midlife crisis." My sister—the newly empowered witch—spoke without a hint of irony.

I didn't want to argue with Alys. We'd spent too much of our adult lives arguing already. Mentally, I tagged on an agree to disagree and changed the subject. "Why didn't Hottie McNibblet come home with you? His time of the month or something?"

My sister's lover was two decades her junior and a werewolf to boot. They were tied for first place as the cutest couple next to Maeve and Kal, the lovebirds who never seemed to stop cooing at each other.

"I wish you wouldn't call him that," Alys sighed.

"Brock doesn't mind."

"Well, *I* mind. It's disrespectful."

"You can make it up to him for me." I made a catlike claw with my hand and tagged on, "Between the sheets."

Alys rolled her eyes. "To answer your prying question, I suggested that he go home and spend some time with the pack."

She had? That was a first. "Are you getting sick of him or something?"

"No, why?"

I snuggled deeper into my flannel blanket. "Then why didn't you go with him?"

Alys was quiet for a minute. "I don't feel right being over there. Not since Nate…." She trailed off. Her expression turned sad.

Nate was one of the werewolves, a teenage boy who had been stuck in his werewolf form. He'd run off several months earlier after a car accident. There had been no word from him since. Alys had been driving when the accident had happened. And because Alys was Alys, she felt responsible for Nate.

Though I was comfortable and loathed to move, I set my wineglass aside and reached for her hand. "No one blames you for what happened."

"I blame me." She gave me a tight smile. "He's still a kid. He should be going to school, talking smack with his friends, not running around the countryside as a wolf."

"You can't control everything, Alys." Though she always tried.

She nodded, her lips compressed tightly together.

I squeezed her hand. "So get over there and sully that young buck."

"What about you?"

I raised my eyebrow. Though I loved the effect, my piercing had been too cold to wear while sitting outside in the winter. Now it was back and judging by the way Alys's gaze went to it, glinting in the firelight. "What about me?"

She said nothing but I knew.

My sisters had been very careful to keep me occupied over the last few months. Someone was always with me. Maeve, Alys, Kal, even Maeve's kids. All had been assigned rotations on watch Siobhan duty.

As if I was going to disappear if I wasn't being hovered over every single second of every day.

"He isn't here." I didn't use Sebastian's name. We both knew who I was talking about. "He isn't in Eckhart."

"You're sure?"

I nodded. "According to your real estate agent, that place he was renting up on the hill has been sold. He has nowhere else to stay, at least not where we wouldn't hear about it. It's a small town. I have no reason to run."

Alys nodded, as though accepting my words. "If you want to talk about it, I'm happy to listen."

"I don't." The tone came out harsher than I'd intended so I pasted on a smile. "Stop stalling and go shag your werewolf already."

"If you insist." She stood up and handed me her still full wineglass. "Are you coming to the closing party tomorrow night?"

Alys and Maeve ran their own business, *Silver Demo and Design.* They bought run-down houses and fixed them up, sometimes taking the structures down to the studs. The Mid-Century Modern that they had just sold had been a huge project and had taken a long time to finish. To celebrate the closing, Alys and Maeve were throwing a party for everyone who'd helped on the house at the ski resort and their families. It was a thank you to the whole team.

"Yeah, I'll be there."

"Good," was all Alys said. "See you there."

I watched her back her brand-new full-sized white Yukon up until she had the room to turn the massive vehicle around. Though Alys lived simply here at the cottage that only recently had been wired for electricity, the woman had piles and piles of money.

Rich, accomplished, and with a much younger lover. And at fifty she had an ass that still hadn't quit.

I'd never told her, but she was kind of my hero.

After finishing Alys's wine, I took up my own glass and stared at the fire. I didn't see it though. Instead, I kept seeing that tarot reading and wondering what it all meant.

It meant nothing. Just like the stupid feminine nightgown I'd bought at Target and had decided to wear tonight. It was sheer and sexy, not at all my usual counterculture style. Yet I had been drawn to it.

Not everything had to have a purpose. Overanalyzing the crap out of life was more of an Alys activity. I just went with the flow.

The wind shifted and the smoke wafted closer to me. I set my second empty glass down and shut my eyes. My head felt light and the wine, a quality Riesling, had mellowed my dark mood. I'd go inside in a minute. Just one more minute of enjoying peace.

Sebastian stared up at the ceiling of the small room. Everything was ready. Afterward, he would take off, leaving no trail for the magic hunters to follow. He hated being still, feeling trapped. It was ironic. He had once been the greatest hunter the magical community had ever seen. Now he was the prey. He hadn't spent two nights in the same place for months.

All because of *her*.

Siobhan Silver. She hated him. He knew that. Deserved her scorn. He had been sent to track her down. Her and her sisters. Three more targets on a long list of them.

It should have been straightforward. Just another job. But when the chance arose, he couldn't do it. He couldn't take her magic. Couldn't destroy her soul.

Instead, he had tried to protect her. Protect all of them. It had morphed into a full-time job since someone had raised the bounty on the three of them. And added Sebastian's name to the list.

One of the reasons he hated being still was because it gave him time to think. To mull over his actions and dwell on his mistakes.

Sebastian had made many. Continued to make them.

He shifted and his arm bumped up against something solid.

He let out a slow breath. Part relieved sigh, part frustrated groan. She was there. Alive beside him once more. She smelled of a campfire and clean mountain air. These little nocturnal visits were pure torture at the same time as he savored each one.

He couldn't wake her. She hated him. The last thing he wanted was to fight with her. If he left her alone, eventually she would travel back to where she belonged as she had done every night.

And he would leave before the magic hunters tracked the illegal use of magic to this small motel room.

He rolled onto his side, propped a hand under his head, and drank her in. She wore that bit of metal above her eyebrow again. There was a blanket wrapped around her shoulders. Her hair was still purple, though she had cut it short with the bangs angled to frame her impish features. The fantastical symbols that once adorned one-half of her scalp had grown out months ago. Her cheeks were flushed, her pale pink lips parted with her every breath.

He wanted to wrap his arms around her, to feel her. He didn't dare touch her. Sebastian doubted Siobhan knew she had been coming to him every night. It was her body, her wellspring of desire that made her magic happen. A desire she fought, even as she teased and coaxed it.

Her contradictions fascinated him. Strong and soft. Sweet and tart. Lusty and reserved.

"*Annwyl,*" he whispered the endearment to her. It fit her because he never cherished anyone or anything until she had come into his life.

Soon it would stop. In less than a week, she and her sisters would be sanctioned by the council of elders and become registered magic users. Once that was done, once she was safe, Sebastian would turn himself in and face his punishment.

But not until Siobhan's position was assured.

She let out a breathy sigh and rolled toward him. The blanket fell away and he saw she wore a long sheer night-gown beneath. It was so unlike her usual style it gave him a jolt. He'd seen her in sweats, jeans, tank tops, and leather. This garment was so much softer. More feminine. The dusky outlines of her nipples were visible.

He'd seen every part of her body. She slept in the nude more often than not and often appeared that way. Typically, he covered her up, after taking a good, long look at what he would never have.

Something about the sweet, barely-there covering tempted him beyond reason. He imagined she had been thinking of him when she had donned the garment, imagined what it would be like to have him slowly peel it from her luscious form.

Her hips were rounded, her breasts and thighs full. Her pale skin seemed to glow in the softly lit room. Beneath the smoky fire smell, he scented her desire. A rich, thick aphrodisiac of warm vanilla and all things edible.

For a man who had spent many of his early years half-starved, she was fantasy-made flesh.

His pulse picked up when she tossed a leg over his hip. He didn't resist as she burrowed closer to him. Didn't fight her when her lips found his pulse point and brushed a soft kiss over the spot.

"Sebastian," she moaned those succulent lips a hairsbreadth from his own.

So warm, so soft, so welcoming. And she wanted him.

He was lost.

Siobhan

On a scale of one to ten as far as erotic dreams went, this one was a solid eleven.

I could feel my lover's hands as they roved down my arms and up the smooth expanse of my leg. Heat radiated off him in waves, more intense than fire, the taste of his skin more appealing than any wine.

It must have been the wine that brought on this delicious fantasy. That plus all of my thoughts about Sebastian and the tarot reading. I'd manifested a dream and was fully prepared to enjoy it.

All the reasons that Sebastian and I couldn't be together didn't matter in my imagination. I couldn't hurt him here and he didn't have the power to hurt me. I could open myself up to the pleasure of feeling.

"*Annwyl,*" he said again as his fingers threaded through my hair. "I am lost for you."

His words were pretty but I didn't want words. I wanted action. Pressing myself tighter against his erection, I ground my hips against his. He groaned at the contact and his hand tightened in my hair, pulling a few loose.

"Ow," I said. And then frowned. Ow? A dream wasn't supposed to hurt.

Unless….

I pulled back, panting for breath, and stared. There wasn't much light in the room but Sebastian's amethyst eyes lit up the space around the bed.

This wasn't my bedroom. Not at the cottage. Not at Maeve's house. There was a scent of stale cigarettes and the cover I was laying on was a scuzzy polyester. My sisters would have gutted this dump in a heartbeat.

It was real. I had traveled to him. Stupid wine. Stupid freaking hormones. I swore viciously.

"Siobhan." He reached for me again.

"Get the hell away from me," I flung myself out of bed and pressed up against the far wall. "Don't you *dare* touch me."

I was more worried for him than I was for myself. God, if we had kept going I could have killed him.

18

He rolled onto his back and stared at the ceiling. "I don't, usually."

My gaze locked onto the bulge in his jeans. Dear sweet dark chocolate, was that him just semi aroused? What sort of pants python was he packing? Then the words registered. "What do you mean *usually*?"

He turned his head to the side and I could feel those eerie eyes boring into me. "You've come to me every night since we last parted."

I shook my head. "Not possible." I would know if I was traveling in my sleep.

Wouldn't I?

"It's the truth," he insisted.

I laughed without humor. "The truth. You wouldn't know the truth if it bit you on the ass, Sebastian."

He sat up and scowled at me. "I've never lied to you, Siobhan. Never once."

The fact that he could say that with a straight face..."Are you kidding me? I thought you were a divorce lawyer. A *human* divorce lawyer, not some dark fae magic hunter who wanted to rip out my soul!"

He got out of bed, clearly unwilling to sit there while I attacked him and reached for his shirt. "I never lied. I let you believe things that weren't entirely true, but I never once spoke an untruth."

Laughter bubbled out of me but it was a hollow sound. "You're arguing semantics, Sebastian. You pretended to be something you're not. That's lying. You hid the truth from me every time we talked. That's lying!"

My hands balled into fists at my sides and tears stung my eyes. I was angry with him. But not just with Sebastian. The rage was directed at me too. For being so willing to trust him. For wanting the impossible so badly that I hadn't even tried to see the truth.

"You took advantage of me," I breathed. "Of all the things I didn't know. You used me."

He nodded once. "I did."

I blinked. I hadn't expected him to own it.

"I did," he said again. "And I had you. I was moments away from trapping you under my soul net and capturing your magic. But I couldn't do it. Don't you see? In hundreds of years of being a magic hunter, I have *never* hesitated. Not before you."

I snorted. "I guess that makes me special."

Either he didn't pick up on my sarcasm or chose to ignore it because he nodded. "You are special, Siobhan. In all the world, there is no one else like you."

"I—"

Sebastian dove for me. He gripped me around the waist and twisted in mid-air to take the impact of the landing on his back.

"What are you doing?" I screeched.

"Magic hunters," he breathed just as the opposite wall exploded.

3

ALYS

"*D*id I mention how glad I am that you decided to come over?" Brock panted as I rolled off his naked body.

"Hmmm." The sound of satisfaction was the only reply I could make. Making love with the man rendered me utterly speechless.

After letting out a contented sigh, Brock snuggled me deeper into his side, sharing his warmth. "I never sleep well when you aren't with me."

Apparently, he wanted to talk. I struggled for words that wouldn't burst the bubble surrounding us. I hadn't been designed to play the part of the romantic heroine. I was too terse, too practical, too driven. Let's face it, I was a big old serving of bitch. But Brock seemed to like that about me. "Not that we do too much sleeping when we are together."

His low chuckle shook the bed. "You have a point."

There was something in his tone. A sort of undercurrent. I turned my head and rolled so that my chin was resting on his sternum. "What is it?"

Golden eyes stared down at me. The wolf was ascendent. "Move in with me."

I froze.

Brock closed his eyes and groaned. "I'm sorry, Lys. I can scent your panic."

"I… I'm not panicked." It might have been more believable if my voice hadn't been shaking.

"I wasn't going to ask you until after the meeting with the council of elders. I know it's safer for you to stay in the convergence for now."

Aunt Jess's cottage was built at a point where ley lines intersected. Within the convergence, my sisters and I could use magic without being tracked by magic hunters. Outside of it, all bets were off.

Funny that the thought of magic hadn't even occurred to me when he'd asked. My panic had an entirely different source.

"It isn't that," I hedged.

Brock opened his eyes. They'd regained their more typical chocolate brown hue. "Is it the pack?"

Brock lived in a house full of wayward werewolves. Some came and went but there were a few regulars who seemed to do nothing more than hang around and gossip most days. As the *de facto* alpha, Brock kept the roof over their heads, and in turn, they followed his instructions. It wasn't the most normal living arrangement, but I liked the motley little crew. Liked that there was always someone to laugh with, to cook with. And even though I wasn't a gourmet like Sibby, they never complained when I made my halfhearted attempts.

I shook my head. "No, I'm fine with the pack."

He hesitated. "Then…it's me?"

It amazed me that this thirty-year-old golden god struggled to believe that I, a woman twenty years his senior, wanted *him*.

"Don't be stupid. I love you." I shoved him a little and then sat up.

Brock sat up too. "Then what?"

I combed my left hand through my hair. My wedding ring was long gone. I'd taken it off the day I'd found out Kyle had been cheating on me. I didn't know what was causing the fluttery feeling in my belly and had no way of explaining it to him. "What's wrong with the way things are?"

His eyes searched my face. "Is that really what you want?"

If I said yes, Brock would respect it. He was an amazing lover, an amazing man. If I drew a line, he didn't see it as a challenge, something to get me to back down from. He accepted my boundaries and at times, even helped me reinforce them.

But did I want to plant my flag on this proverbial hilltop?

"Tell me why you want me to move in here," I asked instead. "What made you even think about it?"

"Your divorce."

My lips parted. My divorce had been finalized over a month before. Despite my ex-husband being ridiculously difficult at the onset, he had moved on in a hurry. In fact, I hadn't seen Kyle since the fall.

"I guess I always viewed you living at the cottage as a weigh station," Brock murmured. "A place to stop and rest but not your final destination. Isn't that why you never bothered to fully unpack?"

He was right. Most of my worldly possessions were still in boxes scattered around Aunt Jess's old room.

"I would offer to move in with you—"

My snort cut him off. "Now that is crazy. This house is amazing. And the pack needs you. Plus, this is your territory. I would never ask you to give that up."

Territory. *That* was what was bugging me. The cottage was my place. It belonged to me and my sisters. The greenhouse was the source of our magic, our tie to our mother and the adopted aunt that raised us after her death. Hell, we even had a guardian ghost that hung around the place.

Thoughts of the cottage filled me with nostalgia. But was it really my forever home?

"Sibby," I began, grasping the first reason that wasn't a lie but didn't admit the truth I wasn't ready to process. "Sibby is in a bad place right now. I don't want to just run out on her."

He stroked my cheek. "I know you have a lot on your mind. The last thing I want to do is put pressure on you. Just know that I would love to have you here all the time. The idea of knowing you would be in my bed every night…."

He didn't need to complete the thought. A certain part of his anatomy finished it for him. *Behold, exhibit A.*

My brow lifted. "Again?"

His grin turned wicked. "Let me show you exactly what the thought of having you here does to me."

I had to give the man credit. He could be *very* persuasive.

Siobhan

*M**agic hunters.* Plural. Three of them filled the space that had been a wall a moment ago. Two men and a woman, all wearing black leather, and armed to the teeth. Their skin looked an unnatural shade of green as though they all suffered from seasickness.

"Goblins," Sebastian muttered.

"How—?" I didn't get a chance to finish before the female, who was head and shoulders taller than her male counterparts, uncoiled the whip on her belt and cracked it.

A cage made of what looked like forks of lightning formed overhead. Sebastian threw up his hands. A transparent amethyst dome covered us and kept the electric bars from crashing down over our heads.

"They tracked your magic," Sebastian's body covered me like a living shield. "Can you jump back to the cottage?"

I didn't know. Desire, the primary trigger to my magic, could take me farther than either anger or fear. And it was the one emotion I wasn't feeling looking at the goblin hit squad.

"Surrender yourself, dark fae," one of the goblins growled. "We know your magic is almost spent."

I put my hand on Sebastian's shoulder. He might be a dick, but I wasn't going to leave him to face three adversaries alone. I reached out with my mind and struggled to find the cottage. If we were within Eckhart town limits, I would have felt the pull from the convergence. But there was nothing familiar nearby.

"It's too far," I told Sebastian. He was starting to shake, his body trembling with the force of holding the magical barrier in place.

"We need to get into the ley line," he wheezed. "I'll make an exit through the back wall. The closest line runs through the pool. Get ready to run on my mark."

I wriggled out from underneath him and rolled into a crouch.

The two male goblins fanned out, clearly intent on grabbing us the second Sebastian's strength gave out.

With his other hand, Sebastian made a gesture to the wall behind the bed. It exploded out. Plaster and concrete lay strewn across damp asphalt. The owner of this building was going to be really pissed when he got a look at the damage.

"Go," Sebastian said. I shot off the mark like an Olympic sprinter, ignoring the flare of pain in my bum knee as I ran. My bare feet made no sound on the pavement. I could feel Sebastian behind me. He was almost a foot taller than my five-foot-five-inch frame and should have easily overtaken me. But he was struggling to keep up. Using that much magic must have drained him.

Booted footfalls sounded behind us, three sets of them. The motel had gone dark, no lights anywhere. Magic and electricity couldn't work in the same space. "Where the hell is this pool?"

"Left," he wheezed as we reached the corner of the building.

I skidded like a cartoon character, my bare feet taking the brunt of the damage as I tried to round the bend. A loud crack rumbled in the distance and a wall of that eerie lightning appeared right in front of us. It stretched out from the corner of the building to the line of small evergreens. Sebastian slammed into my back when I stopped, almost sending us both careening into the thing.

Through the glimmering bolts, I could just make out the oblong shape of the pool.

I turned to the trees, just as another lightning fence went up.

"Travel to it," Sebastian said. "Before they close the cage and cut you off from your magic."

I reached for his arm but he withdrew. "Leave me."

"Don't be stupid," I snapped.

Lightning crackled along the brick wall of the building. The cage would be enormous.

"They're hunting me too." Those amethyst eyes bore into me. "They'll be content with one of us."

Another lightning barricade went up between us and the goblins.

"And what happens when I travel to you the next time I fall asleep, huh? Then your noble sacrifice won't mean jack shit. So just shut up and take my hand already,"

He did. I traveled half a second before the goblins closed the top.

We splashed into the pool. The frigid water stole my breath. I went under. Water went up my nose, filled my senses. I flailed about and broke the surface just in time to see the goblins sprinting toward us.

If they used that whip while we were in the pool, we'd be electrocuted.

A hand wrapped around my ankle, pulling me down. I fought out of reflex. Amethyst eyes glowed at the murky bottom of the pool like a great water beast and beneath him….

It wasn't something I saw as much as felt. The pull of power. I forgot my struggle for air and even the need to breathe, the fact that the goblins were after us and let that monster pull me down.

And my body began to….dissolve.

There was no other word for it. I became more and less, was part of everything but absolutely nothing all at once. Sebastian was there too. I couldn't see him. I no longer had eyes to see with. But he was there. I felt him nearby.

Others were there too. Swirling in the river of power. I had a sense of them all. I was them and they were me. What a wonderful way to travel. To explore everything.

After a time—and even the word time had lost all meaning—I realized we were being pulled toward something stronger. Something more. Swirling currents overlapped and we traveled faster and faster. Pure joy pulsed in what remained of Siobhan Silver. I was everything and everything was me. I couldn't get enough.

Until I was violently ripped away.

Soaked to the bone, I collapsed onto the ground in front of the firepit. The fire had burned down to embers. Sebastian was beside me, still sputtering and coughing up water.

My whole body cried out from the loss. "What was that?"

"The convergence." Sebastian turned his head to look at me. "You were almost lost to it."

I stared at him, still feeling the ache of the loss. "I don't understand."

He closed his eyes, shook his head. "Don't ever go in there again."

The thought of never feeling that glorious freedom, seeing those swirling colors. Of being part of the whole magical ecosystem.

Suddenly Sebastian rolled on top of me, pinning my arms to the side. "You must never go in there again, Siobhan. Promise me."

"Why?" I breathed. "It's beautiful."

"That's the allure. All that power, there for the taking. But your body can't channel it. Those others that you felt? Those were witches and fae and other magic users that thought they could channel directly from the lines. But their bodies can't hold the magic. It destroyed them. They became part of it."

He was breathing hard, that eerie gaze intent. A muscle jumped in his jaw. "Do you understand me? You think you want to be there but once you lose yourself to the convergence, you lose everything you are. You serve magic instead of magic serving you. One soul can't last very long within. Vow to me you will never go in there again."

He was so intent and the words escaped before I had thought them through. "Okay."

Sebastian closed his eyes and I saw a moment of relief before he slumped on top of me.

"Sebastian?" I asked. "I said I wouldn't go in the stupid convergence. No need for the drama."

I put my hand on his back and then moved it, intent on putting it on his shoulder to roll him off.

But the moment my fingers came away I knew that they weren't just wet from pool water. The color was darker and when I pressed my trembling fingers together, they felt sticky.

From Sebastian's blood.

4

MAEVE

*W*ith my head positioned as it was on Kal's lap and my eyes glued to the television, it took me a while to realize something was wrong. Gimli and Grogu had finished their game of tug-the-towel and were curled up together in their bed. The shredded bit of navy terrycloth lay limply before them. Bella and Philip had gone to bed an hour ago. This was our time to just be together. Husband and wife. Usually, we put on a movie or sometimes listened to an audiobook but after the excitement of the carnival, we were both content with an old episode of *Good Bones*.

Usually, Kal combed his fingers through my hair when we lay like this. But his hands were still. That was my first clue. I turned until I could see his face. He wasn't looking at the TV. His expression was distant as though his gaze was locked on something only he could see.

I sat up and scrounged in the couch cushions for the remote. That broke him out of his trance. "What's wrong?"

"I can't find the remote. The couch ate it again." Frustrated, I got up and shambled over to the set, turning it off manually like a savage. Hands-on-hips, I spun to face my man. "Okay, what's going on with you?"

Kal didn't try any of that macho BS pretending like nothing was amiss. It wasn't his style. "I was thinking about the wedding."

"It's in June, right?" Slowly, I eased myself down beside him. Though my Multiple Sclerosis wasn't flaring up at the moment, I was much more aware of my every move than I had been a year ago. Kal too, if the way his gaze followed me was any indication.

Kal nodded. "June 21. The summer solstice. The official invitation arrived today."

That explained his pensive mood. Before, he could have kicked the mental can on down the road. But not with an RSVP looming.

"I don't know what to do," he murmured when I was seated beside him. "On the one hand, I'm glad Harper told me. It's nice to be invited to a family event after so long."

"Makes sense," I threaded my fingers through his. "And you're right, it was nice that she reached out."

Even if it had sparked a massive misunderstanding at precisely the wrong time in our lives. But I wasn't the sort to shoot the messenger.

"And on the other…. he will be there."

He was Kal's father. The man hadn't acknowledged a single call or letter or email from me. I had tried. Over the years I'd sent pictures of the kids and long newsy letters catching him up on our lives, hoping something would break through the deep freezeout. Nothing. Pilip had a thick layer of permafrost on his heart. I'd kept reaching out for Kal's sake until MS or Miss Priss, as I'd dubbed my autoimmune disease, took over all my free time. Then I'd gotten angry. What sort of father, what sort of grandfather, behaved that way?

But Pilip refused to acknowledge his middle son. Worse he ignored his grandchildren.

Kal shook his head. "What do I do, Evie?"

This was the first time he'd brought the subject up for discussion. We'd had plenty of other things to talk about. The children, the dogs, work, town events, school events, my MS, and even my enchantress magic. Kal knew all my secrets and I knew his. But at the same time, my husband needed time to process.

The fact that he was asking me meant that he really was at an impasse.

"You want to know what I think?"

He nodded.

"Okay. Well, this is your olive branch. Harper has reached out and you can either extend yourself or shut them out for good. If you can't or don't want to deal with it, that's understandable. We'll send a nice gift and that will be that. But I don't think you're going to get another chance to know your youngest brother as an adult."

Toklo had only been nine when Kal had struck out to find his own way in the world. With almost a decade between them, they hadn't been close as children. Now he was getting married. I had to believe Harper's actions were because Kal's brother wanted to reach out but didn't know how to overcome the distance.

Men were stupid like that.

His dark gaze searched my face. "Would you come with me?"

I blinked. The question stunned me into total silence. Never once had I imagined making the journey *with* Kal. I was the outsider, the non-Inuit woman who had deepened the wedge between him and his family.

"I know it's a lot to ask," Kal said quietly. "That traveling will be exhausting for you. But Evie, I don't think I could handle this trip without you."

That took a lot for him to admit, even to me.

I sucked in a deep lungful of air, then released it. "Are you sure? I don't want to make things more difficult with your family."

"You're my family." Kal pressed his forehead to mine. "You and Bella and Philip. No matter what happens with any of the others."

His words touched me. Kal wasn't a big talker but he somehow always managed to say exactly what I needed to hear. "If you really want it, we'll make it happen. Will we bring the kids? They'll be out of school for the summer."

He frowned. I knew him well enough to understand his inner debate. On the one hand, he would love for Bella and Philip to see the place where he'd grown up and get to know his side of the family. On the other....

"If your father says anything shitty to you or the kids, I will annihilate him," I vowed.

The corner of his mouth twitched. "Verbally?"

I didn't comment. I was a witch and by the time the wedding rolled around, I'd be a fully sanctioned one. If anyone hurt my husband or kids, they would pay.

Kal's dark eyes were full of amusement. "Have I ever told you how sexy you are when you go all mama bear?"

"You have strange and unusual taste." I fought the smile but when he reached out and started to tickle me, I ruined the prim effect with a shriek of laughter.

"Ssshhh," Kal whispered as he lay on top of me. "You'll wake the dogs."

"Chocolate forbid. You better find a way to shut me up."

My cellphone started playing music just as things were heating up.

"Ignore it." Kal was working to unhook my bra.

"That's Sibby's ring tone." I flailed an arm toward where I'd left it on the coffee table. "It might be a witch emergency."

Since his arms were longer, he retrieved the phone and handed it to me. He didn't move though, probably on the off chance that my youngest sister's interruption was nothing more than a butt dial. It had happened before.

"Hello?" I gasped, still out of breath from laughing.

"He's bleeding. I don't know what to do." Sibby's voice wobbled.

"Who's bleeding?" I locked eyes with Kal and he rolled off me, then extended a hand to help me sit up. "Sibby, you need to call an ambulance."

"Sebastian," she sobbed.

No humans then. I had no idea what hospital tests would reveal about a dark fae. I hunted around for my discarded sneakers. "Where are you? And where's the injury?"

"At the cottage. Outside. We just got here. And I think it's the back of his head."

Head wounds could be tricky. "Is he conscious?"

"In and out of it."

"Try to keep him awake. Apply pressure to the wound with fabric if you can. Maybe a clean towel. Is Alys with you?"

"No." Her voice sounded small and broken. "She went to Brock's."

"I'm on my way." Just as soon as I found my keys.

"Maeve—"

Kal was holding the keys out to me.

"I'll be there as soon as I can," I said into the phone. "And I'll call Alys on my way."

The call disconnected and I looked up into Kal's worried eyes.

"What's Sebastian doing there?"

I shook my head. "I guess we'll find out after I save his life."

"Always the hero," Kal said and gave me a final kiss to see me on my way.

●

Siobhan

I really didn't want to call Alys. Maeve had medical training and wouldn't judge. Alys would pepper me with questions about what Sebastian was doing here and what was I thinking, bringing a known magic hunter to the cottage. We'd end up in a huge fight with me playing defense.

But she was closer. And I really was afraid Sebastian would die before Maeve got to Witch Way.

Not wanting to leave Sebastian long enough to go get a towel, I'd already whipped my nightgown off and held it against where I thought the wound was at the back of Sebastian's head. In the dark, I couldn't be sure I covered the correct spot.

"Don't die," I whispered.

Those amethyst eyes blinked open again. His gaze was unfocused, the pupils blown wide almost engulfing the eerie light.

"Sebastian," I called his name.

He didn't respond.

"Can you hear me? You need to stay awake."

His eyelids fluttered down.

"Shit," I muttered and reached for my phone once more.

Ten minutes later, Alys and Brock skidded to a stop in the gravel drive. Alys left the headlights on to illuminate the spot where I sat naked, holding the blood-soaked nightgown against Sebastian's head.

"What happened?" Alys barked.

"I sleep traveled to him. There were magic hunters. I didn't know he was hit until he passed out." It came out in a rush.

"Do you want me to move him inside?" Brock asked. Even though Sebastian was larger, Brock was a werewolf. He could easily manage to carry the bigger man.

Alys was frowning down at Sebastian. "Let's wait."

"Alys," I began. I knew she didn't trust Sebastian. Neither did I. But we couldn't just let him die on the front lawn.

Not after he'd gotten hurt because of me.

She held up a hand. "We'll wait and see what Maeve says. It might do more harm than good to move him. Go inside and get dressed."

I bristled at the tone. "I'm not leaving him."

Our gazes locked and the battle of wills commenced. Alys knew I would sit out here all night, bare-breasted in the moonlight in front of her boyfriend. Not that nudity bothered the werewolf.

"I won't hurt him, Sibby," Alys said quietly. "You don't need to protect him from me."

I didn't say anything, just looked down at Sebastian. A few moments later, Brock handed Alys a blanket which she draped over my shoulders.

"Maeve said I needed to keep him awake," I told them. "But he hasn't opened his eyes since you got here. What if he slips into a coma?"

Alys made soft, soothing sounds and rubbed my blanket-covered back. She didn't tell me it would be all right, for which I was grateful.

Tires on gravel and then another set of headlights rounded the bend.

"Make sure she doesn't fall," Alys said to Brock.

Any other time I would have made a quip about how she ordered the alpha werewolf around, but my gaze was too focused on projecting one thought to the unconscious man in my lap.

Don't die. Don't die. Don't die.

Maeve came up alongside me. Brock set a small suitcase beside her, one of those ones with the rolling handle that could fit in the overhead bins of an airplane, no sweat. She unzipped it and pulled out rubber gloves.

"What is that?" Alys asked, nodding to the suitcase.

"My first aid kit." She flicked on a penlight and then lifted Sebastian's lid. He groaned and tried to turn away from the brightness.

"Hold him steady," Maeve ordered.

Alys placed her hands on either side of Sebastian's head to keep him still.

"Pupils aren't dilating properly. He definitely has a concussion," Maeve snapped the light off. "Let's get him inside so I can have a better look at the injury itself."

Brock hefted Sebastian up in a fireman's carry and moved toward the cottage.

My legs felt like jelly and without Sebastian's weight holding me in place I was worried I would float upward until I vanished into the night.

"Is he going to be okay?" There was a wiggle in my voice as I asked the question.

"I don't know, Sib," Maeve said as she let Alys lead her into the house. "Grab my bag, please."

The task helped me focus. Slowly, I got up and once I was sure I was steady on my feet, went to the medical bag. The little wheels wouldn't be much help on gravel or lawn. I zipped it up and then hefted it up the front steps.

Brock had laid Sebastian on the dining room table. Maeve

37

had taken the shades off of several lamps to increase the wattage in the dim cabin. With no overhead lighting, it wasn't much of an improvement from the lawn.

Maeve turned Sebastian's head to the side and hissed. "Shit. This looks like a burn wound."

"They were tossing magic at us." Still holding my ruined nightgown covered with Sebastian's blood, I moved closer to inspect the damage. "It looked like lightning."

"Get me warm water," Maeve instructed the room at large. "And a razor. Shaving cream if you've got it. Soap if you don't."

I set the nightgown aside and ran for the stairs. After digging out a fresh Lady Bic and a can of the cream that came out as gel but then turned into a sweet-smelling foam, I scurried back to my sister's side.

"It's not very manly," Brock muttered as he looked at the pink instruments. "Remind me to tell him about this when he wakes up."

Alys shot him an irritated glare as she carried a huge bowl of steaming water from the kitchen. "Because machismo is important right now."

When Sebastian woke up. Not if. When. I knew that had been a deliberate choice on Brock's part and I suddenly saw him as more than Alys's boy-toy.

He nodded at me and then chucked a thumb at the door. "I'm going to go turn the cars off. Call if you need anything."

"What can I do to help?" I asked Maeve.

"We need to shave the area around the injury as best we can. Then clean it, see if he needs stitches, and then bandage it."

I nodded and reached for the foamy gel. My hands shook as I caught sight of the hideous injury.

"Give me that," Alys snatched it out of my hands. "You stay in front where he can see you if he wakes up. I'll assist."

For once, I was grateful for her bossy streak. Pulling up a chair, I lowered myself down until I was sitting right in front of Sebastian. It seemed natural to take his hand in mine and I pretended not to see the look my sisters exchanged.

Please don't die.

Alys shaved the back of Sebastian's head and then fetched a clean bowl of water as the liquid turned red. Sebastian's brows pulled together as they touched him but he didn't wake up. Maeve worked with a single-minded focus. Cleaning carefully, assessing the damaged scalp.

"I don't think he has a skull fracture," she murmured at one point. "But there's definitely internal swelling."

"What does that mean?" I whispered.

"That's the concussion. The blood that normally pools with a lump swells under the bone instead. It puts pressure on the brain. Sometimes a doctor will have to drill a hole in the skull to relieve the pressure before permanent damage is done."

All the blood drained from my face. "You're not going to…?"

She shook her head. "No. That's above my pay grade. I don't have access to an X-ray and very little knowledge of how the brain works and where the important parts are. Add to that the fact that he's a dark fae. Who knows what is normal for him?"

I squeezed his hand tighter as she smeared some gel across the back of his head. The bleeding had slowed and I watched as she applied a huge white gauze bandage and then secured it with medical tape.

"That's the best I can do." Maeve stepped back, snapping off her gloves. "We have to wait and see what happens when he wakes up."

When I thought fiercely. When he wakes up. Sebastian was going to recover from this. I remembered him with his magic sword, storming the tent where I'd been held. He was too strong to die from a head injury, even one caused by magic.

"But what if there is swelling?" I asked her. "What if he doesn't wake up?"

She shook her head. "I don't know."

Please don't die.

5

ALYS

"*W*hat are you doing?"

I'd been out on the porch talking to Brock. He and his wolves had been patrolling the area around the cottage on the off chance that the magic hunters would have a way to track Sebastian's movements, even in the convergence. It had taken us hours to convince Sibby there was nothing she could do for Sebastian and that she should take a hot shower and try to get a little rest. Maeve had already turned in, but I'd spied the flash of movement in the greenhouse and came to investigate.

"Looking for a spell. A healing spell." Sibby didn't bother to look up from thumbing through one of the massive magical tomes that were the witchy legacy we'd inherited from our mother and Aunt Jess. She had a towel wrapped around her hair and another one tucked under her armpits. Her bare arms and legs were free of blood but still glistened with water. She hadn't bothered to dry herself, as was evident by the wet footprints on the floor.

The greenhouse had a way of taking care of itself. I had no doubt that whatever magic protected the place would keep any stray moisture for the plants while keeping the books bone dry.

"Sibby," I took a step closer.

She lifted her chin, her blue eyes, the same shade as mine and Maeve's, filled with determination. It wasn't a look I usually saw from her. Stubborn and contrary for the sake of it, yes. But not determined.

"I can do this. We're in the convergence. So don't tell me it isn't safe."

"It *isn't* safe."

She glared at me. "You don't listen very well."

"It's not safe for him." I reached out, intending to close the book but she body-blocked me. My hand fell to my side. "We don't know the first thing about healing witchcraft. It's a skill, just like regular medicine."

Her chin went up to that classic Siobhan stubborn angle. "Sebastian used magic to heal Maeve."

"Yes and he could have killed her." I didn't mean for the words to come out as a growl, but I was still pretty pissed about that.

Sibby turned her back and refocused on the book.

I moved to her side. "Listen to me. Even if you found something and we had everything here that we need, we're all exhausted. Maeve especially. Sebastian is strong. Give him a chance to come out of this on his own before we start dabbling with magic."

"It's my fault." The three words were said so quietly that I barely heard her whisper.

"What do you mean?"

She hung her head, making her hair towel droop. "I've been sleep traveling to him. Every night for months. He was staying in some fleabag motel. He must have waited for me to travel back here each night and then left to find a new hiding place. But I woke up. I stayed too long. He was hurt because of me."

I put my hand on her damp shoulder. "It isn't your fault. We didn't ask to be hunted."

She shook her head and was in immediate danger of losing the towel. "Neither did he."

My temper, never far from the surface, sparked. "Oh yeah? Did we ask him to betray his kind? To come after us in the first place? Don't go painting him as some sort of romantic hero, Sibby. He's an opportunistic dark fae bastard. We're lucky he didn't kill you."

"He won't hurt me. I know that. In here." She thumped her balled fist over her heart.

"He's *already* hurt you. He lied to you."

"He didn't tell me the whole truth. That's different from lying."

I stared at her. "He's a frigging magic hunter. Have you forgotten that little nugget?" It was a low blow but I wasn't about to play forgive and forget with Sebastian just because he was incapacitated. "If not for the hard-on he's got for you he would have killed us all!"

"But he didn't. He protected us."

"Oh please."

Sibby stared up at me with what looked a lot like pity. "I'm not like you, Alys. I can't hold on to all the grudges and view everyone as a potential threat."

"I don't do that."

She leveled a look, her eyebrow ring glinting against the overhead lights.

"Okay well, I don't *always* do that. But when someone's out to get you, paranoia is just smart thinking. You make it sound like I don't trust anyone."

"You don't."

Stung, I took a step back as though I could put some distance between myself and her cutting remark. "That's not fair. I trust you and Maeve with my life. You know that."

"What about anybody else? What about Brock?"

"I trust him." With my business and with my heart. That was a much larger concession than I had ever made for anyone.

"Then why are you still sneaking him in here like a dirty little secret every night?"

I put my hands up. "I don't want to fight with you."

"Which is what you always say when you're about to lose an argument."

I huffed out a breath and turned to look out the window. The sun was just rising over the lake, making the still surface glisten like a perfectly clean window. What could I say to her that wouldn't result in more bickering? In the past, I'd always walked away from Sibby. She pushed too hard for things I wasn't ready or able to deal with. But she was hurting. Guilt-ridden because her actions had hurt someone she cared about.

It was an emotional whip that drove her down here before she could get dry or dressed. Picking a fight with me was just another way for her to delay dealing with her feelings.

Braced for round two, I turned back and saw her hands splayed on the table. The towel that had been draped over her hair was now pooled on the floor and her shoulders shook as her body trembled with emotion.

I grabbed her to me and held on as she began to cry. "It's not your fault. Siobhan Eloise Silver, do you hear me? You didn't do anything wrong."

She clung to me and sobbed without sound. It was an eerie experience. Sibby was loud and vibrant in almost every aspect, but when it came to this outpouring of sadness and fear, she didn't make a peep.

I hated seeing her this way. Part of me wanted to blame Sebastian. Sibby was so different when he was around. He was hurt yet she was the one who seemed vulnerable. Breakable. It was as though being near him shredded her walls completely.

If she couldn't guard herself around him, I would have to do it for her. That's what big sisters were for.

Slowly, the body-jarring sobs eased and turned to the occasional sniffle. I released her long enough to scoop the forgotten towel up and hand it to her to dab her tear-stained face. "Better?"

She shrugged but there was a twitch at the corner of her lips. "Thanks."

Sibby was half a head shorter than me and half a head taller than Maeve. I studied the oddness that was her purple dye job while she continued to pull herself together. The side that she had been shaving was about six inches long now, though still almost a foot shorter than the other. She looked off-kilter and lopsided to me.

"Maybe you're right. I might have OCD."

She snorted. It was a watery sound. "What made you think of that?"

"Your hair." I reached out to either side, demonstrating the differences in lengths. "Before it was intentional. Now it just looks like someone played a mean prank on you at camp."

Another snort of laughter. "Maybe I should start shaving it again. I can draw witchy symbols on the shaved side. Or maybe one big old moon dyed yellow on the light side and blue-black on the dark. Then I'll have a twilight head."

"You're nuts," I told her.

"Speak for yourself." She let out a long sigh and then turned back to the book. "Just let me finish this one and I'll…."

I looked over her shoulder at the page that had caught her attention. The title along the top read *Shadow Work: Past Life Regression.*

"Sibby?" Whatever it was that caught her interest wasn't apparent.

"Do you remember Maeve telling us about that dream she had? That we all had lived before? We were dancing around a bonfire in some sort of ceremony?"

I did, though I hadn't given it much thought since. I could tell my youngest sister had, by the way, her fingertips skimmed across the page.

"Why do you think she saw that?" Sibby whispered as though afraid of the answer.

"Not a clue."

"It has to mean something," she insisted. "In the middle of everything we were going through she has this bizarre dream. She dreamed her memories. I wonder if it really was a past life."

"Considering I have enough trouble with my current life, I don't feel the need to go spelunking into the ones that are over."

She exhaled audibly and then shut the book. "You're probably right. I'm going to go get dressed and check on Sebastian."

I watched her retreat, an uneasy feeling in the pit of my stomach. In Sibby speak, *you're probably right* often translated to, *this isn't over.*

The throbbing in his skull dragged Sebastian out of sleep. He hoped he wouldn't vomit. The cell where he slept was small and the last time he'd been sick from a beating, the stench had permeated the space for a week.

He didn't dare open his eyes. Didn't move. Some sense told him he wasn't alone. Was it the queen come to see her handiwork? Or one of her perverse circle of courtiers wanting to laugh at the changeling's very human response to pain? Or worse…?

No. If he thought of that he *would* vomit.

The feel of his bedding was wrong. He lay upon something soft. No straw poked him in the back. And the air was warm and scented with green and growing things, not the icy chill of the palace that made his nostrils stick together when he breathed too deeply.

Where was he? Terror filled him at the thought that he had been deposited in one of the noble's chambers.

"Hey." A soft hand stroked his hair. "Sebastian? Can you hear me?"

That voice. He knew her. Mortal. Witch. *Siobhan.*

"Where?" The word came out as a croak. His memories were a jumble. The childhood he kept under lock and key seeping through the cracks to fog the present. He dared to blink open his eyes and hissed as the brilliant sunshine cooked part of his gray matter through his eyeballs. He rolled away from it. Vertigo made the bed spin.

"Our cottage." There was a rustling and then the sound of curtains being drawn.

"Sorry, I didn't think. You can open your eyes now."

Sebastian did. This time the room didn't tilt. With great care, he rolled back over.

"Can you sit up? You ought to drink some water."

She sat on the bed again, careful not to jostle him. Slowly, he eased himself into a sitting position. There was a glass in her hand. He reached for it. His fingers brushed hers as he took the glass.

She had no idea. Not a clue the level of trust it took for him to accept something from another living being. He

47

didn't eat in restaurants, never kept a supply of food lying around in case someone tainted it. With no natural immunity to the deadly fae poisons, he was always vulnerable.

The water slid down his throat cool and clean. He didn't disgrace himself by sicking it up.

"How long?" he croaked.

"Three days," Siobhan's blue eyes were filled with an emotion he didn't recognize. Was it…concern? Over him?

That couldn't be right. He'd lied to her. Hunted her and her sisters. She hated him.

She sniffed. "We didn't know whether to bring you to a hospital. What blood tests would say."

"They would say I am human."

She blinked. "But, your eyes? I thought….?"

He waited. Offered nothing. He wouldn't lie to her, but even if she had been tending him, centuries of distrust didn't just go away.

She trailed off and shook her head. "Never mind. It can wait. Do you think you can eat something? Alys made some tasteless soup earlier."

Sebastian was confused. "You've been caring for me?"

"Of course. You saved me from those magic hunters." Her eyes filled. "I'm so sorry I've been putting you at risk. All these months, every time I slept. Believe me, if I could have stopped it, I would have."

He heard the note of anguish in her voice. "I stayed ahead of them. Left as soon as you did."

She exhaled a shaky breath. "Which meant you were always on the run. I didn't mean to do it."

He knew that. But he wasn't sorry. Because he had lived for the moment when she had appeared beside him. Had known she was safe and whole. Then her earlier words registered. "Three days you said. That means Beltane is less than a week away."

She nodded.

He set the water glass down on the nightstand and then turned to her. "For both of our sakes, I am requesting sanctuary in the convergence until after you and your sisters are sanctioned by the council."

"Sanctuary?" One eyebrow, the one with the metal hoop, lifted.

"My magic is spent, Siobhan. Moving through the ley lines consumed the precious little that was left of it. If I leave and you travel to me again, I don't have the means to protect you."

"I…." she stalled, shook her head. "I need to talk to my sisters about it."

"Of course." He leaned back into the pillows and shut his eyes.

A moment later. "I'll let you get some rest."

He listened to her move to the door. Heard it click behind her. The witches would relent, for Siobhan's sake. Even with his head pounding and the threat circling, Sebastian smiled.

He had a handful of days of freedom. But for those days, he would get to be with Siobhan.

And after….

He wouldn't think about after. Some things were too cruel even for his twisted soul to endure.

6

SIOBHAN

"*H*e wants *what?*" Alys barked as the three of us congregated around the firepit. Coward that I was, I'd waited until Maeve had arrived to bring up Sebastian's request.

"Sanctuary. *Temporarily*," I emphasized the last word as I opened the wine.

"It does make sense. After all, he's just looking out for Sibby's welfare." Maeve paused in sipping her green smoothie. It looked like the product of a cow's digestive tract but Maeve and Kal were playing around with Maeve's diet to see what combinations of foods gave her the most energy. I kept my observations to myself.

"And his own skin. I'd feel safer to have a venomous snake under our roof." Alys glared at the charcuterie board as though the cured meat and cheese and olives had wronged her.

"You have somewhere else you can go," I snapped at her. "He doesn't."

"You want me to leave you alone with him?" Alys's eyes narrowed to blue slits. "Fat chance."

To keep from escalating into another bickering match, I reached for the plates I'd set on the low table between our chairs. I was starving. Alys's soup had tasted like dishwater. My sisters were amazing in so many ways, but their disinterest in food made me sad. Food was life. It was culture and harmony and all the good things in the world. I would try anything at least once and had consumed things that would probably blow their small-town minds.

Knowing that Sebastian wasn't going to die from his skull fracture had brought my appetite roaring back. Maeve had picked up the deli platter from the market in town. Too bad I didn't have any stone ground mustard or maybe a spicy jam. That would make the meats, cheeses, roasted nuts, and pickled vegetables pop.

"He's laid up," I told Alys after swallowing a mouthful of prosciutto. "It's just for a few days."

"Who knows what he's plotting?" Alys said. "We don't even know *what* he is. Having him stare at you like you're prime picking on the dessert cart does not make him a good guy, Sibby. Have you forgotten that he could have killed Maeve with his little stunt after the car accident?"

How many times was she going to bring that up? Knowing Alys, whenever it suited her purpose. Of course, I didn't want to just shrug that off as though it was inconsequential but I needed to diffuse my oldest sister before she went nuclear. Clouds were already gathering over the lake. Before I could decide how to respond, Maeve spoke up.

"I don't blame him." Her tone was quiet, even.

"*What?*" Alys whipped her head around as though Maeve had spoken in tongues.

"Well, I don't." She took a sip of her smoothie, wrinkled her nose, and then waved at me to pass the charcuterie board. "Look, I've thought about this. If I was going to die anyway, it would have been better that it happened right away instead of me hanging on for a week in the hospital and both of you being put at risk because of it."

Alys appeared nonplussed by her logic. I couldn't blame her. Maeve's matter-of-fact manner in discussing her possible death was a little unsettling.

"I was either going to get better…or I wasn't. Sebastian just sped things along. He's always looked out for Sibby's best interest."

"Are you kidding me? He's a *magic hunter*," Alys's nostrils flared. "He's sucked out witches' souls and used their magic to trap other witches. Witches like us who didn't have a clue about the danger."

"I'm not saying he's some sort of white knight." I spoke slowly, trying to dislodge the image of Death on his pale horse from my mind. "Believe me, I still don't trust him."

"And don't forget about Maeve's vision," Alys knocked back the rest of her wine, a sweet muscadine that I had given her for Christmas. "Even in a past life, he was a dark fae. According to Brock, that means he doesn't have magic of his own so he *steals* it."

"Believe me when I say this, Alys. I haven't forgotten any of it." My thoughts wandered back to the shadow work spell I'd found in the book.

She got up and began to pace around the fire. "It has to mean something. We were all there. Us and Brock and Kal. You're sure it was Sebastian, right Maeve?"

Her head bobbed. "It was definitely him."

"But who was the other man?" I asked. "The one that you said was trying to dance with me?"

"No one I recognized." Maeve set the empty board back on the table and then leaned against the back of her chair. "It was a warning. Like a cautionary tale of some kind. It felt important but I don't know what the message was. I think…I think maybe there was more to it but I woke up and got pulled out of it."

"Maybe it wasn't a message for you." The words slipped out before I'd thought them through.

Alys stopped pacing and pivoted to face me. "What do you mean?"

"You were with Brock, just like you are now. Maeve is with Kal, just like she was then. You two are in tune. Settled with your mates. But I...." I shook my head. "I think Maeve's vision was a message meant for me. That there's something I need to know about that life. Something important."

"You think it's about... you know." Maeve's gaze flicked down to my crotch, and color rose in her cheeks.

"About my vag of doom, you mean?"

"Don't be crude," Alys muttered without heat. She sank back into her chair and refilled her wineglass.

"It could be. I want to do the shadow work spell for past lives. To find out."

"Fine. After Beltane, when we're sanctioned." Alys said.

"When it's safe you mean," I grunted. "No problem, it's not like it's *your* curse."

"Even if it were, I wouldn't risk it. Not when we're so close to being safe."

I folded my arms over my chest. "Fine then. I'll wait if you agree to let Sebastian stay."

She glared at me. "That's blackmail."

"No, that's life. You need to give something to get something, Alys."

"It's only a few more days," Maeve patted Alys's arm. "I really do think Sibby will be safe with him."

"Fine. But I am going to be here the whole time."

I frowned at her. "What about your job?"

"I can afford to take a little time off."

Maeve and I stared at her, both open-mouthed.

"What?" she sounded defensive.

"You never take time off," Maeve pointed out. "Not for holidays or sick time. None of it."

"I took time off when we went to the Amazon."

"That was hardly a vacation," I said.

"Part of the joy of being your own boss." She twirled her glass before her, watching the firelight through the rose-colored liquid. "I take the time I want for the reasons I want and don't have to explain a damn thing to anybody. And I want some answers from him. You are not to go back in there unless I'm satisfied."

I started humming the Stones *I Can't Get No Satisfaction* and she growled at me.

"What? It's kinda my theme song." I was doing my level best to make light of it because the truth was, I was scared. My sister had seen me cry over Sebastian. That alone put his life in jeopardy.

"Is it safe to wake him up?" Alys knocked back the rest of her wine, her gaze on Maeve. "I want to do this tonight before Sibby pops up in his bed again."

Maeve sat forward. "Yeah. I think so. Want me to come with you?"

Alys cracked her knuckles. "I need to do this alone."

We watched her disappear inside.

"Why didn't you stop her?" I hissed to Maeve

She sipped at her smoothie, made a face, and set it back down. "Do you really think I could have?"

Point taken.

Maeve's gaze was intent on my face. "Sibby, what happened to you in Peru?"

My heart hammered in my chest. "You were there. You know it all."

"I'm not talking about our trip there. I think you know what I mean." She offered me a reassuring smile. "You were jumpy, on edge. You had that money. Don't tell me you hadn't been there before."

I wouldn't lie to her.

"You never mentioned it to me," Maeve said. "That must have been the first year after you left Eckhart. You were probably nineteen."

"Leave it alone, Maeve."

One eyebrow went up. "Like the way you leave me alone when I'm pushing myself too hard?"

"My secrets are in the past, not the present."

"Can you look me in the eye and tell me that whatever it was that happened to you there isn't having an effect on you now?"

I swallowed past the lump in my throat. *Just say the words.* But I couldn't.

"Can you at least promise me you'll talk to me when you're ready?" she asked.

I cleared my throat. "Sure."

Maeve searched my face as though she didn't believe me. I couldn't hold her gaze so I stared out over the lake.

I felt more than saw Maeve turn and look over her shoulder at the cottage. "At least there's no lightning raining down. That's a good sign, right?"

"Unless she decided to give him some pillow therapy." I meant it as a joke but neither of us laughed. Our eyes met and as one we lunged for the house.

Alys

*S*ebastian was asleep when I walked into the room that had belonged to our mother. I hated seeing him there. In her bed. As though his very presence befouled the space. Sullied her memory.

I stepped inside, the first time I'd crossed the threshold of this particular room since she'd died. I tried not to let it distract me from my task as I shut and locked the door. Turning, I ignored the bed and moved to the armchair that sat in front of a standing lamp.

He was our enemy. It didn't matter what Sibby said, or what he had done that had worked out in our favor. We had been his targets and he only changed sides because he wanted something from my sister.

"She deserves better than you," I muttered.

"She'll have it."

I stared as his head turned on the pillow. Our gazes locked. Those creepy amethyst eyes glowed in the dim room but I refused to back down.

I was the first to break the silence. "Sibby said you requested sanctuary."

He tried to nod and winced as though the motion hurt him. "For her sake as well as mine. As long as I remain in the convergence, she won't need to travel to me."

"Maybe I should just kill you now." My tone was easy as though I were weighing all of my options.

Sebastian said nothing. There was no sign of fear on his face. His expression remained blank.

"What would you do in my place?" I asked.

"If I were you, I would have let the threat die." He struggled upright. "It's more difficult now because I survived."

"Then we understand each other. You are scum."

"No, Alys. Your ex-husband is scum."

I jerked. He wasn't wrong. Kyle was a spineless bottom-feeder. "So why did you take on his case?"

"To get close to you and your sisters. Why don't you ask me what you really want to know?" His eyes glowed brighter.

I held my breath. The divorce had been too easy, especially after the way it had started. I hadn't drawn a deep breath until the papers had arrived, signed and sealed. "Do you know what happened to Kyle?"

"I do. He's been enthralled by my fae essence. He will serve in the fae court for a year and a day until the magic wears off. I made sure he signed your divorce papers promptly."

I shook my head. "Why?"

"Because he was making too much trouble for me here."

"So noble of you." I leaned in close. "You use people until they no longer serve your purpose. You disgust me, magic hunter."

Those eyes flashed with temper. "Hate me if you choose. You're not the first and undoubtedly won't be the last. But magic hunters are necessary to the continued existence of all magic users."

I snorted. "Is that how you sleep at night? You tell yourself that you're performing a necessary service? That killing innocent people is important?"

"Not killing. Depleting. And it *is* essential."

I opened my mouth to respond but he wasn't done. "Consider what would happen if there were no magic hunters. If every energy worker and witch could roam freely without consequences. In the age of information, widespread technology, and the global internet. The human backlash against the supernatural community would make the witch trials look like a garden party. Hate the player, Alys, but do not hate the game. Because it's one of survival."

The doorknob rattled and then someone began hammering on the wood. "Alys?"

Sibby sounded desperate. What did she think I was doing to the bastard anyway?

Sebastian struggled upright as if just having Sibby closer gave him strength. "You told me once that you don't like me. And you don't need to. I no longer pose a threat to you. My magic is depleted and I am being hunted as well for abandoning the guild. As soon as you and your sisters are sanctioned, I vow I will turn myself into the council of elders and accept my punishment. We want the same thing, Alys. To protect Siobhan. Please let me do that much."

I tipped my head. "Brock told me dark fae can lie. Give me one reason why I should believe you."

"Because," Sebastian said quietly. "It's more dangerous for Siobhan to send me away."

The pounding ceased and a moment later, Sibby had traveled inside the room.

"He can stay until Beltane," I growled and then stalked to the door, turned the key, and exited past a startled Maeve.

I didn't have to like it. Or him. But the bastard was right. Sibby's safety mattered more than my anger. And even though I still didn't trust him, it wasn't up to me.

●

Siobhan

*M*y breathing was uneven as I watched Alys storm from the room. "I thought that she was killing you in your sleep."

"I'm certain she thought about it."

I moved closer to the bed and studied Sebastian's

complexion. He looked better than he had earlier. The green tinge had left his skin. "How's your head?"

"It hurts, but given time it will mend." His gaze was fixed on me as I moved closer.

"Can I get you anything? Are you hungry?"

"No."

"You're not really a foodie are you?" The clues had all been there. The lack of groceries in his refrigerator, the pizza he left untouched at the restaurant. Had I ever seen him eat?

"Food was used as a punishment during my youth. Another way for the fae queen to torment me. Sometimes the court would add poison to my meals. I have learned only to eat when the hunger grows overwhelming and never show that need to another."

My brows drew together. "That's awful."

His lids lowered. "I survived."

I said nothing for a minute, just studied the smudge of shadows under his eyes. It was hard to reconcile him with the being of blazing glory that had rescued me from the Headhunter. Without thought, my hand went to the underside of my arm where the other magic hunter had impaled me with shards of bone.

"Let me see them," Sebastian murmured.

I moved forward and held out my arm. Sebastian traced the marks lightly, sending a cascade of goosebumps along my skin.

"I never thanked you," I breathed. "For saving me."

"I'm sorry I didn't get free sooner," he dropped his hand and his eyes held mine. "That you had to endure it at all."

"You've done worse though," I held his stare and hardened my heart. "Haven't you?"

"You don't become the best magic hunter in the guild by being a nice guy, Siobhan."

A strange sensation threaded through me. Pride at his

words. Sebastian was still a mystery in most ways. I knew so little about him and the things I did comprehend were horrific.

"What exactly is a dark fae?" I asked him. "And why are you all magic hunters?"

"A dark fae is a fae born without the magic to make bargains. We have no power of our own, though our souls can hold it, same as yours. We are helpless unless we siphon soul magic from others."

"So that's why you became a magic hunter?" My tone held a note of hope that I couldn't hide. "To protect yourself?"

"I became a magic hunter to earn respect." His full sensual lips compressed into a tight line.

I leaned in close, ignoring his pique. "I think you're lying. If not to me then to yourself. There have been times when I've been in danger." I tapped my arm to indicate the scars.

"That's not the same as—"

Cutting him off I continued, "Going to sleep afraid. Waking up afraid. Remembering what was done. Imagining what else could be done. Jumping at shadows. I know, Sebastian."

That gaze glowed brighter, searching my face. There was fear in his eyes but hope too.

"I would do anything if it meant I never felt that way again. *Anything*. So tell yourself that it was for prestige and respect all you want. But I know the truth." I rose from the bed. "I'll be right next door. Call out if you need anything."

I exited the room before he could ask for more than I was able to give. My shadows were riding me too hard to say more.

7

SIOBHAN

I paused at the door to Sebastian's room. Funny how fast it had gone from being mom's room to his in my mind. The sun streamed in from the open window in my bedroom, indicating it was after eight, but there was no sound from the other side of the door.

Maeve had reassured me that he was going to be fine. He was alert and talking with no signs of memory loss. That was a good thing. He was also watchful, those amethyst eyes always assessing. My worry over him had kept me focused on his recovery. But now that he was on the mend, all the bad shit between us resurfaced like a leaky septic system.

The lies. The danger he'd put the three of us in by not telling us the truth. Of course, if he had way back in the beginning when we were so freaked out by just the thought of a magic hunter, we might have killed him. Hell, Maeve had taken the three of us out to learn how to fire a gun so we had a way to protect ourselves without magic. Could I really blame him for keeping his true nature on the down-low?

Troubled by this new line of thought, I didn't hear the bathroom door. And there he was, naked other than the small powder pink towel wrapped around his waist. The girly color provided a striking contrast to his cut abs. His chest was all smooth skin covering bulging muscle. No hair other than on his head. Was that a fae thing?

My pulse pounded in my ears. Damn it, I was a sucker for a fit male body.

"Siobhan?" He put his hands on my shoulders. The loosely knotted towel was all that stood between his naked body and my probing gaze. And by the way, the wet terrycloth drooped, gravity was doing its best to help a sister out.

"Are you all right, *Annwyl*?"

Annwyl. The one I cherish. The endearment snapped me out of the lusty fog.

I moved away from him, putting a decent distance between our bodies and trying not to miss the heat that radiated off of him in waves. "You shouldn't be out of bed. And don't call me that."

"You wanted the truth from me. And I do cherish you. As to the other matter, I am healed." He reached behind his head, probably to touch the bald patch.

"I didn't do that," I blurted. "Shave your head, I mean."

"Oh?" The smug bastard shouldn't look that amused. "Why not?"

"My hands were shaking. I was worried I would make things worse. Alys had to do it."

I couldn't tell if the idea of my sister holding a sharp object to the back of his unconscious head unnerved him. It should. "You need to be careful while you're here. She's not happy."

"Is she ever?"

I stood up straighter. I may pitch Alys a rash of shit whenever the mood struck but that was because she was my big sister. "What the hell is that supposed to mean?"

"Only that unlike you, joy isn't your sister's natural state."

He shrugged, letting his hand fall back to his side. "I, more than most, understand the depth of her power. And of yours. The three of you will be a great addition to the magical community."

I couldn't tell if he was being sincere or sarcastic. And that was the worst bit. Sebastian had managed to hide a huge part of his identity from me. With him, I couldn't trust my instincts. I wanted to believe him too badly.

That stupid tarot reading popped back into my head. The Fool card. Trusting my judgment was harder than it sounded.

"You better get dressed." I cleared my throat. "There are some clothes and shoes in a bag in the closet."

"I can't wear another's possessions."

Why? I bit off the question. Half of my shopping was done in thrift stores. Was the dark fae too good for hand-me-downs?

"They're yours. I popped into your apartment and packed a bag."

"You did what?" Before I knew what he was doing, Sebastian had gripped me by the arms and shook me hard enough that my teeth clacked together. "Siobhan, you mustn't go there. Not there, or my former house in Eckhart. It isn't safe."

"I was quick. Less than ten minutes. They couldn't have tracked me."

"They could have been lying in wait!"

"It was only—"

"No, not for any reason." His amethyst eyes glowed brighter. "Vow you will never do so again."

God, he was fierce. And practically naked. My pulse picked up and I was aware of how close our bodies were. How much I loved his touch. Strong, firm, yet still tender.

Lust blazed through me. I wanted to touch him. To rip

that towel off and explore his body with my hands. With my mouth.

"Let her go," Alys snarled.

Peeking around Sebastian's shoulder I spied my sister. Blue white energy crackled in her fingertips and her normally neat bob stood up as though electrical current was passing through every strand.

With another shock, it dawned on me that was exactly what was happening. When had she learned to do that?

Sebastian didn't turn a hair, his gaze fixed on my face. "I will have your sister's vow on this, witch. You can't release your magic without harming her."

The look in his eyes. I saw it then. The magic hunter capable of stealing a soul. He knew our powers better than we did and had used familial ties as leverage before.

My stomach acid churned even as I craved his touch. If I'd eaten I would have vomited on the spot. Damn it I had known what he was but it hadn't mattered before. He was a killer. A soul stealer. I'd kissed him more times than I could count and conveniently forgotten that.

But I couldn't afford to keep putting it aside. Because using his past as wedge to pry us apart might be the only thing that would keep him safe.

If I let my hormones rule the day...

The thought made me sick.

I lifted my chin and stared him in the eyes and lied. "I vow I will never set foot inside any of your previous addresses again. In fact, I vow that I'm done helping you in any way at all. You disgust me."

His hands fell away and I immediately slid past him and headed for the stairs.

"Siobhan."

"Fuck off, Sebastian," I called and headed out the door, pausing only long enough to scoop up the keys for my motorcycle. Alys would grill him like a steak and he wouldn't follow me.

It was safter that way.

●

Sebastian stood frozen. The look on her face. He didn't know what had occurred in that complicated mind of hers but whatever it was, he'd seen it there. The same expression he'd seen on countless faces over his long life.

Hatred.

"Looks like you just pissed off your only advocate," Alys said. "In fact, I don't think she would even be all that upset if I roasted your nuts over an open flame."

"Bring it on, witch." Sebastian squared his shoulders and looked down his nose at her. "I've endured more torture than your small mortal mind could ever envision."

She stared at him a long moment, her gaze assessing. To his surprise, the crackle of energy faded away and her hands fell to her sides. "Meet me downstairs in five minutes. I have questions for you."

He watched her straight-back stance march away. She had the advantage, so why would she back down?

Sebastian headed into the room and shut the door. The clothing Siobhan had mentioned was in a powder blue nylon duffel bag that he'd never seen before. It must be hers.

He opened it and found two pairs of jeans, three black t-shirts, two white ones, socks, sneakers, and boots. His toothbrush, comb, and razor were packed in individual Ziplock bags. His leather duster was hung carefully on a lone coat hanger.

A week's worth of clothing, packed carefully by her hand. Sebastian had had a few lovers. None had ever done such a thing for him before. Considered his needs and went out of her way to meet them, especially at great personal risk to herself.

The thought of the magic hunters lying in wait for him and catching her while he lay unconscious brought the icy fear he'd suppressed rushing back to the foreground. And on its heels, a tidal wave of scalding hot temper.

He dressed quickly and then stormed downstairs to where Alys sat at the dining room table. She sipped from an oversized mug with the logo *Silver Demo and Design*.

"How could you allow her to go to my apartment?" Sebastian raged. "After what happened?"

Alys tilted her head as though she were a bird eyeing a particularly juicy worm. "Have you *met* Siobhan?"

Was she jesting? "Of course."

"Because anyone who has ever met her knows within the first five minutes that no one allows Siobhan Silver to do anything. She does what she wants, whenever the mood strikes. And to hell with the consequences."

"But it was dangerous. And pointless." To risk her life over a few articles of clothing?

"We were discussing your situation. Brock told us that a dark fae won't wear anyone else's clothes. Is that true?"

Sebastian gave a reluctant nod. "Did he tell you why?"

"Something to do with the energy field attached to clothing messing with your *stolen* magic." Her lips pursed. "Sibby was there and back before we knew what she intended to do."

Sebastian sat down hard. His eyes slid shut and he felt the urge to bang his head against the table. "Is there no stopping her?"

"She made you a promise. Sibby doesn't make those lightly. That's not to say that she won't do something else to make you crazy. Just not that."

He gave her a dark look.

Alys got up and retrieved a second mug, filled it with coffee, and then set it in front of him. When he glanced up at her, she was considering him very carefully. "I don't know if your being in love with my sister makes you more or less dangerous."

He stared down at the coffee. "I never said I loved her."

"You don't have to. You're ridiculous for her. The same way Kal is with Maeve." After refilling her own mug, Alys sat down across from him and waited.

He took a sip. The coffee was strong and bold, not unlike the woman who had made it. Or her sister. He'd known from the beginning that these witches would be the death of him. He hadn't envisioned aligning with them though. Or sharing coffee with them.

Somehow, he doubted Alys was the sort of woman who would resort to poison. If she wanted him dead, she would use her hands.

He finished the mug and then folded his hands and waited for her questions to begin.

"How old are you?"

That surprised him. "Two hundred and thirty-seven."

Alys stared at him for a beat.

"What?"

"And here you don't look a day over two hundred and twenty-five." She shook her head. "How long have you been a magic-hunter?"

"Since I reached my majority. When I turned eighteen."

"And how many…targets do you go after in a year?"

"Depends. As the population expands more of the unsanctioned crop up. Ten to twenty in an average year."

She blew out a long breath. "That's a lot of dead witches."

"And how many would survive if the unsanctioned were to reveal magic to mankind? How many innocents would be accused of wrongdoing and punished as was done in your witch trials?"

Alys was shaking her head. "What does being sanctioned have to do with magical misconduct?"

"Everything. A sanctioned witch binds a piece of their soul to the collective and takes an oath never to use magic in a way that can put the rest of the community at risk. The oath anchors the bit of soul to the magical network and forms what we call ley lines. Even after your mortal life ends, a piece of you lives on within the network."

Alys got to her feet and then turned to stare at the greenhouse. "How come no one told us this?"

"It's forbidden to tell the unsanctioned more about magic. You'll find all this out once your petition to join the collective is accepted."

"Why does the council of elders only meet twice a year?"

"That I don't know." When she shot him a disbelieving look he added in an exasperated tone, "I'm a cog in the system. I didn't design the damn thing."

She considered that and then asked. "You said it's forbidden to teach the unsanctioned. Yet you told me about it. Why?"

Sebastian gave her a droll stare. "Regardless of how many rules I break, they can only punish me once."

8

MAEVE

"*A*dam Sandler?" I asked Kal as we strolled arm in arm through the park. It was a gorgeous spring day. The kind when the intense Carolina sun warmed you to the bone and a breeze kept the humidity from making your hair stick to the back of your neck. Perfect mountain weather. I wore a loose dress and the hemline flapped lightly around my calves. I carried the wicker picnic basket Kal had packed and was happy to just be out with my family.

Bella and Philip were on their bikes, circling us on the paved walking trail like eager little sharks. They would ride ahead until Kal or I called out to them and then turn back to find out what was taking their parents so long before speeding off again.

"Alive. Though the internet sometimes likes to claim otherwise. Bill Paxton?"

We were playing the celebrity alive, alive, dead game. It was something we had started after my casual remark that you couldn't turn on the computer without seeing the death notice of some famous face. Half of them were scams on social media and it was difficult for my MS fatigued brain to keep track. Kal had admitted that he couldn't either though so sometimes we quizzed each other with random names.

No doubt about it, we were going to hell. But as Kal liked to point out, at least we'd be together.

I thought about it for a minute. "Hmm, I'm not sure. I always get him confused with that other non-descript middle-aged white guy. Oh, what's his name...?

"Bill Pullman. Or Tim Robbins?"

"Dead, alive, alive," I said, though I wasn't sure. "Oh. Oh. That guy. He was in that movie with the thing?"

"Dead." Kal was stone-faced.

I paused to glare up at him. "You have no idea who I'm even talking about."

His lips twitched. "How could I miss it when you are so specific?"

The corgis yanked on the leashes, eager to catch up to the kids. They made this odd high-pitched whimpering noise whenever the twins rode bikes. Kids on wheels was definitely not a corgi favorite. Bella and Philip rode around the town green, circling a woman pushing a stroller.

"Guys!" Kal called and pointed to a spot. "Over here." He led me to a battered picnic table that sat in the shade of a sprawling live oak.

I glared at it dubiously. "I'll have splinters in my ass if I sit on that."

"I'll pull them out."

I gave him a dirty look and he dropped a quick kiss on my forehead. "Promise."

Gingerly, I smoothed the back of my skirt and then lowered myself onto the bench. Once secure I set the basket on the table. "Next time bring a blanket."

"Yes, ma'am. I'll go corral the kids if you take the wee beasties." Kal handed me Gimli and Grogu's leashes.

The dogs tugged but with me seated they might as well

have been tethered to an anchor. "Picnicking in the park would probably be more enjoyable without these two yapping at every squirrel they see."

"Where's the fun in that?" Kal winked and then headed off.

I smiled to myself. He was just as attached to the badly behaved critters as me.

From my position, I could see the sun reflecting off the windows of *Silver Demo and Design*. It was my lunch break and one of those random off days for the school so Kal had decided we should have a picnic. All my witchy problems, work snafus, and health issues were a million miles away. I closed my eyes and turned my face up to the sun.

"Maeve?"

My peace evaporated at the sound of that voice. Missy freaking Hargraves. Of freaking course.

I opened my eyes and pasted on a smile for Missy. Her bottle-blond hair was cut in a long bob that reached her shoulders and she wore a blue V-neck and pearls paired with designer ripped mom jeans.

Mom jeans. High-waisted pants that ended at the ankle bone and gave the wearer a flat ass. Even my plus-size booty. There was a look that should have stayed buried in the past. Instead, they came screaming back with strategically distressed ventilation as though the wearer couldn't afford undamaged pants. With pearls. Unironically.

Missy wouldn't know irony if it bit her on her flat ass.

Shit, were those bitter old lady thoughts? If so, well, then okay. I would own my inner curmudgeon.

"We've missed you at soccer," Missy said. "And Philip of course."

My smile turned brittle. She hadn't missed me. What she missed was having another minion to do her bidding. Missy was married to Dale Hargraves, who coached soccer at the local park and she treated the other parents like we were her toadies. It was all bake-sale this and fundraiser that.

"We've been otherwise occupied," I said. I hated that I felt the need to explain anything to Missy freaking Hargraves. Philip hated soccer, mostly because on the rare occasion when the coach did let him play, he sort of sucked and the other kids made fun of him. The other parents too. One time he had accidentally kicked the ball towards his team's goal instead of down the field. I'd overheard the women sitting in front of me muttering about him not knowing which team he was playing for.

The jury was back. People sucked.

"I heard." Uninvited, Missy sat on the bench beside me. "MS. You poor thing."

"Well, yes," I said as I tugged on the leashes. The corgis had found a wet patch beneath the shade of the oak and were chest deep in what I hoped was mud.

"You look great though. Everyone is saying it. You don't even look sick."

I felt a little sick at that. Everyone? I knew gossip had spread. Gossip was currency in our small town. But to hear that my chronic illness was being discussed in my parental social circles was different. Parents I was going to have to look in the eye any time the schools had an event were talking about me. Saying things like *Poor Maeve. At least she doesn't look sick.*

I opened my mouth but before I could find any sort of reply someone else beat me to it.

"Then she must be faking it."

I jerked my head around in time to see Sibby dressed in her motorcycle duds, a helmet under one arm.

Missy's hands took off like they were startled birds, all fluttering in her haste to explain. "I didn't mean…I was just saying…"

"That Maeve looks great. She does. My sister is a class act." Sibby thunked her helmet down on the table. "Nice of you to stop by, Muffy."

"It's Missy," Missy stood right as Gimli decided that it would be fun to pop a wheelie and land on her lap. I tugged but it was too late. Her designer mom jeans were covered in the same muck that coated the corgi's fur.

Missy let out a dismayed cry. "Look what your dog did!"

"Oh sorry," I said. "I'd be happy to pay for the pants."

"Maybe next time you can find some that don't have holes," Sibby added.

Missy's jaw dropped and she whirled away.

"You are my hero," I said to my baby sister.

"I had help." Sibby scratched Gimli behind his pointed ear. "These things are growing on me."

She winked and then slid the picnic basket over to peer into its depths.

"Oh, oatmeal raisin cookies, my favorite."

"You can have mine," I said. "After that performance you deserve them."

"You know she was all of two seconds away from telling you that you are an inspiration and inviting you to be the guest of honor at some fundraiser or something." Sibby raised her pierced brow.

"Either that or she would offer to set up an MS walk in my honor." I let out a sigh. "It's just like when we were kids. We were the weird girls who lived out by the lake and didn't have a TV. No one knew what to make of us. I never wanted that for Bella and Philip."

Sibby put her hand over mine. "Did you ever think your fight to fit in and be normal isn't actually worth it? I mean we survived. Hell, even made some friends along the way."

"I know. Bella and Phillip are happy. They have everything they need and plenty of what they want, too." I blew

73

out a breath and then squared my shoulders, determined not to let Missy Hargraves ruin my afternoon. "So, what are you doing here? You haven't left the cottage since...."

"Since Sebastian. I know." Sibby jabbed her fingernail into the top of the picnic table. "He's awake now. And I...needed some space."

Which meant she was running. That's what Sibby did when things got uncomfortable. She'd first taken off after Aunt Jess was diagnosed with ovarian cancer. She'd stayed away for years, only coming back for the funeral and our weddings. I'd always thought that Sibby didn't like Eckhart, but over the past few months, I'd begun to realize that she did. She just didn't want to compromise who she was to live here.

She'd begun to settle in for good. And then Sebastian returned.

I spied Kal and the kids on their way back to us. "Do you want to talk about it? We can go back to my house and—"

But she was already on her feet. "No, I don't want to spoil your outing. I was thinking I would head over to the new project house. Maybe take some measurements? Do you have the code?"

I took out my phone and texted it to her. "Okay. I'll meet you back at the office in a bit."

Sibby's smile was tight. "Make sure Kal bathes those dogs. They smell like an open sewer."

I watched her walk away and hoped she was right. I didn't like that scared look in her eyes. Sibby wasn't fearless.

Now if only she'd realize that.

●

Siobhan

*T*he old hunting cabin sat on a rocky outcropping nestled between towering pines about twenty miles from downtown Eckhart. The road leading up to the place was long, winding, and full of switchbacks. Perfect for a motorcycle ride. Less ideal for construction vehicles. I had faith that Alys and Maeve had thought that through before buying the place. They knew their business and would make accommodations for any challenges.

The hum of my Ducati Monster drowned out the thoughts in my head. There was nothing like being on the open road with this sort of power and speed at my command. Riding it was one of the few times I actually felt fully in charge of my destiny. I had a sudden urge to pass the drive that led to the cabin. To keep going. It was strong but not overpowering.

Besides, I would just wind up back at the cottage when I fell asleep. Probably in Sebastian's bed.

I slowed and then set my feet down and rolled to a stop in front of the project house. The view from the outcropping was killer but the house itself was a wreck. The roof sagged and the porch listed to one side. Alys had said it had been abandoned for years. The previous owner had been a part-timer, using the place as a vacation spot. After his wife died, he hadn't had the will to maintain it. But seeing as it had been in his family for years, hadn't wanted to sell it to just anyone. Alys had convinced him that Silver Demo and Design would work hard to restore the cabin to its former glory.

She had her work cut out for her.

Stowing my helmet in my saddle pouch, I took the tape measure from the bag along with my phone. I had only been up here once, before the closing and hadn't been inside. I wanted to get a feel for the place and maybe give Maeve a few ideas and snap a few before shots for the website and Instagram.

I paused with a hand on the doorknob. All the small hairs were standing on the back of my neck. Maybe coming all the way out here by myself wasn't the best idea. I'd acted on impulse, first by needing to get away from Sebastian and then determined to do something useful. Alys was missing work because I'd lobbied for the magic hunter to stay with us. I didn't like how guilty that made me feel, especially when my feelings regarding the dark fae were so scattered.

I craved him. I was afraid for him.

That stupid tarot reading popped back into my head. The Queen of Cups crossed by the Magician reversed. Scattered, confused, frustrated.

That summed up our relationship.

It was only a few days more. Less than a week and we would be sanctioned, magical practitioners. No more being hunted. And as for me drifting to wherever Sebastian was....

Well, I'd figure that out too. There was the shadow work spell to consider. Maybe if I knew what had caused the curse I could figure out a way to break free of it.

Squaring my shoulders, I marched into the cabin. The interior was dark, the windows too small and facing north so there was no direct sunlight on the faded wood floors. The place smelled damp and musty and a bit like a dead mouse.

I'd stayed in worse.

The old woman's rented room in Peru flashed in my mind. I staggered a step and braced myself on the rough-hewn wood. No. I was not going to think about that now. Not now. Not ever again.

Shoving the darkness away, I refocused on the task at hand. Measurements. Alys had taken general ones of the entire floorplan. I was after more specific dimensions so we could plot the design. The kitchen wasn't much more than a galley pass thru with only a few rickety open shelves for storage. Knowing Maeve's pragmatic streak, she would gut the thing and create a pantry. The problem was there wasn't anywhere to steal the space from except….

I headed into the kitchen and eyeballed the outside through the warped pane of glass. Maybe we would need to expand this side of the house out farther over the outcropping. If that was even possible.

My heavy motorcycle boots thunked against the dusty boards as I checked out the rest of the space. A teeny tiny bathroom that wouldn't have been out of place in an RV and an equally mouse-sized bedroom that, oddly enough, didn't smell like a mouse. Someone had tacked down a piece of indoor-outdoor carpeting, the only protection from icy floors during a frozen mountain winter.

So, dark, dank living spaces. Only one bedroom and one minuscule bath. I tried to imagine the person who would buy this place. Would it be a full-time resident or a part-timer who needed to escape? Certainly not a family with more than one child. A couple. With a dog. Not ridiculous dogs like Maeve's but a big yellow lab. Or Golden Retriever.

It was a love nest. A place where two people could go to reconnect with nature and one another.

A picture of me and Sebastian and a big goofy dog popped into my mind. I shoved it down and mentally stomped on it for good measure.

There would be no nesting, no lovemaking. I was cursed and he was a bastard. More than a bastard. A bastard and a half. No, a bastard and three quarters. Almost two full bastards.

The dark alley... There had been two of them….

"No," I shouted and clapped my hands over my ears as

though I could somehow physically block the memory before it swamped me.

I was in Eckart. In a cabin. Not in that alley where those men had grabbed me and ....

My adrenaline spiked and before I knew it, I had traveled.

Back to where I felt safe. To the cabin. And into Sebastian's bed.

●

Sebastian heard a sound coming from the room where he'd been staying. He leapt to his feet and charged up the stairs, ignoring the residual throbbing in his head.

Alys was right behind him. "You have no magic. Let me go first."

"It's Siobhan."

"Are you sure?"

"Yes." He would recognize that cry of distress anywhere. It haunted his dreams, the sounds that she made when the Headhunter had tortured her.

He hit the top step, barely pausing to peer at the spirit of the cottage who drifted just outside the door.

Siobhan was curled on his bed in a fetal position, her hands covering her ears and tears streaming from her blue eyes.

Sebastian froze and Alys barreled past him. "Sibby? What happened? Sibby?"

"She was bewitched," the ghost said from behind them. "Cursed to relive the worst thing that ever happened to her. I can feel the magic still on her."

"Ethan?" Alys turned but it was obvious from the way her gaze moved over the empty room that she couldn't see the ghost, even if she could hear him.

"Bewitched by who? And how?" Sebastian asked the phantom.

"I don't know," Ethan murmured. His gaze was full of sorrow. "I can't leave the lines, so I can't follow her."

"Sibby?" Alys shook her sister's shoulder. "Can you hear me?"

Siobhan's eyes squinched shut and her whole body trembled.

"What can we do?" Alys looked up at him, her own blue eyes full of worry. "How can we help her?"

He let out a breath. "Memory charms are tricky. Once the spell is enacted, the mind powers the vision, and the victim relives the event in her mind. It's a sort of punishment magic wielders will use on violent criminals."

"But why would someone do this to Sibby?" Alys cried. "She's never hurt, anyone."

He put a hand on her shoulder. "Call Maeve. Have her come here. Perhaps the two of you will be enough to bring her out of it."

Alys gave him a desperate look. "My phone's downstairs."

"I'll stay with her," Sebastian vowed. "I'll keep her safe."

Alys swallowed and then hurried from the room.

"You didn't tell her all of it," Ethan murmured.

He picked up her cold hand and brought it to his lips. "No."

Alys didn't need to know that sometimes the victims of such memory spells never recovered.

He slid onto the bed and pulled Siobhan until she was nestled into his chest.

She would come out of this. She had to.

Sebastian wouldn't give her another choice.

9

ALYS

"*T*hank chocolate," I murmured when Maeve and Kal pulled up into the driveway. "Where are the kids? And why are you all dressed up?"

Maeve wore a long paisley skirt paired with a sparkly top and a lightweight cardigan. Her hair was piled into loose ringlets on her head and she wore make-up. Kal too was dressed to the nines in a charcoal gray suit cut to fit his large frame.

Maeve gave me a funny look. "The closing dinner? We were on our way there when we got your call."

Mental forehead smack. We'd rescheduled the dinner after the crisis with Sebastian and it had slipped my mind. "I totally forgot about it. And it's too late to cancel."

"Then don't cancel." Maeve wobbled on her heels. Part of me wanted to snap at her that she shouldn't be wearing the foolish things and putting herself more at risk.

"You have a lot going on. People will understand." Kal offered his arm to escort Maeve up the steps, preventing me from bitching at one sister while stressing about the other.

People, like Brock. Who I needed to call. But I wanted

to be back at Sibby's side, yanking her free from the magical mind trap, not playing have you heard on the phone.

Maeve turned to Kal. "Love, would you call Lara? Just tell her we have an emergency and ask her to play hostess in our stead. And if she sees Brock, let him know we are at the cottage, code Silver."

"Will do, if you take off those shoes."

"I like these shoes. When I'm wearing them I can almost look you in the eye."

Kal just smiled at her. How could they be so at ease when Sibby was in trouble?

Immediately I felt bad. Maeve and Kal were just being Maeve and Kal. They were both calm in a crisis and kept each other grounded.

My gaze slid to the phone. I wanted Brock here. But what could he do? Was I leaning on him too much?

Maeve tottered a moment more and then relented. "Fine. I suppose they aren't practical given the situation." She kicked them off, then gathered her skirt and headed up the stairs.

I hesitated a moment more.

"I'll call, him, Alys," Kal promised. "Go."

I went.

Maeve had made it to the top of the stairs when I caught up with her. "She was heading out to the cabin on the ridge. Planning to take some measurements the last time I saw her. Do we know where whatever it is, started?"

"No. She came in about twenty minutes ago by her magic."

Maeve entered the room first and headed straight for Siobhan who was nestled between Sebastian's spread legs. Her eyes were closed and her breaths escaped in shallow pants.

"You know what this is?" Maeve asked Sebastian as she peeled one of Sibby's eyelids up.

The dark fae nodded. "It's a form of punishment the council of elders uses on the sanctioned who violate the oaths of magic."

"What are the oaths of magic?" Maeve removed her hand and Sibby's eye closed again.

"To become fully sanctioned magical practitioners, you must abide by the oaths of the community before the council of elders by making a blood vow. You must promise never to use magic for personal gain, to not harm another magic wielder unless in defense of your own life, or the lives of others, and to keep magic hidden from the world at large. Once these oaths are bound in blood, you become sanctioned and the magic hunters can not touch you."

"What if someone breaks the oaths?" Maeve sat back on her heels.

"It depends. Small indiscretions are often overlooked. There is a gray area where a witch might use a spell for personal gain and lose her ability to channel white magic. Over time she can regain her former position by keeping to the letter of the law. The bigger ones require rehabilitation. The memory charm is one form of rehabilitation used on those who have harmed others."

"So we, the unknowing, can have our souls sucked out. And no one will tell us why because that's also against the rules. But someone who deliberately hurts another gets the magical equivalent of a bad acid trip down memory lane? How is that fair?" I stared down at Sibby's slack face.

"It isn't meant to be fair. It's meant to keep us hidden and safe from the persecution of those who fear magic and our powers."

"You've broken all of those rules, haven't you," Maeve asked quietly.

I jerked my gaze up in time to see Sebastian's amethyst eyes turned to chips of twilight ice.

He nodded but didn't speak.

"For Sibby. For all of us. That's why the magic hunters are after you too. But you said they can't take your soul."

"They can't. It's against guild law to attack another sanctioned hunter."

And he had done that too.

Part of me wanted to ask what they would do to him when his sanctuary was up. But we had a more immediate concern. "You said having Maeve here would help Sibby. How?"

"She is caught in the ephemeral strands of memory. It will repeat on an endless loop until the one who placed the curse removes it or she is pulled into another by a stronger force." He looked up and I could see the determination in his glittering gaze. "Except for the former fae queen and her oldest son, there is no one stronger than the three of you. That's why the bounty on you has been raised. You pose a threat to those in power."

"How do we pull her into another memory?" Maeve shook her head.

"The past life regression spell," I murmured. "Sibby found a book downstairs that had a spell for looking into past lives. That was the one she wanted to try. Would that work?"

Sebastian's brows drew together. "It might. But you need a focus from this life to go in there with her. Right now she thinks she is whatever age she was when the memory occurred. She might not realize she's a witch. Or an adult. A focus that is part of her recent history can help tether Siobhan as she is now to the spell. And she needs a reason to come back. Something she wants very badly. The focus can deliver the message and we have to hope that her desire for whatever we offer her is strong enough to overcome the charm."

"How do we do all that?"

Sebastian ran a thumb between Sibby's eyebrows which were drawn tightly together. "Cast a sleeping spell on me. Your ghost can act as a bridge between our minds. It's up to the two of you to decide what to bait your hook with. To tell me what she wants more than anything."

Sibby wanted Sebastian. I refused to tell him that though. The arrogant dark fae didn't need the ego boost and I wasn't going to betray Sibby's confidence. Besides, she was still cursed…

"The shadow work regression spell."

I looked to Maeve who nodded. "I'll go get what we need from the greenhouse. You stay here and let me know if there is any change."

Maeve bowed her head and I headed downstairs.

Kal was texting on his phone. "Lara is all caught up and Brock should be here any minute. I should get back and relieve the sitter. Unless you need me?"

"No, thanks." I shook my head

He patted my shoulder. "She's strong. She'll come out of it."

"Thanks." I gave him an impulsive hug.

Kal started and I released him and looked away. We'd never hugged before. But desperate times and all that. He offered me a small smile and headed up the stairs to say goodbye to Maeve. Alone, I turned toward the greenhouse.

Sibby was the best with magic. I didn't even know which tome she'd been scouring when she'd come across the shadow work spell. And then I needed a sleeping spell for Sebastian….

I felt dizzy and braced my hands on either side of the work table. Could I do this? Sure, I was powerful, but the finesse of spellcraft was so different from the crackling energy that bubbled out of me whenever I was lost in the heat of anger or passion or the cold grip of fear.

Headlights appeared and I turned just as Brock's truck bumped up the rutted drive. I ran for the door and flung myself at him the moment his feet touched the gravel.

"It's okay, Lys." He murmured as he stroked my hair. "Whatever it is, we'll figure it out, together."

My knuckles were white where they gripped his shirt. "It was meant for me. That magic trap. Maeve said she went up to the cabin. I was supposed to be there today. If not for Sebastian, it would have been me."

"It's not your fault," he said.

And suddenly the weight I carried wasn't so heavy. Because two people could bear the load. I wasn't alone anymore.

I allowed myself one more moment to relax in his embrace and then headed back into the greenhouse. Brock hesitated at the door. "Is it okay for me to be in here?"

It dawned on me that even though he spent almost every night with me in the cabin, I'd never invited him into our witchy space before. He was respecting a boundary that I hadn't set. The greenhouse had been Mom and Aunt Jess's big girls-only club. That was how they needed it to be. No children, no men, just women's space. Witches only.

I knew that Maeve wouldn't hesitate to bring Kal inside though. Sibby would probably invite that bastard Sebastian into the source of our power without a second thought.

Time to shelve the old rules.

I reached out a hand and without a moment's hesitation, Brock took it.

"Here's what we need to find."

Siobhan

I loved Peru. I loved the food, the people, the rapid-fire Spanish being spoken all around me. It was so much better than Eckhart. So much better than the whispers all over town that there was something wrong with my family because we lived in that hovel out by the lake. We were poor, charity cases even before Mom had died.

Being different in Eckhart was an unforgivable sin.

In Lima, the air was warm and damp. The buildings were brightly colored in golden saffron hues even though the architecture was clearly old. Traditional. That's what the city was. I'd snapped a thousand photos already, of everything from the Archbishop's palace to birds flying over the historic downtown fountain, to the dish I'd had for lunch at the Chinese-Peruvian fusion or "chifa" in Lima's own version of Chinatown.

A week in the city, I was running low on cash. It hadn't helped that Lima hadn't been my first stop. I'd been to Argentina and Chile, the Galapagos Islands. Then Cusco and Machu Picchu before landing in Peru's capital city. My Spanish had gotten progressively better and I was sure I could find work in one of the restaurants that catered to English-speaking tourists as I had done in other places.

The room that I was renting was paid up for the month. An elderly lady who had all of three teeth left in her head had been adamant that I pay in advance, which I had been happy to do. The room was small with a narrow cot and the walls were made of cracked plaster but I'd stayed in worse places during my travels. I didn't need a five-star resort, just a landing zone to dump my rucksack and crash for a few hours at a shot.

I'd been so careful with my budget before Lima. Mostly US currency, but with some Sol mixed in. It was just my appetite that was the problem. The urge to consume drove me. Food, sights, sounds… I wanted to swallow it all whole. Every last little bit until it filled up the cold places left by Aunt Jess's diagnosis.

Ovarian cancer. And according to Maeve, she didn't have long.

A cloud dampened my good mood along with that pervasive feeling of guilt. I should head home. Be with her. But the thought of seeing her frail and fading scared me. Aunt Jess was the most colorful person in my life. She had encouraged my love of food and taught me how to make Creole dishes where flavors burst on the tongue. I wanted to remember her like that, not eaten up by the disease.

Lost in thought, I turned down an alley, a shortcut I had found between the historic center of Lima and where I was staying.

The small hairs rose on the back of my neck. Someone was watching me. I turned but couldn't spot anyone in the crowd. Shaking off the weird feeling, I returned to traversing the alley. Just my imagination. I'd been warned not to take this shortcut but it took twenty minutes off the walk and I could feel a blister forming on my big toe.

Hands grabbed me and yanked me into a doorway. "What did I tell you?"

I gasped and then melted against Alejandro's big, warm body. "That you're lucky to have me."

He grinned, his dark eyes alight with mischief. Alejandro was a few years older than me. I'd picked him up outside of Cusco, where he'd been working at his family's llama farm and dreaming of traveling to a larger city and one day opening his own restaurant.

Our plan was to start one together when we were finally ready to settle down. Which wouldn't be for a very *very* long time if I had anything to say about it.

"I thought you had work tonight?" Alejandro had been hired by a friend of his older brother to help in the kitchen at a hotel. In exchange, he was given a small room in the hotel as well as three meals a day.

"Paulo is covering for me." He pulled me tight into his body, smelling of cumin and coriander. "Come back to my place, *querida.*"

I shook my head even as the way he was kissing along the side of my neck heated my blood. "I can't."

"Sure you can."

It took all of my strength of will to push him away. "Sure, I can, but I'm not ready. We've talked about this."

He ran a hand through his thick, dark hair. "When will you be ready? It's been weeks."

I huffed out a sigh. "Look, there's nothing less sexy than pressure, so just back off, okay?"

He clenched his jaw. "Fine. Then let me walk you home. This way isn't safe after dark."

"I'm fine," I insisted. The heat we generated when we were together was more dangerous than whatever could be lurking in this alley. "Go take a cold shower."

I thought he'd insist. He didn't though. Instead, he straightened up and squared his shoulders. I saw it then, the same look men got when I refused them one time too many. If the woman in front of them wouldn't give him what he wanted, he'd find another who would.

"See you later?" I asked though I knew we would probably never see each other again.

"Sure," he said and then headed in the other direction.

I swallowed the lump in my throat. It was inevitable. I didn't put out. Some men found that exciting, at least for a little while. But eventually, they would realize that I would never be ready and they would move on.

Maybe I was paranoid. Maybe the fact that the five men I

had shared my body with had died was nothing more than a coincidence. The first had been a drunk driving accident with my high school boyfriend the summer after we'd graduated. He'd been on his way home from the party where we'd given in to our carnal passions not even an hour before. That had shaken me badly enough that I hadn't been willing to try again until Steve, a fellow wandering soul from the states. He'd left my small room with a kiss and had his throat slit on the street out in front of my room, his wallet, full of US dollars taken.

Roger had been a sailor on leave and had succumbed to malaria. Bo, a handsome and flirtatious Scottish bartender and been poisoned by a vindictive ex-girlfriend. And Tomas….

I had witnessed his demise firsthand. There wasn't much left of him after the zipline broke in Ecuador. Sometimes I woke with his scream ringing in my ear.

All young men. All in relatively good health. All dead after one time with me.

Coincidence? Maybe, but it wasn't worth Alejandro's life. It had been fun while it lasted.

I broke from my musings when I realized that I didn't have a clue where I was. I must have missed a turn. The sun was completely down and I didn't like the feel of this alley. The sensation of being watched was on me again. I shivered and turned in a circle, utterly lost and feeling the first pang of unease.

Oh well, I would just have to retrace my steps back to familiar territory.

Two men appeared in the alley in front of me.

"*Disculpe*," I tried to excuse myself but the larger one caught my arm.

His breath reeked of fried onions and the look in the dark pits of his eyes made my stomach twist.

"*Quieres dinero?*" I would happily fork over the little bit of money I had left if it got me out of this alley unscathed. Never taking this way again.

His grip on my arm tightened and he said something in a low, guttural voice.

I shot a glance at the other one and was nearly sick. Emilio, Alejandro's brother's friend. I could almost see the liquor fumes wafting off of him as well as rage.

"American *puta* thinks she's too good for us," Emilio slurred.

"That isn't—"

I didn't get a chance to finish before the man who held me backhanded me. My lip split on contact and I was knocked to the ground.

I could still feel those unseen eyes on me as I fought. As I lost my shorts and my underwear was ripped from me. As I had my arms pinned.

As I cried while they took turns. Cursing me, using me.

And those eyes watched as both men died, as though struck down by an unseen force. A gurgle, a shudder, and then the glaze of death in their eyes as they collapsed in a heap.

The unseen watcher looked on as I ran, torn clothing hanging from my damaged body and more certain than ever that I was cursed.

And wondered what I had done to deserve it.

10

*S*ebastian was horrified as the scene—that awful gut-wrenching memory he had just witnessed a second time—reset again. Siobhan was back in the historic downtown of the city, looking happily around as she took pictures and completely unaware of what had just happened. What was about to happen again.

This was torture of the most acute kind. Not being able to speak to her, to warn her about the danger. To save her from it. He bore silent witness to the brutal attack.

"Why can we hear her thoughts?" he asked the ghost.

"This is happening in her head," Ethan murmured. "It's her story as she recalls it."

"She thinks she's cursed because those two drug addicts died after assaulting her." Sebastian shook his head. "She thinks she *deserves* to be cursed."

This scene explained so much about his spitfire witch. Why at times she was brave and bold and self-assured as though nothing could hurt her. Why she shied away from intimacy.

Why desire was her magical trigger.

His hands clenched into fists as that young, foolish mortal kissed her again. How could the man let her wander unescorted? Had he been in on his friend's plan to assault Siobhan?

He couldn't watch it again. Not her expression as the mortal turned from her, the sad longing mixed with grim acceptance. According to her thoughts, the chance that he would die after being with her was not worth the mortal's life. Instead, she put herself at risk.

She truly was cursed. He saw the deaths of the other two, the men who had raped her. By all appearances, they were young and healthy. There had been no one else in the alley and Siobhan's powers hadn't manifested.

"Have you ever felt foreign magic around her?" he asked Ethan. A spirit could sometimes see things that an embodied person could not.

"No," Ethan said. "I would have warned her if I had."

"And you're sure her mother didn't cast this?"

"I would know the feel of Laney's magic. And Jess's. It wasn't them."

No obvious magical signature. Every hex left a trace, undetectable by most, but it was there. As a magic hunter, he'd been trained to find it, to follow it to the source like a bloodhound. But for Siobhan to carry a curse with no signature, she must have been born with it.

"I need to talk to her," Sebastian said to Ethan. "Tell Maeve and Alys they need to give my body another dose of the potion."

Ghosts didn't usually wear expressions. Being dead removed the animation from a soul. But Ethan's face turned grim. "Another dose could kill you."

"I am aware of the risk. And Ethan? Do not say a word to either of them about this scene."

Ethan held his gaze. "It is Siobhan's choice to reveal or to conceal." He vanished.

Sebastian followed Siobhan down the alley, trying to ignore the feeling that he was overstepping and that the damn ghost had called him out on it. It was true, Siobhan hadn't been given a choice in sharing this memory. And as much as he could tell himself that what he was seeing was to save her life, it still felt like a violation.

"Siobhan," he called her name. Would the second dose help him penetrate the memory charm? An anesthesiologist knew that there were many levels between awake and asleep. Siobhan was deep enough that her state was akin to a coma. "*Annwyl*, hear me."

She stopped. His heart beat faster. Had she paused here before or had she heard him.

He reached out and put his hand on her shoulder. She didn't jerk or turn. Her eyes searched the spot where he stood the same way Alys had with the ghost.

"Hear me," he repeated. "You are not in this place. You've been trapped in memory but you need to fight. Your sisters are looking for a way to get you out. Fight this, Siobhan. Fight your way back to me."

She turned and there were the men.

Sebastian had never felt so helpless in his life. No magic, no body. He could do nothing but stay with her and pray that she knew she wasn't alone.

Maeve

"*A*nother dose could kill him," I said to the mirror where the apparition known as Ethan appeared. Every hair on my body stood on end. It was all the magic swirling around the small bedroom. The conjuring spell for the ghost with a rune-marked mirror and candles. The waft from the sleeping potion which allowed Sebastian to delve into Siobhan's memory and the cauldron that steeped water that had reflected the full moon along with various herbs and stones we had added to the brew. A second, larger mirror was hung on one wall, the symbols etched into the glass.

That was our traveling mirror. The one that we were supposed to step through to revisit the past. Just as soon as Sebastian dragged Sibby back to consciousness.

For the moment the glass remained dark and still, but it felt like a sleeping dragon. One wrong move and it would wake and devour us all.

"He can't talk to her any more than I can." The ghost said. "He can't drag her from the memory trap if she doesn't know he's there."

"What memory is it?" Alys asked as she ladled the brew into a small glass vile.

Ethan hesitated. "Something from her travels."

I narrowed my eyes on his mirror. "Does it have to do with her curse?"

He nodded, his eyes pleading for me not to ask more.

"That means we're on the right track," Alys said, eyes fixed on measuring the proper dose. "She wants to understand why she's cursed more than anything. Knowing what we're doing should pull her out of this."

I looked at Sebastian's sleeping form, not liking the idea of doubling up on the sleeping potion. Sibby was the witchy one and we'd brewed the stuff without her. Sure, I could recognize herbs and Alys was a pro at following directions but it wasn't the same as my youngest sister's innate understanding of how magic worked.

Alys caught my gaze. "He wants this. He asked us to send him deeper. We need to trust him."

"Do you?" I asked "Trust Sebastian?"

She hesitated. "I trust him not to do anything that will hurt Siobhan. He believes he is in love with her."

I put my hands on my hips. "What do you mean, *believes* he loves her?"

"It means that I don't know if someone who has done all the things that Sebastian has done can actually understand unconditional love. He's a hot mess."

"You've said the same about Sibby a time or two," I pointed out.

"That's different." She didn't elaborate on how. "Sebastian has convinced himself that he will do anything to keep Siobhan safe. And that's good enough for our purposes. If this second dose kills him, my conscience is clear."

I crossed my arms over my chest and watched as she sat on the bed and held the vile to Sebastian's lips. Waited as she tipped it back and the blue potion—which looked like Windex—disappeared down his throat.

I moved to his side and laid my fingers against his neck. His pulse was a little fast, but maybe that was par for the course for a fae changeling watching the woman he loved relive the worst experience of her life.

I had no basis for comparison.

"He's not foaming at the mouth. That's a good sign, right?" Alys's gaze dipped down to where Sibby was snuggled against his chest.

She didn't move. Hadn't moved or made a sound since our vigil began. Her pulse was so slow I'd panicked at first, thinking her heart had stopped. Her eyelids didn't dart back and forth like a person caught in the throes of a dream.

"That's what you looked like." Alys nodded to Sibby. "When the hospital had you in that medically induced coma. You barely looked alive."

I swallowed. "I'm glad Kal didn't see me like that. It would have freaked him out."

"He's only human," Alys's mouth twitched.

"Are they?" I asked nodding to the couple on the bed before meeting her gaze. "Are we?"

It was a thought that bothered me a little. Ever since we'd knocked back the empowerment brew our lives had become freakier. Some days started normally. Kids having breakfast and dashing out the door to catch the school bus. Kal and I lingered over a cup of coffee before heading to work. Hell, we'd had a perfectly normal walk through the green and picnic lunch.

And now this.

"Of course. We're just human plus." Alys got up and returned to the spell book.

"You're sure?"

She turned to face me. "What is this, Maeve? Our path is set. Get Sibby back, figure out why she's cursed, go get magically sanctioned, and Bob's your uncle. This has been the plan for months. Why are you doubting it now?"

"I don't know. Believe me, I've made peace with my Enchantress gifts. It's just…I don't feel like I fit in around town anymore."

"You never did."

I glared at her. "What's that supposed to mean?"

She flung out her arm, gesturing to the cottage walls. "We grew up here. In this cottage with no electricity. No television. No neighbors. Most of the people in Eckhart were afraid of Aunt Jess. Mom too."

"They weren't." No one could have been afraid of our mother. She was so gentle and soft-spoken. A true Southern Belle.

"Yes, they were. You don't remember those early years. The name-calling, the shunning. I do. Right up until you started working as a nurse and I slowly bought up half the town. That changed opinions quick."

I snorted. "So that was your evil plan? Go make tons of money and rub their noses in it?"

"I never wanted to rub their noses in it. I just wanted respect for our family. There was no way Aunt Jess would ever leave this place. You either, not after you met Kal. You have never lived away so you don't know what it's like to go about your life anonymously."

She was right, I didn't. "Is that why you left? You and Sibby?"

"I wouldn't presume to speak for Sibby. Her reasons are her own. But yes, I needed to not feel everyone's eyes on me all the time. Judging me. And it's better now because we're a part of the community. We've done great things. Hell, you saved lives. Some of the old warhorses are gone and new people have moved to town. Things are different. We're different." She reached over our younger sister's body and Sebastian's so she could squeeze my hand.

I squeezed back and gave her a smile. "Thanks."

"Okay then. Help me get this thing ready." She cast a side-long glance to the dark mirror. "Who knows how different things used to be?"

●

Siobhan

"*Annwyl,* please."

There it was again. The man's voice. I stopped and scanned the alley. My instincts were clamoring that something wasn't right. Was it him? The faceless male voice that echoed in my ear?

Something about it was familiar. Lilting with an accent

that was distinctly not Peruvian. He seemed to know me. What was that word he kept saying?

"Hello?" I called out, humiliated when my voice broke. "Is someone there?"

Something touched my shoulder and I whirled around.

Nothing. No one.

"Siobhan? Can you hear me? You're in danger. You need to leave this place."

"That's what I'm trying to do." It felt ridiculous, talking to this person I'd conjured out of nothing more than fantasy. "Be a good delusion and point me in the direction of home, kaythanksbye."

Nothing. I blew out a breath. Okay, I should probably retrace my steps until...

"Not that way!" A hand clamped down on my arm. And I could see it. Long sleek fingers, much paler than the natives of Lima. As pale as my own. There was warmth too. But the hand simply...ended. No wrist or arm. Disembodied. It held me with desperate strength. When I looked up to where the voice came from, I saw no chin or mouth, only eyes.

Eyes that glowed with a deep purple hue. No, not purple. Amethyst.

Something tickled along my brainstem. Primal. I recognized those eyes. I was as sure of that as I was that I had never seen them before.

"Listen to me, Siobhan. This isn't real. It's a memory and you need to rouse yourself from it. Your sisters are waiting for you."

"You know my sisters?" My brow furrowed. Maeve and Alys didn't know where I was. I hadn't had a chance to call home in several weeks.

"I know them. And I know you don't remember me but I know you too." Half of his face appeared and then vanished again, though those eerie eyes remained. "You're forty-one and a newly empowered witch. We met in Eckhart. You've changed my life."

Was it possible to be sane when your delusions spoke nonsense? I shook my head.

"I saved you from the Headhunter. In the Amazon."

An image of a hut, a man with a painted face. Another man with a blazing sword. He looked like the angel of death. His face was fierce and beautiful. The picture vanished like smoke caught up in a tornado.

My heart was beating too fast. The alley tilted. What was happening?

"You're a witch. So are your sisters. You walked into a magical trap and are caught in this memory. Leave now."

He had the tone of someone who was used to issuing commands and being obeyed. Part of me wanted to jerk my hand free and tell him to fuck off. No one ordered me around. But the way he was looking at me, with intense desperation. Almost pleading.

He solidified and his grip on me loosened. A hand rose to stroke my cheek. "Please, *Annwyl*. Leave this place behind. Force yourself to wake. Your sisters will help you find the answers you seek. They are preparing a spell even now to help you find out the origins of your curse. But you must accept that I am telling you the truth."

I shook my head and the alley wavered. Then solidified. "How do I know you're real and not just some bizarre figment of my imagination?"

I wasn't prepared for his answer. Not when he cupped my face and lowered his mouth to mine. The heat of him blazed through me. His need, his desire, melding with my own.

He stole my breath as the kiss deepened, grew hotter, more intense than anything I'd ever felt before. It seared me clean of the cobwebs that clung to me, then bizarre tendrils that had anchored me in this place. I pulled away from the kiss as memories surfaced and dove, and surfaced and dove. Like dolphins ready for a new adventure.

"Sebastian," I breathed against his lips.

He smiled. And in the next instant, began to fade. I reached for him, only to discover that it was my body that was losing form.

"You deserve so much better," Sebastian said. "*Annwyl*, you deserve everything life has to offer. The whole world."

And then he was gone.

11

ALYS

"She's coming to," Maeve said as I finished drawing the final rune on the standing mirror.

I turned in time to see Sibby move her head and groan. Her eyelids fluttered and one of her hands went to her forehead. "What happened?"

"Quick," Maeve urged me, unnecessarily. "Sebastian said we had to get her invested in something real as soon as she woke so she doesn't fall back into the mind trap."

"I know that," I snapped and then stepped back. I wasn't really angry at Maeve or Sibby or even Sebastian.

I was angry at myself. It should have been me at the hunter's cabin today. I shouldn't have let her leave. I should have done it all differently. Anger crackled through my veins in an uninterrupted circuit. Probably a good thing since this particular spell called for a mother nature witch to do the unthinkable. "Are you ready?"

Maeve, as the Enchantress, had to add three drops of her blood to the mirror's glass. I wish I knew why but there was no one to ask and no time to lose.

"Stay with us, Sib." Maeve snipped a lock of purple hair

from Sibby's head with her pinking shears. She tied the purple strands up with a white ribbon. White for amplification, just like the pillar candles we had scattered about the room. This part of the spell was meant to hold Sibby to us.

After placing the hair in a ceramic bowl, she began to sterilize a sewing needle. Who knew sewing supplies could be so useful in witchcraft?

"Ouch," Maeve winced as she pulled the needle back. Blood welled on her finger and she met my gaze. "Ready."

I nodded and then closed my eyes. Embraced the crackling energy.

"Guys?" Sibby groaned. "What are you doing?"

"Getting you an answer sleeping beauty." Maeve spoke in a low, soothing tone. "Though I'm the one who pricked her finger. But it was on purpose so I can't complain."

There was a rustling on the bed and then a tentative question. "Sebastian?"

"He went in so he could get you out," Maeve explained. The quintessential middle child, always ready to make peace and offer clarification.

Outside thunder rumbled.

"Alys?" Maeve put a hand on my arm.

"Quiet," I snapped. "This is harder than it looks."

"That's what she said," Sibby quipped and I knew she was back with us all the way. A bit of tension eased from my shoulders and I redoubled my efforts.

Wind blew through the room, blowing my hair across my face. Behind my closed lids, the light dimmed as the gusts blew out the candles.

There. I could feel it, the charge of raw power.

I opened my eyes and pointed at the mirror. "Stand back."

Lightning struck.

Me.

The bolt sizzled down my spine to my toes. It didn't hurt.

It felt wonderful. Hot like a lover's caress. As wild as my werewolf.

In the mirror, my eyes glowed a brilliant white, and my hair whitened as I watched. I thought I'd have to fight with the lightning to get it to do my bidding. Instead, I reveled in it. It lit me up. My veins glowed with the thrum of power. I could feel the convergence. The ley lines that fed into that one central point. With so much power I could go anywhere. Do anything. I was a conduit. A part of it all. I wanted to travel with it. Lose myself in it.

"Alys!" Maeve shouted. "You have to let it go!"

Let it go? I never wanted this feeling to end. I turned my head to tell her so.

And saw Sibby. My baby sister. Her blue eyes were huge, the whites seeming to glow in the candlelight. Her lips were parted in shock. Her lopsided hair was damp with sweat from the fever dreams we'd just freed her from.

The sight grounded me. Magically. I recalled my purpose and turned back to the mirror and let loose the bolt. My body pulled taut as a bowstring and the lightning became the arrow fired at the mirror.

The glass exploded with a deafening crack.

I stumbled back away from it, instinctively raising my arm to keep fragments of glass from flying at me.

But there were no shards. The mirror hadn't splintered. Instead, it had come apart, down to its elements. Grains of sand glowed with the power of the controlled bolt of lightning. They swirled in a rhythm completely apart from the wind. And then, as we watched, reformed into the mirror.

Instead of seeing reflections of ourselves, we saw a huge bonfire.

"That's it," Maeve whispered. "That's the scene from my dream."

Sibby got off the bed and came to stand between us. Her fingers threaded through mine. "What now?"

"Now, we step through," I told her.

She didn't say anything.

I turned to look at her. "This is what you wanted, isn't it? Answers?"

Her teeth sank into her lower lip. She turned her head so she could see Sebastian. "Will he be all right?"

"All his vitals are steady," Maeve reassured her.

"But—?"

"Brock and the pack are patrolling the woods," I said. "And Ethan will make sure he wakes up after the sleeping potion wears off."

Still, she hesitated.

"Sibby, this isn't as easy as I'm making it look. If you want to do this we need to do it now."

She let out a shaky breath and then pulled me into a fierce hug. "Thank you."

I hugged her back with all my strength.

"Are we ready?" Maeve said. "Do we have everything?"

She was such a mom. I was half expecting her to ask if anyone needed to use the bathroom before we left the house.

Sibby reached out and dragged Maeve into the hug. And then she pulled away, wiped her eyes. "I love you guys."

As a unit, we step forward into the mirror.

To explore our shadows.

●

Siobhan

I tripped over something and landed face-first in a muddy puddle. My jeans were soaked to mid-thigh. My left palm stung and I picked it up and saw a trickle of blood. A stone had embedded itself in my skin. "Ouch."

I half expected to hear my sisters' voices asking me if I was all right. When I didn't, I glanced around and called out. "Maeve? Alys?"

No answer.

Staggering to my feet I tried to make sense of my surroundings. There was no bonfire like the one I'd seen in the mirror. We'd been holding hands. Where could they have gone?

"Not good, not good, not good," I chanted as I slogged toward dry ground. My motorcycle boots would be ruined but I didn't care. The air was humid and smelled of green and growing things, much like the greenhouse. Above me the waxing moon shone down, casting the budding tree limbs into stark relief.

Using the hem of my t-shirt, I blotted the cut on my palm with the fabric. If Maeve were by my side she'd be bitching at me to show her the wound so she could clean it out properly before it got infected.

But she wasn't.

Where the hell were they?

I wasn't sure exactly what had happened. My memories were all jumbled up. I'd been at that cabin and then…what?

Sebastian. In bed with Sebastian with my sisters hovering over us and doing magic like there was no tomorrow. What had prompted them to change their minds?

The missing pieces were almost as frustrating as being abandoned in the middle of nowhere. Okay, though, I did know some things. This was supposed to be a past life shadow work spell. Maeve had recognized the bonfire that she had seen in her dream. That meant that scene did have something to do with my curse.

"Are you here?" A voice called out from the darkness on my left. One I knew intimately.

"I am here, my love." The voice came from my right.

Shit, what should I do? I had no idea who these people were or if they were part of the magic council or whatever. Before I thought better of it, I traveled behind a tree.

And watched as Sebastian emerged into the clearing beside the bog. Even though I couldn't make out his features, I knew it was him because of the way his amethyst eyes lit up the night. My lips parted when I recognized the woman who emerged to meet him.

It was me. But it wasn't. Her hair was dark for one thing and I saw no tattoos or piercings. Saw it all because she was buck-ass naked.

What the hell? Had I been cursed for streaking through the woods like an idiot? That seemed like it should be its own punishment.

"You shouldn't be here." Not-me smiled when she caught sight of the man even as she chastised him. "The others might have seen you."

"I needed to be with you," he said. He stepped forward into the moonlight and I was relieved to see it wasn't Sebastian. He was fae, those eyes told the story for sure, but it wasn't my Sebastian.

"But it's Beltane," not-me told him. "You should be with your people."

"You are my people." His look was intense as he pulled her toward him.

I wanted to roll my eyes at the drama. Okay, so really not Sebastian and I were star-crossed lovers. Not exactly a shocking revelation. Some people theorized that souls fated to know one another met again and again, reliving the same sort of situations until they got it right. Whatever "it" was. So the angst unfolding before my eyes was familiar but I could laugh at the ridiculousness of it because I wasn't invested in these people. It was like watching a badly written play.

The kiss went on and on and I was about to pop away and leave them to the horizontal mambo when not-Sebastian murmured something to not-me and then put a hand low on her stomach. For a second, I thought he was going for the gold, but then he cupped the small mound there. It was a very protective gesture.

And lightning struck. Both behind me in the world and the crackling pop of thought fully realized.

After giving the lovebirds one final once-over I turned away, using my magic to travel through the woods toward the source of the lightning.

The night had been still a moment ago so that bolt could only mean one thing.

My big sister was nearby. And she was pissed.

●

Maeve

I stood in almost exactly the same place as I'd stood when witnessing the dream. Only now, sights and smells were sharper. I could feel the heat from the fire.

And the frustration that rolled off Alys in waves.

"Where the hell is she?" My big sister seemed completely uninterested in the PDAs going on before the fire while I could barely tear my gaze away from them. Me and Kal, her and Brock, the leaping flames, the rhythm from unseen drums that pulsed like a heartbeat under my skin. If not for Sibby's disappearance, I wouldn't have room in my head for anything else.

"I was holding her hand when we stepped through." I told Alys for the third time. Not that repetition would make a difference.

"So was I."

I pointed to the empty spot on the side of the bonfire. "That's where past Sibby was dancing. She's not there now. Perhaps she stalked off into the woods already?"

"What does that have to do with...?" Alys trailed off as she caught sight of what was going down—literally—by the fire. Brock was on his knees and past-Alys had her leg hooked over one of his broad shoulders. "They aren't...out in public like this?"

"Looks like they're in good company." I nodded to where the other version of me and Kal were doing the same act, just in a different position. Past me was flat on her back, writhing under his ministrations.

I was glad I'd changed out of my slinky party dress into a pair of borrowed black sweats and a hoodie that allowed me to better blend in with the night. Didn't want them to look over here and see us.

Not that the foursome at the fire had eyes for anything but one another.

Alys swore as a bolt of lightning lit up the night. It touched down beside her past self's head.

Past Brock took that as his cue to round third base and blaze a trail for home. Past Kal seemed completely content where he was. I watched, mesmerized as past me stretched out her hands, and wisps of purple sparks were released into the air. They swirled like spores around the fire. All the small hairs on my body rose up.

"What the hell is this?" my sister whisper-hissed.

"I'm not sure," I said, uncomfortably aroused and embarrassed all at once. "Some sort of ritual. But it explains why the guy Sibby rejected was so irritated. He thought he was going to get some and then she shunned him."

A crashing from the woods behind us and then, "Damn it, Alys. That temper of yours is going to give us away."

"Sibby," Alys and I turned to see our youngest sister emerge from the dark forest behind us. "Are you all right?"

"Just wet," she indicated her jeans.

"You aren't the only one," I muttered with a sideways glance to the fire.

"What do you...oh!" Sibby's final word was one of surprise. "Damn Alys, I didn't realize you were that flexible."

"Hush," Alys said and then grabbed us by the arms pulling us farther from the clearing. "What happened to you?"

"I ran into my other self. With her version of Sebastian."

"Did they see you?" I asked.

She shook her head. "No, I hid before they knew I was there. And they were very caught up in each other. I did find out a few interesting things. One, it's Beltane here, wherever here is. Sebastian is persona non grata at this festival. I gather he has people of his own and that those people and our people," Sibby gestured at the clearing. "Don't exactly gel."

I caught sight of what looked like blood on her hand and caught her by the wrist even as I shucked the first-aid kit from my bag. "We need to clean this out before it gets infected."

Sibby's lips twitched as though the thought of gangrene amused her.

Alys cleared her throat. "Did you learn anything else?"

"Yeah. I'm pregnant."

SIOBHAN

"**W**hat the hell do you mean you're pregnant?"

I should be grateful that Alys didn't start in with the interrogation until after we had found shelter for the night. Shelter was a rather optimistic word for the small narrow cave that was about three miles away from the clearing where the Beltane fire still blazed.

"Don't be ridiculous, Alys," Maeve snapped as she squatted beside her backpack. She had a few emergency road flares cracked so that the chemicals glowed a bright orange providing light but no heat. "She was talking about the other version of her."

"Oh," Alys said and then clamped her mouth shut.

"I guess she's the pre-curse version of me," I murmured. "Since the Sebastian stand-in is still alive."

I'd taken off my jeans and spread them on a large boulder to dry. The wind picked up causing goosebumps to rise along my damp skin. I shivered and tried to rub some warmth into my chilled body.

Maeve handed me a shiny thermal blanket that she had

pulled from her pack. "I guess that answers the question about where we are."

"Huh?" That statement knocked Alys off whatever train of thought she'd been riding. "What does?"

Maeve gestured toward the mouth of the cave where we could see dark treetops bending almost at a ninety-degree angle. "Where else does the weather change as fast as in the mountains?"

She had a point. The temperature had plummeted like a stone into a pool, surging from the mid-seventies to the upper forties.

"It might have had something to do with the Beltane rite," Maeve added.

"What do you mean?" I pushed the question out between chattering teeth.

"Oh, move over. We need to share body heat." Maeve lowered herself gingerly down to a spot to my left. She scooted in close and I sagged against her. After a moment's hesitation, Alys took up a similar position on my right side, pulling my arm up so that the arm holding the shiny blanket draped over her shoulder. My sisters bookended me and provided much-needed comfort as well as warmth.

We were silent for a long time, each of us lost in our own thoughts. Then Alys asked, "Sibby, where were you?"

"I told you. I was in the woods."

I felt more than saw her shake her head. "No, I mean in the memory charm. Sebastian told us it's some sort of punishment spell. That it catches you in your worst memory and makes you relive it again and again."

"Alys," Maeve's tone held a note of warning.

"She's well out of it now." My oldest sister murmured. "She's not going anywhere." Her fingers wrapped around my arm. "She's safe with us."

"Right," I said. Bits and pieces of the in-between time

were coming back to me, like a puzzle cut from sheet metal, sharp with a sinister edge. I hadn't fumbled with them too much for fear of slicing open a barely healed wound.

"I was in Lima. A city in Peru. It was a few months after I left...." I stopped and cleared my throat. "I made a bad call. A really bad call."

Why was it that seeing not-me with not-Sebastian barely registered but just the thought of that alley made my stomach flip over?

Maybe a part of me was dead. The part that experienced real genuine positive feelings like joy and love. All that remained was the darker stuff, like the scunge at the bottom of an unwashed coffeepot.

"You don't have to talk about it if you don't want," Maeve cleared her throat. "But we're here for you. If you want to."

I thought about Sebastian's eyes in that alley. *"You deserve so much better,"* he'd said. *"Annwyl, you deserve everything life has to offer. The whole world."*

That was real. The way he'd looked at me.

The guy in the swamp though....

"It isn't Sebastian," I whispered.

"Of course, it's not." Maeve patted my arm. "Just like it wasn't us out there demonstrating our exhibitionist tendencies."

"No." I stood up, needing to move as I thought this through. "The guy in the swamp wasn't Sebastian. I'm sure of it. He was similar and he was saying all the right things and the eyes were the same but something was off."

I began to pace, the cold forgotten. The more I thought about it the more sense it made. Sebastian wouldn't have come to the Beltane fire and lured me away. That wasn't the same man who had been running from magic hunters while trying to give me the space I needed to grow into my powers. He'd wanted me to stay in the convergence with my sisters.

He risked everything for me.

"Sebastian is a changeling," Alys whispered.

I rounded on her. "What?"

She met my eyes. "A changeling. He was born human. He said that if we had taken him to the hospital all the tests would reveal that he's human."

I blinked at her. "So you're saying that not-me is in love with something pretending to be Sebastian? So much so that she's considering running off with him?"

"It makes sense," Maeve said. "Sebastian concentrated on you first, tried to drive a wedge between us. Another dark fae might do the same."

"So he's using her," I sank into a crouch and ran my hands through my hair. "Trying to trick her. Why?"

My sisters shook their heads in unison. They didn't have any more answers than I did.

The tarot reading popped into my mind. The King of Wands reversed. An asshole male authority figure. It wasn't someone I knew, at least not from my current life.

But what about a previous one?

"We need to warn her," I said staring out into the darkness. "She needs to know she can't trust him."

"Sibby, think this through," Alys urged. "What if it were you? I mean, it actually is you, just a you who has been living a different life. If three strangers came out of nowhere and told her the man she is in love with is using her but had zero proof, how would you respond?"

"I'd laugh in her face," I said and took a moment to enjoy their stunned faces caused by my agreement. "That's why we won't go to her directly. We'll go over her head."

Both of Alys's eyebrows shot up nearly to her hairline. "You mean...?"

"At first light, we'll go find your counterparts," I

explained. "Because if anyone is going to look out for me in any lifetime, it'll be the two of you."

●

The storm had passed by the time the horizon lightened. My lips were dry and cracked. I got up and shuffled to Maeve's backpack. In addition to her first aid kit, there were several protein bars, packs of trail mix, and three aluminum water bottles.

Taking one of the bottles, I unscrewed the cap and took a long slug, savoring the delicious flavor. I didn't have to pee, which was a little worrying. Women my age *always* needed to pee, especially when surrounded by cold air.

How long since I'd had water? Time was warping in my mind but by a rough count, I'd probably gone a full day without drinking anything. I was definitely dehydrated.

The bottle was empty. I eyed the other two but decided to leave them for Alys and Maeve. With any luck, we would complete our fact-finding trip and be home for a late break-fast. Maybe it was overly optimistic, but I knew handing the Sebastian poser over to Alys and Maeve was the right thing to do.

And what about the baby? My mind floated the question out there. I couldn't dismiss it. My hand went to my own midsection, and, not for the first time, I wondered what it would feel like to actually be pregnant. Because of my curse, I hadn't entertained the idea. Some women rocked the single-parent life. But that was never the sort of pressure I'd wanted.

Besides, it was probably too late. At fifty, Alys was on the far side of menopause, and at five years younger, Maeve was already wrestling with perimenopausal symp-toms. The end of the fertile part of my life was approaching like an express train and even if I did somehow manage to make it happen, there would be so many complications.

But the other me was charging forward into motherhood. She would have a baby, with or without her lover. At least she would have her sisters to help her through it.

If she could do it, why can't I?

Tons of practical reasons. I didn't have a steady home. Or a steady source of income. I was a witch who tended to disappear. Bringing a baby into my nomadic magic-filled life seemed so irresponsible.

Annwyl, *you deserve everything life has to offer.* Sebastian's words wrapped around my heart and planted the seed.

The thought of going through it, feeling the baby grow, giving birth, and holding it in my arms. An image flickered in my mind. A daughter, a daughter with amethyst eyes.

I squeezed my eyes shut to dispel the thought.

"Sibby?" Alys sat up and raised her hand to shield her eyes against the morning light. "You okay?"

"Yeah," I said and forced a smile. "Why wouldn't I be?"

Maeve rolled over and groaned. "Coffee?"

"Sorry." I knelt and dragged the other two bottles of water out of the pack and handed them over. "This is the best we've got."

"There's dark chocolate in the trail mix," Alys said.

"When did you have time to make trail mix?" I asked her.

"I didn't. Brock made it."

"Wow, and here I thought chocolate was bad for dogs."

Maeve snickered and Alys sent me a dark look.

She was such an easy mark and I decided to needle her a bit more. "Can I ask you something?"

"As long as it's not about my sex life."

I made a disappointed sound. "You're no fun."

"What is it, Siobhan?"

"Does Brock ever sleep on the end of your bed? You know when he's a wolf?"

She made a strangled sound and then said, "Excuse me."

"Because you know how cold your feet can get in the winter."

Alys was too classy to give me the finger. But I could tell by the stiff set of her shoulders that she considered it. I'd call that a win.

"You're terrible," Maeve said, though her shoulders were shaking with barely suppressed giggles. "Don't ever change."

"Why would I change when I've mastered perfection?" Though I kept my tone light, the words sounded hollow as they echoed in my ears. "Just got one pesky little curse to unravel and then there will be no stopping me."

Maeve reached out a hand and I helped her up. She rolled her neck from side to side.

"How many spoons?" I asked her, referring to her MS. Maeve's energy could come and go without warning. And that was when she woke in a warm bed instead of a chilly cave.

"Half a dozen at least." She smiled and I was glad to see there was no resentment at my question. "I'm good to go as soon as I see to nature. You should drink more. I'm worried you'll get dehydrated."

She handed me the rest of her half-filled bottle. I took it with thanks, knocking back the rest.

The flares were mostly burnt out so we decided to leave them behind. My jeans were still damp as I struggled to get back into them. After doing one final check of the space, which Alys insisted upon, we headed out into the misty morning air.

It took us almost an hour to find the site of the bonfire since it was nothing but ash and charcoal. No signs of life. Our counterparts were long gone.

"Can you feel it?" Maeve asked as she stepped into the clearing.

"Feel what?" Alys said.

"The ritual. Something happened last night, at the festival. A connection."

I paused and took stock. I did feel something in the ground beneath my feet. A stirring perhaps. Like an invisible giant waking out of a hundred-year sleep.

"Maiden, mother, crone," Maeve muttered as she strode around the pile of charred wood. "I could feel the rhythm of it, could hear those words in my head in time to the drum. The phases of life."

"Does that mean I'm the crone?" Alys asked dryly.

"From what I saw, the other you was in imminent danger of breaking a hip," I winked at her. "What with being bent like a pretzel while getting her groove on."

"Sibby, I swear to chocolate—"

"Guys, I'm serious." Maeve snapped. "The phases of a woman's life are maiden, mother, and crone. I think each one of the dancers was here to represent a phase, to make an offering. That's what the guys and the…er…consummation was all about."

"An offering to who?" Alys asked.

Maeve shook her head. "I don't know. But the pieces fit. We don't know what year we're in. We don't know the culture or belief system. But this has to be connected with Sibby's curse because this is her shadow work past life spell."

"Not-me left the party early," I muttered. "Do you think that's why I'm cursed? I offended some witchy deity with my hubris?"

Maeve shook her head again. She had no answers for me.

There was a throbbing pain behind my eye that threatened to turn into a full-blown migraine. "Okay, well we won't learn anything more just standing around here. So which way did they go? After it was over?"

"Not a clue," Maeve said.

Alys was poking around the outer edge of the clearing. "I see footprints over here. Lots of them."

Maeve and I met up with her and stared down at the partial footprints scattered across a rocky outcropping. A small cascade of water spilled out beneath the outcropping, dropping down fifty feet into a pool below.

"If I were setting up a primitive village," I mused. "I would do so near fresh water. They can't be too far off. Come on."

The trail was little more than a goat path that wound between rocks. The incline was so steep that a person would have to lean very far forward and maybe use her hands to help her climb up.

Maeve eyed the rock dubiously. "I'm not sure I can make it down there."

"Me either," Alys said.

I scouted the area, poking through bushes and looking for a more convenient path. Nothing.

I looked back at my sisters. "I think they jumped."

"Jumped?" Maeve squeaked.

"The pool's probably plenty deep." I was already toeing off my squishy boots.

"You're not serious." Alys's tone was flat. "We have no idea how deep the water is. You could break your neck. Or paralyze yourself."

It was true. The pool was dark, the water still. There could be boulders just beneath the still surface.

Instinct prodded me that this was a test I had to pass. I always trusted my instincts, for good or ill. It was my code of life. That damned Tarot reading was in my head again. The Fool, about to go over a cliff.

"Sibby, please." Maeve implored. "We can look for

another way down. We don't even know if the people we are looking for are down there."

I gripped her hand and squeezed. "Trust me."

"I do," Maeve said. "We do. But we don't want you to get hurt."

I shrugged and pulled my t-shirt over my head. "You can wait here if you don't want to risk it."

"Sibby, come on, this is reckless. There has to be another way." Alys tried again.

I raised my pierced brow at her. "Maybe, but this is my way."

And without another word, I flung myself off the cliff.

13

SIOBHAN

The water was cool and crisp, the pool much too deep to see the bottom. I plunged in deep and then kicked until my head surfaced and then turned to wave at my panicked sisters on the jutting rock above. "Water's great."

Alys threw up her hands in exasperation. "You're insane, you know that, right?"

I shrugged and took the opportunity to slurp down some of the water. It was sweet and clean and hopefully didn't contain any nasty microbes that would make me sick. I was almost too thirsty to care.

Though I would like nothing more than to drift around on my back all day and let the sun that snuck through the budding tree limbs make shadowy patterns on my face, I needed to find my sisters. Well, the not-me version of my sisters.

"We're going to try to find another way to get down," Maeve shouted down to me as I swam to the edge of the pool. "If we don't find one, meet back here with us at sunset."

I hauled my carcass out of the pool and shivered as the breeze picked up. "Toss me my stuff."

Alys, for all her skills, threw like a girl. My jeans went sailing overhead and got caught in a tree branch about eight feet above me. One boot thunked down twenty feet behind me and the other landed in the water.

I winced. Those puppies had been expensive and deserved better treatment. Picking my way back to the water's edge I went in after it.

"Sor-reee," Alys sing-songed down.

"You did that on purpose," I shouted up at her.

"That's for scaring ten years off my life!" she hollered back.

Holy crap, she *had* done it on purpose. Maybe I ought to be grateful it was only the one. I never knew Alys had such a vindictive streak. I snagged my boot laces and then held the thing aloft. It dripped on my head all the way back to shore. By the time I climbed out, my sisters were gone.

I stripped off my shirt and underwear, wringing them out as best I could, and then laid them on a flat rock in a patch of sunshine next to the poor, abused boot. I wasn't too worried about being in the raw out in the open this way. Not after what those naughty Nellies had been doing by the bonfire the night before. Saucy minxes.

What I was concerned about was actually *finding* anyone. My world was covered in concrete and steel and there were people everywhere to ask for directions. Even out at the cottage, we could hear sounds of trucks passing on the road or the occasional motorboat around a bend in the lake. But here everything was oddly quiet. The odd bird twittering, the splash of water as it slid over the rock and into the pool. Nature, unfiltered.

When exactly was this past life? I'd got the impression that it was a long time ago. Centuries. Was it my last life or had there been several between? These were the kinds of questions I was dying to ask someone. After my sisters and I became fully sanctioned, of course.

For now, I needed to get to the bottom of my curse and figure out a way to keep faux Sebastian away from not-me and my unborn child. Then I needed a long, stiff drink because this shit was confusing as all-get-out.

My instincts had told me to jump off the cliff and I had. I trusted them again to pick a direction and they did so at random. The ground was damp and mossy beneath my bare feet. Keeping an eye out for sharp rocks, or worse, snakes, I headed along the path. I would walk a half-hour in one direction before turning back. Give or take since I didn't have my fitness tracker or phone to tell me precisely what time it was. My stomach rumbled but I ignored it. When all this was over, I was going to reward myself with a big juicy steak.

"So that's what the kids are calling it these days," I muttered as a mental image of Sebastian, the real Sebastian, popped into my mind. Naked and in bed, those amethyst eyes glowing with lust. I was definitely hungrier for him than for a New York strip with a side of twice-baked potatoes. Part of me worried I had turned into that twit who was risking everything for the love of her life.

But no, I wasn't that woman. I was Siobhan Silver, an extreme badass witch and, convention flouter extraordinaire. Figuring out why I was cursed was about me, not just some random dude.

Except that he wasn't random, was he? He'd defied his code, had sacrificed everything, risked himself to protect me again and again. And yeah, I was still pretty pissed about the innocent witches whose souls he had destroyed. Those women, men too I supposed, they mattered.

Breaking from my troubled thoughts, I decided that my half an hour was up. I glanced around and saw nothing but thick ferns and big stinking rocks. "So much for witchy instinct." I groused to the empty forest.

I was about to retrace my steps back to the waterfall when I heard something. It sounded like someone calling for help. But the sound was muffled, as though the person was gagged.

"Hello?" I called out, wondering if that was a mistake.

The cry came again, louder and more insistent.

"Do you need help? Where are you?"

Another call, but this time I was sure I could make out the garbled words, *over here.* It sounded as though it were coming from a big tree with massive roots that jutted up out of the ground.

I paused and then looked around. "Keep calling out so I can find you."

Again the noise and I jolted as I realized it was coming from underneath the root. Dirt had been packed loosely against it. Had someone been buried alive beneath this tree? The thought made me shiver.

I didn't pause to consider what the person had done to end up this way. Getting to my hands and knees, I used my hands to pry away the loose soil and shoved it out of the way. Soon my hands and arms and legs were covered in mud and two of my fingernails had ripped clean off when I'd snagged them on roots, but doggedly I pushed on.

I saw a collarbone first. With a tattoo. A three-pronged fork. The symbol of the magic hunter.

"Sebastian," I breathed and increased my speed. Something in me knew it was him. Well, not-him. And not the doppelgänger faker. The actual not-him. Keeping it all straight was making me dizzy. Ignoring the twinge in my bum knee as I worked on removing the dirt to reveal his face. Adrenaline sang in my blood as I dug until I had exposed his bound arm and his face.

Gagged, as I'd thought.

His eyes opened and I saw them. The same amethyst eyes.

It wasn't Sebastian, at least *my* Sebastian. His nose wasn't as sharp, his chin less chiseled, his face gaunt to the point of emaciation. His hair was darker, brown rather than dirty blond, and much longer. But it was him. Somehow, I knew it was Sebastian.

He stilled when he saw me, the dark brows pulling together. Did he recognize me too?

I wiped my hands on the grass behind me and then reached out to lower the gag away from his mouth so he could speak. "Who did this to you?"

The only problem was he didn't speak English. A torrent of...something spilled from his lips.

I shook my head. "I can't understand you."

He kept going as I worked to shift dirt off his torso and free his legs. The limbs were bound and he was laying on his arms. I dragged him free of the impromptu grave and then set to work picking the knot loose. The words continued to spill from him like water sliding downhill after a deluge. I made soothing noises and noncommittal sounds.

Was that Welsh? Other than the endearment Sebastian used, I didn't know a single word in the language. It was entirely possible no one in this strange land would understand me, including not-me and my sisters.

Wait. I remembered coming across a magical translation incantation. What were the words again? Latin, I'd thought at the time. A luxury car brand. Lexus? No...

Clearing my throat I tried, "*Audi et intellege.*"

"...have to help her. He'll kill her once the child is born."

I blinked. Great green guacamole, it had worked!

Then the meaning behind the words registered. "Who will kill her?"

He huffed out a breath and then knocked my world off its axis. "My brother."

●

*T*he story unfolded as I worked at the ropes around his wrists with my bleeding fingers and a sharp rock. His name was Owen, not Sebastian. And he was a changeling, the product of a mortal and fae coupling. His brother, Cedric was a full-blooded fae, son of the queen and her consort. As a mortal, Owen could serve as Cedric's anchor to this realm.

Magic hunters, according to Owen, were the law keepers for their people as well as go-betweens for the magic dwellers who lived in the human settlement.

"Is that how you met…." I trailed off since I didn't know not-me's name. "Um, your woman friend?"

He turned to look at me. "Aoife. She is my lover."

"Okay then," I refocused on the bindings. That answered the is she cursed yet question.

"She is the maiden of the human tribe."

Maybe the translation spell wasn't working. Didn't maiden mean virgin? But then I recalled Maeve's telling me about the three faces of the triple goddess. Maiden, mother, and crone. Perhaps the term maiden wasn't referring to her phase of life but more of an office that she fulfilled.

Owen confirmed this when he added, "She is very important to her people. And to mine. Cedric knows this. Our mother has been trying to arrange a union between Cedric and one of the priestesses of the temple for ages. But the two elder priestesses are already wed."

"And you probably kept your relationship with her on the down-low, huh?"

Owen glanced at me over his shoulder. "You speak strangely."

No time to teach him slang. Finally, the outer coil of rope frayed enough that I could pull it apart. "I mean, you kept your relationship with, um… Aoife a secret. And I'll bet mommy-dearest wasn't too happy when she found out."

"No. I am not of the queen's lineage, just an ungrateful whelp who should have been left for dead."

The way he spoke those words, so matter-of-factly made me wince. It was said by rote, like something that had been repeated to him every day of his life and he accepted it as the truth.

"If she didn't derive so much pleasure in torturing me, she would have killed me outright." Owen wore a loose shirt that once upon a time had probably been white along with dark brown trousers. His eyes fell to my breasts and then without a word he removed his shirt and handed it to me.

"Thanks," I mutter and then hissed when I caught sight of the ribbon of scars. They cover his arms, his chest, his back. Like he had been gored by a mountain lion. "What happened to you?"

"The queen," he said.

"The queen sounds like a rank bitch." I winced as I tried to stand and my bum knee sang out in protest. "Why didn't the two of you just leave?"

"We planned to, after Beltane. She is training a new maiden to take her place in the rituals and couldn't leave until she passed the torch to her replacement."

I was starting to get the full picture. "And Cedric found out."

Owen nodded. "I must get to her. Thank you for your assistance but I must go."

"Wait," I called out, but he was already on his feet and jogging down the trail. "Damn fool man."

I pulled myself up, wincing as my knee screamed in protest. A large branch hung from the tree, partly broken off. I staggered over to it, Owen's shirt hanging loose around me. After balancing most of my weight on my good leg, I gripped it with both hands and pulled. With a crack, the branch broke loose and I immediately planted the sharp end on the ground to help me balance.

Walking stick in place, I hobbled on down the trail after Owen.

The path was worn and obvious so I didn't stray from it. An hour passed, then another. I reached a fork in the road. The changeling is nowhere in sight. Now what, eenie, meenie miney mo?

An uneasy feeling swelled up in my chest. What if not-me doesn't believe he is who he says he is? She hadn't known the difference the night before. Pregnancy brain? Or did she not know her lover had a full blown fae brother? What if Cedric got to him before he could reach her?

Too keyed up to hear my instinct, I stood, frozen in indecision. Then I heard their voices. Feminine, familiar and bickering.

My sisters.

"You need to rest," Alys was saying. "Have something to eat. Chocolate knows how long it will take us to backtrack to that pool."

"I'm fine," Maeve bitched.

"Guys," I called out and raised my hands, waving the stick above my head. "Over here."

They turned and then Alys sprinted forward and gave me a hug so fierce she practically lifted me off the ground. I let out a lungful of air and then squeezed her back.

Maeve took her time approaching us, choosing her footing carefully. She eyed my walking stick with a frown. "What happened?"

"Abused my knee when I dug not-me's significant other out of his unmarked grave."

They stared at me.

"Long story. Did you see a man run past? Shirtless and covered in scars?"

"No," Alys was digging in the pack and thrust one of the protein bars into my hand even as Maeve was unspooling an Ace bandage for my knee. "We haven't seen a soul."

That answered my question of which path led to the village. "Come on. I can catch you up on the way."

Impatiently, I waited for them to finish fussing. Bandage secure and Maeve nibbling on a protein bar of her own, we moved toward the opposite trail, in the direction of what I hoped was the human settlement.

"So Sebastian, er...Owen, he has a brother?"

"Half-brother is my understanding. Full fae. But they look alike, at least enough to convince not-me that one is the other."

"But I don't get it. Why is the fae queen so obsessed with uniting her son with one of us. The other us, I mean?"

I shook my head. "No clue, but I bet it has something to do with magic."

Alys paused. "Do you smell that?"

I stopped and sniffed. Woodsmoke. "The settlement must be close."

It appeared around the next bend and it was clear to see that the place was in an uproar. People were emerging from small wooden huts with thatched roofs and surging toward a larger building at the top of a hill that was made out of stone. A main gathering place perhaps? We got caught up in the crowd and moved along with the flow down the well-worn dirt street. My sisters were glancing around, probably taking in the primitive architecture. I was more interested in finding our counterparts.

I stopped dead when I spied the three of us, all wearing white robes and sitting on what appeared to be thrones on a raised dais outside the stone building. Not-Brock stood at not-Alys's shoulder and Not-Kal flanked Maeve. But not-me….

Her chin was up, her eyes glistening with tears as she looked down at something. I couldn't see what it was.

"We need to get closer." I hissed to my sisters.

"Lean on my shoulder." Alys reached for my walking stick and used it to clear a path by whacking the unsuspecting. It worked though as the crowd parted to let us through.

"Kill us both," I heard a male voice say. Owen's voice. "If that is the will of the triple goddess."

He was on the ground his hands bound once more. Beside him was an exact replica of him in the exact same position. His doppelganger. That must be Cedric.

"No," Cedric squirmed in his bonds. His eyes grew wild with panic.

Aoife had her arms wrapped around herself in a protective gesture. She looked so vulnerable, sitting there with her hair loose around her shoulders, her gaze rimmed in red.

"The fae have tricked us," a man called. "Seduced our Maiden."

"That's the dickhead from the ceremony." Maeve hissed in my ear. "The one who was trying to get it on with not-Sibby."

Three men, fighting over little old not-me. Being consort to the Maiden must be a good position to be in. I felt dirty and a little sad for Aoife. But didn't she know that Owen really loved her?

Judging from the blank look in her eyes, she totally didn't. I could see her lip tremble, her shoulders held with military precision to keep from collapsing.

Owen was watching her face, his own expression

reflecting her pain. He stared up at her with resolve. "Kill us both if it will bring you peace."

"No," I whispered.

Not-Alys put a hand on her youngest sister's shoulder. "It is the will of the triple goddess that both these tricksters be put to death. For betraying a priestess of the temple. For using her for their own wicked ends."

"No," I cried, my gaze going from Owen to Aoife. "That's not how it happened!"

But my protests were drowned out over the roar of the crowd. The seething mass surged forward, some carrying clubs or rocks. The mass bloodlust was palpable. A cry of pain. The meaty sound of bodies, the spray of blood.

"No," I shouted. Then louder, directed at the platform. "Do something!"

She turned away. Unwilling to look at the destruction she had wrought.

"Come away, Sib." Alys had her hand on my shoulder. "There's nothing we can do."

I yanked myself free from her grip and addressed not-me sitting there, letting this evil thing happen. Not fighting for the man she loved. Watching him die because someone else had tricked her. Because she was hurt and confused.

I hated her at that moment. Rage bubbled up inside me and I traveled to her side.

She stumbled back but I reached out and put a hand over her womb. The words came unbidden. "You deserve everything that's coming to you. Your soul will suffer no man, you will not know love, or satisfaction, or satiation because you have turned your back on it this day. You are doomed to wander the world alone forever. So mote it be."

She gasped and staggered back. Not-Kal and not-Brock reached for me but I traveled again, back to my Alys and

Maeve. And taking them by the arms, traveled back to the place of ash where a fire had once blazed brightly.

Maeve was gaping at me, her blue eyes huge. "Sibby? What the hell did you do?"

I swallowed, bent over, and threw up.

"She cursed herself," Alys murmured. "Her soul. For all time."

I closed my eyes and bowed my head. So mote it be.

14

*S*ebastian paced the confines of the cottage interior. He'd awoken at dusk and was dismayed to see that the Silver sisters hadn't returned. Outside the howl of a werewolf broke the still night. Probably the alpha singing for his mate.

Sebastian knew how he felt.

The ghost hovered nearby, still and silent.

"Are you sure she was well?" Sebastian asked Ethan once again. "That her mind was intact?"

The ghost sent him a pitying smile. "She'll be all right. She's with her sisters."

That was what he was afraid of. The spell had drawn a great deal of power. If they had been anywhere other than within the convergence, the magic hunters would have already come and obliterated the structure and any who lived there. Even now he could still taste the bitter residual of magic from their casting.

Sebastian had been a magic hunter for a very long time. Yet he had never felt anything like it. And those had been spells from *two* of the three witches. With their strengths combined, they would be unstoppable. So much power when he was completely drained. The temptation needled at the back of his mind. He shoved it aside but still, it lingered.

That's not who I am anymore.

Self-preservation was a hard habit to break.

The electric lights flickered. He glanced at the ghost and asked, "Is that something you are doing?"

When Ethan didn't reply, Sebastian made for the stairs, taking them two at a time. The power failed the way human electricity did in the face of magic. He ran down the hall and grabbed a hold of the doorframe just as lightning struck the standing mirror.

Feet emerged. Three sets, two wearing sneakers, one bare. The sisters were grimy, their hair sticking out every which way. Their shoulders slumped in defeated exhaustion.

He spied the purple hair. She was wearing a grubby piece of linen and he feared the worst, that she had been assaulted again. His hands balled into fists and he growled,

"Are you hurt? Should we take you to the hospital?"

Who do I need to kill? He thought wildly and reached for her.

She stiffened and then pushed away from him. "I'm fine." She shuffled out of the room without meeting his gaze.

"Siobhan?" He turned and would have gone after her, but a hand caught his arm.

"Leave her," Alys murmured. "She needs some time alone."

"Did she discover who placed the curse on her?" Desperate for answers he rounded on her sisters.

Maeve let out a long exhale. "She did it to herself."

Sebastian frowned. "I don't understand."

Maeve and Alys exchanged a speaking glance. Were they trying to silently decide how much they could safely tell him without betraying Siobhan's confidence?

Maeve nodded once and Alys focused on him. The eldest witch was more disheveled than he had ever seen her, with mud-spattered across her clothing and leaves stuck in her hair. She seemed more human, somehow. The lingering glow from the mirror they'd emerged from reminded him of her power.

"We met our previous incarnations," Alys spoke carefully. "Let's just say we aren't the women we used to be."

"If you want more details, you'll need to get them from Sibby," Maeve added.

He watched them exit the room and head down the stairs. Slowly, he lowered himself onto the bed. He waited for a moment and heard the gurgle of water in the ancient pipes. Siobhan must be taking a shower. Downstairs, he could pick up the low murmur of conversation, though he couldn't make out their words. The front door slammed and an engine roared to life. Alys must be driving Maeve home.

He let his head hang as he considered what came next. He felt lost and powerless in more than just his magic. He hadn't gone with them, had thought his role was more vital to pull Siobhan from the memory charm. But she had barely even *looked* at him. As though the sight of him repulsed her still.

Something shimmered in the doorway and he glanced up and saw the ghost hovering in the hall.

"What should I do?"

Ethan appeared as helpless as he felt. "There's nothing you can do unless she allows you in. Women of the Silver lineage are easy and impossible to love by turns. You ride out one storm and are hurtled into the next. The only thing you can do is make the most of the lulls in between."

Sebastian swallowed hard. "Is it worth it?"

The ghost's gray eyes met his. "Always."

Siobhan

I stared at my reflection in the bathroom mirror, hating what I saw. My feet were cut and bleeding. I'd forgotten my boots. My arms and legs were bruised from being shoved around in the crowd like a pinball. Those things would heal, eventually.

I held up a damp lock. My hair needed a change. I'd grown sick of the purple. Poison green with a red stripe maybe. Or was that too Christmasy? It didn't matter. I didn't have the supplies to do anything about my hair, other than clip it back. And I was hungry and in desperate need of comfort food. And wine. A freaking vineyard of it.

Swathing myself in a towel, I emerged from the bathroom and jerked to a halt when I spotted Sebastian sitting on the edge of his bed. He rose when he saw me and moved to the door. "Siobhan."

I couldn't look him in the eye. Not after what I'd done. Instead, I scurried into my bedroom and shut the door. There was no lock, so I moved the waist-high bookcase in front of the door. I didn't think Sebastian would try to force his way in after me but I wasn't taking any chances.

A knock sounded followed by his lyrical voice. "Siobhan? We must speak."

My eyes slid shut. The voice was exactly the same as Owen's. He was the same, just as I was.

"Go away." I backed up until my knees hit the mattress.

"You granted me sanctuary, remember?"

That seemed like a lifetime ago. A hysterical laugh bubbled up at the thought but I shoved it back down. I rooted through my closet looking for the least sexy garments I owned. Ragged gray sweats and an oversized black t-shirt with the image of a big copper-bottom pot that said Kiss My Grits.

135

Another knock. Firmer this time. "Siobhan, please. Tell me what's wrong."

Dressed, I glanced around the room. There was nothing to eat. My stomach growled. Besides, the wine was downstairs. Past the dark fae I couldn't look in the eye. I reached for my phone to text Alys to bring it up to me when I saw there was a message from her already.

Alys: Taking Maeve home and going to visit Brock. TALK to him.

"You traitorous little witch," I growled. I couldn't believe they'd just abandoned me with Sebastian without telling me they were going. Alys the overprotective nutjob. And Maeve! After all the secrets I'd kept for her. Whose side were they on?

I paced a moment and Sebastian knocked a third time. "Please, Siobhan. If this is about what I saw in your memory, then let's talk about it. It's been plaguing me since you vanished."

One more thing I didn't want to discuss. I slid the bookcase aside hard enough that it tipped over. Paperbacks went flying but I didn't care as I yanked the door open. "I really don't want to talk about *that*."

He didn't back down at my acerbic tone. "Then tell me what occurred on your journey."

I shoved past him. "I'm making dinner and getting drunk. Talking is not on my to-do list."

I thundered down the stairs and made a bee-line for the kitchen. Comfort food. Something heavy enough that it would take all my effort to digest and leave me zero room to think. To remember.

I slammed cupboard doors until I found the big copper-bottomed pot and filled it with water. There was always pasta in the house. I checked Alys's new fridge-freezer combo. It was mostly empty. Neither of my sisters cooked and with magic hijacking the electricity on a regular basis, it made no sense to overstock on perishable items. There was a brick of gouda as well as one of cheddar, plus a small container of cottage cheese. Perfect.

Sebastian had followed me into the kitchen. "What are you making?"

"Three cheese baked macaroni," I added salt to the water and then covered the pot. The water came to a boil faster at elevation but it would take the pasta longer to cook through.

Normally when I made the dish, I used a food processor to whip the cheese together. But the cottage wasn't equipped with new-fangled tech so I grab a spoon, dumped the cottage cheese into a bowl, and started mashing the large curds against the side to create an even texture.

"Can I help you?" Sebastian moved closer to me.

Was he talking about the food preparation or my unhinged mental state? Didn't much matter. Either way the answer was no. I turned my back on him and focused on my task. Was the gouda smoked? If not, I would add some smoked paprika to the dish to enhance the cheese flavor.

Cooking was good. It was classic me, lost in the rhythms of food preparation. I controlled everything and could toy with ingredients to suit my desires. Food was either good or it wasn't. All it took was a nose to figure out the difference. A witch could count on food.

I knew who I was in the kitchen. A problem solver. A risk-taker.

I stirred faster and faster, trying to drown out those awful memories with action. It didn't work. The thud of rocks hitting flesh. The blood spattering those closest to where he stood. Not-me's impassive face.

So much for star-crossed love.

Sebastian put a hand on my shoulder. "Seeing you like this is breaking my heart."

I jerked away. The bowl clattered to the floor. I put my shaking hands over my face. My whole body trembled as emotion ripped through me. A sob broke free. Followed by another. And another.

Sebastian curled his arms around me. I wanted to tell him to let me go. That he shouldn't touch me, shouldn't comfort me. But the emotion kept the tears flowing, my throat clogged to all but the wracking grief that came out in a wordless cry.

He was warm and solid beneath my hands. So alive. I clutched his shirt with my fists and wadded up the fabric. My eyes streamed. My nose ran. My knees buckled and he sank to the floor with me, heedless of the mess I'd made.

He rocked me until the wave of emotion retreated. Until my breaths became steadier. One hand stroked my hair while the other held me firm against him. I didn't deserve his comfort, but there was no way that I could force myself to pull away from him either.

"It's all right," he was saying. "Whatever it is, it'll be all right."

"You don't know," I forced the words out of my tight throat. Shaking my head back and forth. "What I did."

A finger curled beneath my chin. He forced me to meet his gaze. "It doesn't matter."

My lip trembled. "It was horrible."

He silenced me by sliding his mouth over my lips. It was a soft, sweet kiss. Not asking or demanding, but giving. Reassurance. Strength. Courage. All the things I was fresh out of.

I was a bit dazed when he pulled away. "I don't need to know, Siobhan. I know you. And I trust you."

"Because I'm supposed to be the good one." Slowly, I

pushed myself out of his arms. I stepped in the cottage cheese but didn't care.

"You are good—"

I made a sharp slicing gesture with my hand. "I'm not. I thought I was a decent person. That I was a good witch. You were the bad guy. You're the one who kills people. That's what I knew, damn it. But I was wrong. So wrong."

He didn't say anything.

I reached for the roll of paper towels hanging under one of the cabinets. I yanked and the roll unspooled in a big loop instead of tearing a few sheets free. I cursed and then tore the sheets loose. I was angry and sad and lost all at the same time.

Sebastian took some more towels and without a word, assisted in the clean-up.

I sat back on my knees and muttered, "I thought I knew who I was. Where my lines are."

"Lines?" He frowned. "Like the ley lines?"

I shook my head. "No, my personal guidelines. The ones I would never cross. Right and wrong. Those thoughts kept me together after Lima. After… what you saw happen."

"Siobhan, that wasn't your fault. You didn't deserve to be raped."

I closed my eyes. "Maybe I did."

"How can you say that?" He growled.

I shook my head. "I'm not brave or good or any of the things I believed that I was. And way deep down, in my heart, I knew it too. I'm a coward."

"You're not—"

"I ran. When I found out my aunt, the woman who raised us, had cancer. I ran away. I couldn't deal with it, Sebastian. I'm not strong like Alys or competent like Maeve. She was sick and I just… left."

It was a truth I hadn't even admitted to myself. The core of Siobhan Silver was rotten and cowardly. Self-serving.

"You were young," Sebastian said. "In those memories, you were barely out of your adolescence. Give yourself a break."

He still didn't get it. It wasn't about being a child. Not-me hadn't been a child when she'd turned her back on Owen. It wasn't about youth, it was about the true self. And mine was ugly as they came.

"Siobhan," he reached for me again. "I have seen evil up close. You aren't it."

I couldn't bear to hear him defend me for another second. Throwing the slimy paper towels into the bowl I shouted, "Do you want to know what I did? I sacrificed you. In that other life? I loved you. But when things got too complicated and my precious career was at risk, I offered you up like a fatted calf."

Sebastian frowned. "I don't understand."

"You, the other you, he was determined to save me from becoming a fae pawn. She was carrying your child. But another fae tricked her and it created a big surge of outrage in the human settlement. He gave his life to keep her safe. She let them kill him. And she is me and he is you! So tell me, Sebastian, which of us is the villain here?"

My throat swelled up again and I looked down at the battle-scarred flooring. That was it. He would leave now that he knew.

"Siobhan, look at me."

I shook my head back and forth.

"Damn you, witch look at me!"

His anger startled me into complying.

"This was why you cursed yourself?" Sebastian asked.

I nodded miserably. "I would have killed her if she hadn't been pregnant. I was so angry."

"And you did this…for me?"

He sounded almost, in awe. Not the response I was expecting.

"I did it because I was horrible and no one there would do anything. Alys, Maeve and I…we were the authority. Owen was all alone. He had no one."

His warm hands covered my cold ones. "He had you. No creature could ask for a better champion."

My eyes filled again and my lip trembled. "How can you say such things to me?"

"You say Owen died to protect the woman he loved. He gave his life to keep her and their child safe." He ran his hand over my cheek. "You are worth any sacrifice, Siobhan. Owen knew it and I know it."

A lump formed in my throat. "How could she let it happen?"

His thumb caressed my cheekbone. "You don't know everything about that world. Maybe she had no choice. You said she was with child?"

When I nodded, he murmured, "Perhaps she made her choice not to condemn Owen, but to save their child."

"She should have saved both." I lifted my chin at a defiant angle.

"And I shouldn't have killed hundreds of witches to protect myself from the fae." Sebastian smiled sadly at me. "I shouldn't have let my fear drive me into failing to see their humanity. But I did. Can you forgive me?"

I stared at him. I'd been clinging to some antiquated notion of right and wrong, good vs. evil. But life wasn't black and white. Good people did bad things. Ignorance, fear, or whatever the reason, bad things happened.

It was time for me to grow up and see all the shades of gray.

"Yes, I forgive you."

"Then you need to forgive yourself as well, *Annwyl*. For only then can you do what needs to be done."

I frowned at him. "What do you mean what needs to be done?"

"Isn't it obvious? Only the witch who lays the curse can undo it." He ran his thumbs over my lips. "You are the only one who can lift your curse. If you are willing to do so."

15

MAEVE

I couldn't get to sleep. Beside me, Kal snored like a gang of gorillas crank starting a Model T, but I was wide awake.

Tomorrow. According to Brock, and supported by Sebastian, tomorrow was the first day of the Beltane festival. The day when new magical petitioners presented themselves to the council of elders and were officially removed as targets from the magic hunter rosters.

As Sebastian had put it, "It's a fucked-up system, but it's the only one we've got. We've learned to work within it."

In the morning my sisters and I—sponsored by Brock's pack—would go before this council and pledge our fealty and our blood, to the bass-ackwards system.

And then what?

The question tumbled around in my brain like a load of tennis balls in a dryer. I knew the rules for being a witch the way things were. I knew which could be bent, and which could be broken. The cottage was our home base, our place to rest and be witchy. But when we were sanctioned, would we even bother to go there?

My phone lit up with an incoming text. I rolled over and picked it up.

Alys: You awake?
Maeve: Yeah. Want to talk? Give me five.

I hit send and then rolled out of bed. Gimli and Grogu, always ready to bound into action, poked their heads up out of their bed. Their little pointed ears perked like fuzzy antennae. I pulled on my bathrobe and then headed out of the room, corgi attendants trailing in my wake.

I held onto the railing as I moved into the darkened downstairs and shuffled to the backdoor to let the lads out to do their business. The wind was blowing hard, causing the tips of the trees to creak under the weight of new leaves. I shivered and had just turned to put the kettle on when my phone buzzed.

"Hey," Alys said.

"Hey yourself." I snagged an herbal tea bag that smelled like citrus and clove and plunked it down into my *Silver Demo and Design* mug. "Couldn't sleep either, huh?"

"It's so odd. We wanted this, right?" On her end of the line, I could hear the crackling of a fire and knew she was probably snuggled up in one of the Adirondack chairs by the fire pit. I wondered if her restlessness was causing the wind outside.

"Of course we did. Who wants to have magic hunters on their tails all the time? Worried that one panic attack will end up with you getting your soul sucked out?" Never mind brainwashing the frozen food aisle of the supermarket.

"See, that's just it. We'll be safe. But what about the others?"

"Others?" I opened the back door for Gimli and Grogu, then secured it before heading into the living room again.

"All the witches who don't know about the system. Who are as clueless as we were on day one. Is it fair that their ignorance will mean their deaths?"

"Of course, it's not fair. But what can we do about it?"

"I don't know," Alys murmured. "Something. There has to be something. I mean, you saw who we were in our past life."

"Extreme exhibitionists?" My cheeks flushed as I remembered it.

"We were powerful. Revered and respected. So much so that a crowd pulled those guys apart on Sibby's behalf."

"I'm not sure that's a good thing." I shifted and felt uneasy at my admission. "It wasn't just her fault, you know."

"What do you mean?"

"I could feel it. My gift. I mean, the other me's gift." It had slithered through the crowd like a snake, egging them on. Bending them to do her will.

Alys swore softly. "And Sibby doesn't know."

"Probably not." I hated to think of what she would do if she did know. "How's she doing?"

"I've never seen her like this. So withdrawn and quiet. It's very…un-Sibby-like."

"Things will be better after tomorrow," I said.

Alys made a sound of agreement and then we said goodbye.

"Things will be better," I repeated.

Neither of us really believed it.

Siobhan

I'd never felt my age before. Never thought about it much. Sure, I had the bum knee, the product of my first mishap on my beloved motorcycle. But that was an injury. A battle scar. Young or old didn't matter. It meant I had lived. And survived.

But lying in bed on the morning of Beltane, watching the sun rise over the hills, I felt every minute of my four plus decades. The birds were out in force, singing their little hope-filled songs of love and life. Seeming to mock my inner turmoil. Every ache and twinge, every wound physical or psychic, throbbed.

Twelve hours from now I'd be an officially sanctioned magical practitioner. Whoopee. I'd lost all enthusiasm for the prospect.

After all, what had magic brought me?

A bounty on my head. A man I couldn't keep. A curse that I should just freaking own.

Knowledge of my shadow self and exactly what a coward I truly was.

Downstairs, I could hear Alys moving around the kitchen, most likely making that diesel fuel she called coffee. I should get up, get dressed, go down there.

But I didn't move.

Someone knocked on my door. "Siobhan? Are you awake?"

Sebastian.

He'd been giving me space since that disastrous scene in the kitchen. I knew what he wanted me to do. Forgive myself. Yeah, sure, okay. Like it was that frigging easy. Maybe for him it was. After all, he'd done some truly horrific shit and he didn't have any trouble prying his happy ass out of bed in the morning. No soul searching for the soul stealer.

"Yeah," I said, not bothering to get up.

I heard the creak of the door. "Are you well, *Annwyl?*"

A loaded question if ever I heard one. "I'm fine," I lied.

"You haven't...come to me. At night."

I wanted to make a quip about him being full of himself but it would take too much effort. "Not in the mood, I guess."

He came in and sat on the bed. "I'm concerned about you."

I rolled over to face him. "Why?"

"You are not yourself."

"You don't know who I am." How could he? I didn't know who I was.

"I do." A hand landed on my back. "I have always known. And no matter what happens today, you will always be the brightest star in my sky. My true North."

His words filled me with some unknown emotion and I really looked at him. He wore jeans and a leather coat over his black t-shirt. He'd freshly shaved and the bruises from the attack had faded.

There was a bag by the door.

"You're leaving?" I swallowed. I knew his time was up, that his sanctuary ran out the minute my sisters and I were safe but I hadn't expected him not to be here when we got back.

He raised my hands to his lips. "It has been the greatest pleasure of my life knowing you, Siobhan Eloise Silver."

Something tingled through all the nerve endings in my arm and traveled straight to my heart. I wanted to grab him, tell him not to go. That we would figure something out for him too.

But what? Sebastian had broken magic council law. He was a fugitive. If they caught him, they would punish him, maybe with that memory charm. I shuddered at the prospect.

Something galvanized me as he reached the door. I flung

back the covers and charged after him. "Wait! Will I ever see you again?"

He paused and turned, then caressed my cheek. "Only in your dreams, *Annwyl*."

●

I showered and dressed, trying not to remember the tragic look in Sebastian's amethyst eyes as he said his goodbye. I made an effort with my appearance, donning the long skirt and lacey long-sleeved top I sometimes wore for job interviews. My hair was pulled back in a clip, hiding the uneven strands and I had forgone the eyebrow ring. I didn't look or feel like myself, which was probably a good thing.

Alys was sitting at the kitchen table sipping her coffee. She was dressed in a professional black pants suit and heels. The white line from her wedding ring was gone and the only jewelry she wore was a wolf's head pendant that Brock had given her for Christmas. She looked classy and well put together while I felt like a big fat phony.

"When's Maeve getting here?" I headed to the coffee pot.

"She's coming as soon as she drops her kids off from school."

I took a sip of the bitter brew, winced, and then added a healthy dollop of powdered creamer. "And Brock?"

"He's meeting us there. The whole pack is."

My eyebrows went up at that. "The whole pack?"

"Technically speaking they are our sponsors and wanted to show up to support us."

I nodded absently.

"Sebastian left this for you."

I turned and saw the proffered note in Alys's hand. My heart did a little flip as I saw my name in his elegant scrawl.

"I'm surprised you're giving this to me. I thought you hated him."

"I don't hate him, Sibby." Alys set the note down. "True, I'm not a fan of his former profession, either as the bastard lawyer or ruthless magic hunter, but Sebastian isn't a bad guy."

"Then why did you kick him out?" I asked.

She shook her head. "I didn't. He was the one who chose to leave this morning." Her blue eyes were full of sympathy.

I looked down at the note but didn't reach for it. "I didn't give him any reason to stay."

Alys put her hands on my shoulders. "Between you, me, and the wall? The right guy doesn't need a reason. He stays because his heart doesn't give him another option."

My own heart thudded. "Does that mean he isn't the right guy if he leaves?"

"No. If the right guy has to go, his heart always stays behind." She put her hand over my chest in a very tender way and gave me a soft smile. "You'll be okay, Sibby. No matter what."

She left to go outside and check the fire. Leaving me alone with my note.

I stared at it wondering what it contained. A heartfelt declaration? Information about where Sebastian was headed?

Only one way to find out. I unfolded it and read the two lines scrawled there.

The filmy nightgown was better. But you look best without any clothes at all.

-S

I snorted. And then sobbed. Big dumb jerk. Why did he have to go? It was a good thing I never wore eye make-up. With all the crying I was doing this week, I'd look like Alice Cooper.

Gravel crunched under tires and I looked out the window

to see Maeve's minivan pull up. My sister slid out, the big roses on her dress looking like splotches of blood.

Shoving that thought aside, I slipped the note into my pocket and then went to greet her.

Maeve gave me a hug and then handed me a travel mug of coffee. "That stuff Alys makes could put hair on your chest," she whisper-hissed.

"I heard that," Alys said from her position by the fire.

"Bless you," I murmured and took a sip. It was strong, but not paint-peeling with just the right amount of cream and sugar. I finished it quickly, setting the mug down on the arm of one of the Adirondack chairs.

"Almost time," Alys said.

I held Maeve's arm, letting her lean on me as we joined Alys in front of the Beltane flame. At the heart of the fire, we had sprinkled ashes from our Yule log, to connect the sabbats and our intention to practice magic. There were also the stubs of the Imbolc candles, shells from Ostara eggs, and a withered pumpkin rind from Samhain. Symbols of the pagan holidays we had celebrated since we had become witches. Proof of our dedication. An image of the Three of Cups was imprinted on my mind as I stood there with my sisters.

I stared into the flame, still holding Maeve's hand. Alys came up and took my other one.

"You ready?" Alys asked.

"Yeah." Maeve squeezed my hand.

"As I'll ever be,"

The instructions to get to the festival were simple. No chanting or summoning or potions or spells. All we needed to do was dedicate our focus to the fire and the ley lines would do the rest.

I lost myself in the flickering firelight watching as the licking tongues of fire leapt and played. And when I looked up, the world around us had changed.

The blaze before us was ten times larger than any bonfire I had ever seen. It could have consumed an entire city block in moments. It was contained though.

Music drifted to us on the breeze and the sounds of laugher. Interesting food smells were carried on the breeze from carts and tents surrounding smaller fires. It reminded me of our journey to the midnight market combined with the Highland Games festival that took place on Grandfather Mountain. A gathering of like-minded people intent on celebrating their culture.

"Lys!" Brock's Aussie accent called out. I dropped my eldest sister's hand so she could run to her mate. A smile tugged at my lips as he scooped her up and spun her around, relief clear on his face.

"Sickening, aren't they?" Maeve said, but she was smiling too.

"Like you're one to talk," I chided her.

She squeezed my hand again. "It'll happen for you too, Sibby."

It already did. I didn't say the words out loud, instead, I turned to study the area. "Where exactly is it that the council meets?"

"Over by the stream." Brock had released his grip on Alys and the two of them joined us. "The pack is holding our place. You're third on the agenda."

"Is that good?" Alys asked.

"It means your important. Everyone here is talking about you. I think the council pushed you down to send the message that you weren't the top priority. But your hearing will be observed, there's no doubt."

"We won't have to worry about magic hunters, will we?" Maeve glanced nervously around.

"No. The Sabbats are designated free days. No hunting the unsanctioned." Brock raised his hand and waved to someone. "Come on, we better get over there. The council of elders will be calling things to order any minute."

We headed away from the blaze and the general party-like atmosphere and climbed up a steep embankment. Like the Midnight Market, there was nothing around to indicate human habitation.

A circle of standing stones marked the area at the crest of the hill. There were four people seated on smaller stones within the circle and a fifth stone that remained empty.

"That's the chief gremlin," Brock whispered as he pointed to a man with grayish skin that stood about three feet high. "The head warlock, the senior shifter, and the goblin queen."

He pointed in turn to a wizened old man who looked like a modern-day version of Merlin except instead of robes he wore an Armani suit. The senior shifter was a buxom redhead who looked to be in her mid-thirties. As I watched she…changed into a little old man with liver spots. A true form perhaps?

The goblin queen was beautiful. Unlike the beasts that had come after us at the motel, this woman had smooth skin the color of polished onyx. Her hair was white as the new-fallen snow and she was dressed like a total badass in leather pants and a vest that showed off her toned midriff. Talk about aging well.

"Who is the last seat for?" Maeve asked.

"The fae representative. That's the other reason this gathering is drawing such a large crowd. There has been upheaval in the fae realm since the queen was overthrown. No one knows who will take her place as ruler. For now, one of her sons will take her place on the council."

"I thought it was supposed to be the council of elders. So wouldn't the logical choice be the next oldest fae?" Alys murmured low.

"The fae do things differently," Brock muttered.

"Why aren't the werewolves represented?" I asked.

"We aren't powerful enough. Not in terms of magic. Technically our representative is the senior shifter. But mostly we keep to ourselves."

That didn't sound right to me, but before I could protest, another man entered the circle.

Amethyst eyes fixed on me.

"Sebastian?" Maeve gasped.

But I was shaking my head. That sense of wrongness filled my chest. He wore velvet-lined robes that matched his eyes and his blond hair was cropped short but wasn't shaved in back. Not Sebastian. But...the changeling.

Or rather the fae that Sebastian's changeling was molded from. His doppelganger.

"Cedric." The chief gremlin rose and reached out a hand to the newcomer.

All the blood rushed from my head. A cold lump formed in my stomach. It froze over as that gaze settled on me once more.

It couldn't be the same Cedric from my early life. The one who had tricked not-me. Who had been instrumental in Owen's death? He had died alongside him. I'd seen it.

But in my heart, I knew he was the same fae bastard. Somehow, Owen had escaped. And he was one of the five who would be deciding our fate.

This was not how it was supposed to go. Becoming sanctioned should be quick, a formality. The ball of ice in my stomach grew larger.

The council of elders was called to order. The first bit of business was brought forth by the goblins. They wanted more territory as humans were once again encroaching. I wasn't paying attention, my heart racing as I locked eyes with Cedric.

He was staring right at me. And the feel of his gaze made

me want to hurl up the iceberg that was growing larger by the minute.

"Take a picture it will last longer," I grumbled.

The goblin petition was denied. Then another coven moved forward. To my shock, it held familiar faces, including Tully, the woman who'd done my tarot reading.

"Is that Becca?" Maeve asked when a curvy brunette about our age stepped forward. "I'll be damned. There were rumors that she was a witch but I never believed them."

Becca made her case succinctly for four other women and a preteen girl. There was talk of a demon on Halloween night and an established coven of six.

"Petition granted," the goblin queen said. "Go forth and add your blood to the cauldron."

The five women and girl moved to where an enormous caldron sat on three legs. There was no fire. Becca withdrew an athame and the girl stepped forward. Becca smiled at her and handed her the knife. The girl made a small cut in her palm and then made a fist over the cauldron. She spoke clearly.

"I vow never to use magic for personal gain, to not harm another magic wielder unless in defense of my own life, or the lives of others, and to keep magic hidden from the human world."

Becca nodded and smiled at the girl, took the knife back, cleaned it and then handed it to the next woman in line. Each made a small cut and took her vow as she dripped a drop of blood into the cauldron.

"Our turn," Brock nudged us forward.

Tully waved as she passed and Becca whispered good luck as we moved through the crowd to take our place in the semi-circle before the council.

"Elders, I am Brock of the high country pack and I present to you the Silver Sisters. Alys, Maeve, and Siobhan

Silver are legacy witches from the Silver line. They have proven themselves to be valuable allies to the wolves in my pack, even risking their own lives to help us find a missing child. We hereby sponsor their petition to be accepted into the magical community."

He stopped speaking and waited.

I held my breath as the council studied us.

"Are these the same witches who illegally used magic in the Amazon?" Cedric spoke. "The incident that caused the demise of the Headhunter, a valuable magic hunter and servant of this council?"

"It was done in defense of the Mother Superior of Magic," Maeve protested.

"Petitioners will remain silent!" Cedric barked.

Alys nudged Brock who cleared his throat. "It is as she stated. The sisters traveled to the Amazon at the request of the Mother Superior of Magic."

"Now you wish to entertain us with faery tales?" The elder gremlin snorted. "Only those daffy priestess healers believe there is such a being."

The shifter stood. "If I might serve testimony to the council."

Murmurs in the crowd told me that this was an unusual occurrence.

"The Silver Sisters are known associates of the rogue dark fae known as Sebastian. It is my supposition that they have assisted the changeling in killing not one but two of our magic hunters, including the shifter known as Bane who was sent out after them."

More murmurs as the shifter took his seat.

"The council raised the bounty on these witches," The head warlock spoke up. "Under protest and without quorum seats."

"But they have flaunted their magic at every turn," Cedric

added. "Wherever they go storm clouds gather and dozens of humans become enchanted."

"Don't talk to me about enchanting mortals," the goblin queen muttered. "You and your fae essence. How many humans are serving in your realm even now?"

Cedric ignored her grumblings. "They leave chaos in their wake and then vanish inside a convergence. Is it not the purpose of the unsanctioned time to prove that the magic users can practice restraint? If this is how they behave when under penalty of death, think of the destruction, the havoc if they become sanctioned? I was honored to be chosen to represent my people on this council. And I cannot in good conscience allow these women to practice magic legally."

"Nor can I," the shifter said.

"The Silver line is one of the strongest we have," the head warlock spoke.

"Who among us hasn't made mistakes?" the goblin queen asked. "I say we allow them in."

"Two for, two against," Alys muttered.

We all turned to face the gremlin.

He spoke two words and sealed our fate. "Petition denied."

16

"What's going on?" Sebastian asked a random witch at the heart of the gathering. He had wanted to wait until well after the Silver sisters had been welcomed by the magical community before turning himself in. Then again, perhaps he was fooling himself that Siobhan would care at all what became of him.

But there was something wrong. Normally Beltane was a time of great celebration within their community. Eating, drinking, catching up with old friends. The younger folk had a revel after the sun went down while the elders gathered around the great bonfire to share wisdom, personal news, and make plans for the upcoming seasons. There would not be another gathering of this size until Mabon and all wanted to take advantage of it.

But the air was subdued, almost furtively so. The great bonfire roared but there were no sounds of music or laughter. People were drifting off as though to find a private moment with the nearest ley line to make their escape.

Something must have happened.

The witch did a doubletake when she saw his eyes. "I... that is...." She swallowed hard.

Her hesitance irked him. Had the woman never seen a fae before? But he waited patiently for her to find her voice.

"The Silver sisters have been denied."

"What do you mean?" He gripped her by the arm and she cried out. Several others turned to gawk at them. Sebastian didn't care. He wanted to shake the witch until her teeth rattled if it meant getting answers from her.

"Don't you know this, Sir? You are a member of the council."

Sebastian released her arm and she scurried into the gloaming. Cedric. Of course, that explained her panic. The witch thought he was the fae prince.

Cedric had been appointed to the council of elders? That shouldn't be. Cedric was nowhere near as powerful as his brothers. For that matter, he knew little of the fae's interactions in this realm. Typically, Cedric was content to lounge around the palace, abusing the human thralls to amuse himself. He couldn't recall the last time the prince had left the fae realm. Of course, he could anytime he liked because Sebastian had been born to be the fae prince's anchor, his tether to the human world.

It was the only reason most fae took human lovers. A changeling child acted as a permanent anchor and all the fae needed was to find a foolish human to bargain with.

But why was Cedric here now? Why would he deny the Silver sisters admission to the magical community?

"There he is!" A hysterical female cried, breaking into his thoughts. Sebastian looked up and spied the witch he had spoken with and her....

The goblin magic hunters.

"You can't hunt me on this day," Sebastian lifted his chin.

"Special dispensation for the council's highest priority

fugitive." The female grinned. "You must have really pissed somebody off."

"The hell with this," Sebastian snarled and took off at a run. He headed straight for the bonfire, knowing that the strongest ley line ran beneath it. He could follow that to the cottage and then....

Lightning crackled down from the sky. He staggered to a halt as the cage fell around him. He was trapped.

And tonight, if Siobhan traveled to him she would be as well.

"Let him go," a female voice called out over the crowd.

Sebastian turned and spied a mortal female who looked vaguely familiar. She was middle-aged and plump with medium brown hair threaded through with gray. Her blue eyes were intent as she stared down the trio of magic hunters.

The goblins should have laughed at her. After all, she had no magical aura and her eyes didn't glow with the light of the fae. She was clearly mortal and yet the crowd didn't laugh. If anything, they seemed slightly in awe of her.

"Release him," the woman said.

"But the elders—"

The woman's smile turned up. "If anyone on the council has a problem with this, they can present themselves to me."

The largest of the goblins swallowed and a moment later the lightning cage fell.

He stared at her across the distance, the mortal female who created wariness in the hearts of such jaded creatures. "My thanks."

"Go," she said and made a waving gesture with her hand, blue eyes widening.

Sebastian didn't need to be told twice. He headed for the ley line and lost himself in it.

What the hell had gone wrong?

Siobhan

"What the hell went wrong?" Alys asked as she paced the floorboards of the cabin.

Maeve and I had no answers for her. Neither did Brock in the two hours he had sat and watched his mate bark the same question over and over.

He had been visibly miserable, poor guy. Probably feeling as though everything that had gone wrong was somehow his fault. It wasn't of course. He had been a terrific advocate for us.

We had just fucked up a few times too many.

Maeve studied the purpling twilight reflected on the still surface of the lake. "I guess I can't go home."

Alys paused in mid-stride. "What?"

Maeve turned to face her. "The only reason they let us leave at all is Beltane. Come tomorrow morning the magic hunters will be back at it. And because we filled out the paperwork with our addresses on it, they know right where to look."

Alys sank onto the couch, both hands covering her mouth. "We can never leave. Oh dear sweet dark chocolate, we can never leave the convergence."

"Because if we do, they'll be waiting." I closed my eyes and leaned back in my chair.

We sat in silence for an endless time. This was supposed to be a night of celebration. Instead, we were right back to day one when we drank the empowerment brew. Except that this time, there was no hope for a reprieve.

No one said that this wasn't fair. We knew it wasn't. Yet what could we do about it?

Someone pounded on the cottage door. Our gazes swung to it. "You're sure they can't come into the convergence?" Maeve asked.

I wasn't sure of anything but I murmured. "I doubt the magic hunters would bother knocking."

"Only one way to find out." Alys got up and went to the door, throwing it open. It was too dark out to see our visitor and her tone was baffled when she asked, "What are you doing here?"

"Siobhan? Is she here? Is she well?" I recognized Sebastian's voice and was up out of my seat and pushing past Alys. He stood there, eyes glowing. He was out of breath and his clothing dripped, completely saturated.

I didn't care. I threw myself against him. Relief coursed through me as I heard the steady thud of his heart beating beneath my ear.

He was alive and he was here. That was all that mattered at the moment.

"Are you hurt?" Sebastian gripped me by the arms and held me away so he could see me. "Did they do anything to you?"

"No, I'm fine." I looked him over. "Why are you all wet?"

"Wound up being expelled from the ley line in the lake." His teeth started chattering.

The lake was frigid year-round, the water coming mostly from snowmelt. Early spring it was particularly brutal.

"I'll get him some towels." Maeve was on her feet.

I waved her off. "He needs a hot shower. I've got this."

I helped Sebastian up the stairs and into the small bathroom. I turned on the water and while we waited for the ancient water heater to do its thing, I stripped off his coat and tugged the sodden fabric of his shirt over his head.

I reached for the snap at the waistband of his jeans but he gripped my hands. His were shaking from the cold. "You don't have to...I can manage."

"Don't be stupid. Wet jeans are damn near impossible when your hands aren't shaking." Was he really worried about me judging his shrinkage when he was freezing to death before my eyes?

I worked the button loose and pulled the zipper down.

Commando. I knew he didn't do underwear as I hadn't found any in his apartment to pack. But if this was shrinkage, I didn't think I could handle the full monty at room temperature.

All I could think was, *Holy pants python, Batman!*

"Siobhan?"

I blinked a few times. Right, pneumonia. Got to stop staring at his package and focus on the important stuff. Steam rose from behind the shower curtains and filled the small space. Together we got the wet denim down low enough that he could step out of them and into the shower. And then I was left standing there with the image of his naked body in my mind.

There were scars, lots of them, on his arms and legs. I'd seen them after he was injured with the lightning bolt to the head but had been too worried about him to really pay attention. Now I cataloged them one by one. How had he gotten them? From his time as a magic hunter? Or was it from earlier, the childhood he rarely spoke of but I somehow got the impression was...rough.

I'd traveled the world and seen both the best and worst humanity had to offer. Signs of abuse survivors varied but one thing was common—the anger. Whether it was directed inward to destroy the self or lashing out at others, anger could only be bottled for so long before it came roaring to the surface with a vengeance.

It had to be dealt with or it would consume the bearer whole. And no matter how bad they looked on the outside, I knew firsthand that the worst were the bits carved into the foundation of self.

Now wasn't the time though. But soon, we would talk about his scars. And mine.

Sebastian and I were united by more than just our damaged souls. We were the *same*. Maybe it took a few lifetimes to realize it but it was the undeniable truth.

Without considering my actions, I stripped off my frumpy clothes pulled back the curtain, and joined him in the shower.

Amethyst eyes fixed on mine. "How did you know?"

I tilted my head as I reached for the shower gel. "Know what?"

"That it wasn't me. That I hadn't betrayed you?"

I made a little spinning motion with my finger, indicating that he should turn around. "When you look at me, all my masks fall away."

I put my fingertips over his lips. Words were a weapon we both knew how to wield. Whether a magic spell or barbed rejoinder to keep those we cared about at a safe distance. Better to stay silent.

I let my hand follow the path of his scars. First the one at the corner of his mouth, then down his neck, to his collarbone and the three-pronged mark of the magic hunters. Over his shoulder where a raised and twisted bit of flesh interrupted the skin, then down over his pectorals, where the symmetrical silver slashes that looked like they'd been done by a wild animal. None of them detracted from the broadness of his shoulders, the sculpted slabs of muscle beneath the damaged skin.

I heard him swallow, and lifted my gaze to see his Adam's apple bob. He was studying my face, trying to figure out what my actions meant. *Good luck with that pal.* I didn't know myself.

All I knew was that being together couldn't be as difficult as staying apart.

I moved closer, wrapping my arms around him and pressing my ear over the thunderous beat of his heart. Slowly, his arms came up and wrapped around me, holding me close.

"I'm glad you're back," I said.

●

Alys

"What the hell could be taking them so long?" I muttered, shooting another suspicious glance up the stairs to the closed bathroom door. "The hot water tank isn't that big."

"Do I need to draw you a diagram?" Maeve asked, settling back with a steaming mug of green tea. "It goes something like he's got tab A and she owns slot B...."

I shook my head and reached for my own mug. Herbal because caffeine would probably make my head explode. "She's still cursed, remember? Do you think she's trying to kill him all of a sudden?"

"Talk about going out with a bang," Maeve murmured.

"You've been hanging out with Sibby too much," I grumbled.

"I'm taking that as a compliment."

"As you should." She was quick-witted, our little sis. But I wasn't sure all the wits in the world were going to help us bail our fat from the fire this time.

Footsteps sounded on the front porch and a moment later, Brock strode through the door. He wasn't naked, which meant he'd been stalking around in human form. "No sign of anyone yet. I have the pack patrolling."

Finally, the bathroom door opened and Sibby emerged wearing nothing but a towel. "Be down in a sec."

"Take your time," I said dryly. "Not like we have anywhere to go."

Maeve shot me a hostile glance at the same time Brock flinched. Shit. Maeve chucked her thumb toward my bedroom door. "I need to call Kal. Let him know what's going on."

"Are you going to have him bring the kids over?"

She shook her head. "I want them safe in case we are attacked."

Brock barely waited for Maeve to shut the door before he was on his knees in front of the couch. "I'm so, so sorry, Lys."

His face was filled with regret and I hadn't seen his jaw so tight since my ex was making our divorce difficult.

I stroked his cheek with my thumb. "Not your fault."

He shook his head, unwilling to let himself off the proverbial hook. "I just can't believe it. I had all these plans...." He trailed off, shaking his head.

I tilted my head to the side. "What sort of plans?"

"It doesn't matter now," he said grimly. "It's not important."

"It is to me." I gripped him by the chin and forced him to meet my gaze.

He let out a long sigh. "I was gonna build us a cabin on pack lands. The pack has already cleared trees and we've poured the foundation. It was supposed to be a surprise."

I stared at him.

He blew out a sigh and sat back on his heels. "I just thought that if you had a space that was yours alone you would feel more at home being with me full-time."

I slid off the couch and onto his lap. Our lips met in a scorching kiss. Tears streamed out of the corners of my eyes.

Brock pulled away, his golden wolf eyes narrowed as he searched my face for a sign of threat. "Are you crying?

"Happy tears," I sniffed. "I'm trying to figure out how I got so lucky to find someone who understands and adapts to me so well."

He relaxed, his eyes deepening from yellow-gold to the melty chocolate color. "I'm the lucky one, my beautiful mate. I wish to give you everything. But I didn't prepare well enough. I thought the sanctioning at Beltane was just a simple ceremony."

"It's supposed to be," Sebastian said from the top of the stairs. "This hasn't happened in my lifetime. All who petition are supposed to be welcomed."

I slid off Brock's lap and discretely wiped my face as Sebastian and Sibby made their way down to the first floor. Sebastian wore a set of sweats that I kept around for Brock. They were too short for his tall frame but at least he hadn't made a fuss about wearing someone else's clothes. A moment later my bedroom door opened and Maeve rejoined the party, looking glum.

"Everything okay?" I asked her.

She nodded and forced a smile. "I miss them already."

"We'll figure something out," I told her because we had to. There was no alternative. Past witches might have been content foraging in the convergence and living out their lives in secrecy but we were modern girls. We liked pizza and wine and the occasional trip to the beach. We had jobs, friends, and responsibilities outside of our magical home base. Maeve had kids and doctor's appointments to go to.

In a nutshell, we had to figure a way out of this.

"Tell me exactly what happened once you arrived at the great bonfire."

Sibby started off, with Maeve jumping in to add a detail here or there.

"And that was it. Petition denied."

Sebastian nodded his head. "Cedric. I'm not surprised Blocking your petition buys him time."

"Time for what?" I ask.

"To court Siobhan."

"What?" Sibby asked. "Why would he want to do that?"

"Because you're the only one without a mate," Brock offered.

Sibby rolled her eyes. "So I get the designated creeper by default? Skippy."

I shook my head. "Why would he want anything to do with us? I thought each of the magical factions mostly kept to themselves."

Sebastian nodded. "Some do. The goblins are solitary by nature as are the gremlins. But the witches and shifters often congregate in communities. The fae cannot as they need anchors to stay in this world. That is what I, the changeling child, am for Cedric. My soul connects him to this place. It's why he takes my shape when he is in this realm. It is believed, however, that if a fae mates with a powerful witch who bears him a child to be an anchor, he will be able to stay without the bargains. He will be free to harvest magic at will."

"I still don't see why that's a bad thing," Maeve was fidgeting with the fraying edge of a couch cushion. "So what if some super magical guy gets a little stronger?"

"You don't understand." Sebastian's expression was troubled. "He won't grow incrementally stronger. With a witch-born anchor, he will be able to collect all the magic in the ley lines. Rewrite the world of magic to suit his purpose. And no one could stand against him. Not even the three of you."

17

SIOBHAN

J turned a page in the Grimoire, the family book of personal spells. I didn't know what I was looking for. Hell, maybe I wasn't really looking for any sort of answer. Skimming the pages of these books brought me a sense of comfort and connection. To my mom, to Aunt Jess, and especially to my sisters.

I needed that.

That bastard Cedric. Sebastian had confirmed that he was the same guy that I had seen in the past life spell. Older fae tended to accumulate more power and Cedric apparently was very *very* old. Glamours were his specialty. He could also change his appearance and did to resemble his anchor. First, his brother Owen and most recently, Sebastian.

I remembered that guy that had been so vocal at the hearing, the one who'd accused the fae of messing with the Maiden. Had Cedric switched his appearance with that male and taken out both of his rivals?

In that case, the only thing that was preventing him from having his witch born heir was my curse.

Cedric wanted me. Wanted to trick me, to use me to give him a more powerful anchor.

In a word…ick.

Upstairs in the shower, I'd decided I'd find a way to undo my curse. Because I wanted Sebastian. And I wanted to have all the things I was missing out on. A real life. But knowing that I was part of some master plan for Cedric, that he fully intended to impregnate me….

A shudder gripped me and I wrapped my arms around myself.

Not-me hadn't seemed to notice the difference between Owen and Cedric. But I had known. Would always know. There would be no tricky fae deception mojo to fool me into getting knocked up.

My curse aka failsafe plan B. Even if he did grab me and force me, the curse would take him out before he got what he wanted.

Talk about cold comfort.

A soft shuffling sound dragged my attention to the door of the greenhouse. "Am I disturbing you, *Annwyl?*"

"I'm disturbing me," I muttered and then beckoned him forward.

Sebastian entered the greenhouse and then closed his eyes. "I can feel it here. The Convergence sings in this room."

I hopped up on the worktable beside the book and studied him. "Is that part of what your fae heritage gives you? A sensitivity to magic?"

He opened his amethyst eyes and focused on me. "I have no fae heritage."

I frowned. "But I thought a changeling was half fae, half human?"

"The fae are humans, *Annwyl.* Just as witches are human and shifters too. The way we channel magic is what makes us different from one another. Underneath, we are all the same."

"The gremlins and the goblins too?"

At his nod, I thought it through. "So why do we all channel magic in different ways? And why can you see when Ethan is around but my sisters and I can't?"

"Why are some people taller than others? Why do some have red hair and others brown and still others black or blonde? Some have skin the color of shadows at midnight and others pale as fresh snow and every variation in between. We are all our own creatures. Fundamentally the same yes, but unique in our composition. Some of us choose to focus on developing particular skills and others create blocks that keep us from reaching our full potential." He skimmed his fingers across my cheekbone. "Why are we attracted to some things and repelled by others?"

I hitched in a breath. "I'm pretty sure you're a masochist. Why else would you be sniffing around me and my big closed for business sign?"

His brows drew together. "I do not derive sexual satisfaction from pain, Siobhan. Not mine or others. Believe me."

The look in his eyes made me shiver. I shut my own. "Sorry, it was a piss poor attempt at a joke."

"You jest when you are uncomfortable. To distract those around you from seeing your discomfort."

He wasn't wrong. "Yeah, I do."

"Why?"

"Alys, mostly. In case you haven't noticed she's very protective."

Sebastian made a sound like a stifled snort and I opened my eyes and grinned at him. "Oh, so you did notice."

"I do not want you to think I would speak ill of your sisters. I know how much they mean to you. And oddly, I...," he paused as though searching for the correct word. "I respect Alys."

"Why is that odd?" Alys was a force of nature even before she could command the weather.

"Magic hunters don't respect the unsanctioned."

"But you respect me," I pointed out.

Sebastian shifted and glanced away. "I do not wish to lie to you, *Annwyl*. Not ever again."

"Is that your way of saying you *don't* respect me?" Teasing Sebastian was almost as much fun as getting a rise out of Alys.

He looked so horrified at the thought that I lifted my palms up and pressed them against his chest. "I was kidding. I know you respect me now."

"But I didn't in the beginning. I mistakenly thought you were the easy mark. The one I could use to create a rift between the three of you. I couldn't have been more wrong." He shook his head and then studied my face. "Are you angry?"

"What, you think you're the first guy to ever underestimate me?" The second the joke escaped I realized I was doing it again, deflecting from deeper emotions by lightening the mood. I sobered and asked, "When did all that change?"

"When you gave me this." He reached into his pocket and pulled out a twenty-dollar bill. It took a moment to figure out the relevance to our conversation but when I did a laugh bubbled up. I'd forked over a twenty when I'd thought Sebastian was just an attorney and I wanted the protection of attorney-client privilege to keep our witchy shenanigans under wraps. "What? Why?"

"Because it showed me the way your mind works. It was so complex and yet so straightforward. You did in an instant what others have attempted and failed at for centuries—you disarmed me. I already felt things for you but that moment changed how I looked at you."

I peeked at him through my lashes. Studied the intent way his amethyst eyes focused on me.

"I never know what you'll do or say next, Siobhan Silver. And I find myself holding my breath. Waiting for the next word you speak. The next smile you give. Your every decision is fascinating and I wish to know everything about you. The more I understand the more addicted I become. Discovering why you are the way you are is my greatest joy. Tell me then why you make light because of Alys?"

It was hard not to blush after a speech like that, even harder to pick up the thread from our earlier conversation. It was always like this when I talked to Sebastian, thoughts getting derailed right and left. Part of it was pure animal magnetism. I craved his touch, longed to explore his body and have him map mine.

But there was more to it than that. It was this burning desire to spill out all of my secrets. To share myself in a way I never had before. That wasn't me. I played my cards pretty close to the vest most of the time. I gave people surface things to judge with quippy retorts and counterculture wardrobe. Because once you gave them something to judge, they dismissed you and quit looking.

Sebastian would cherish each and every secret and treat it like a gift.

What had he asked? Oh, the deflection thing.

"Alys is overprotective to a crazy extent. Since I was the youngest and the most likely to act out, she tended to overreact at anything that happened to me. There was this one time when a kid shoved me off the slide and I went over the edge and landed on my wrist. It was not too long after mom died, so her tension was already high and her protective instincts were on DEFCON 2.

"Anyway, this jerk pushed me and I fell. It was a bad sprain and I started to cry. Alys totally lost her shit. She yelled at the kid and then when his mom came up to find out what was going on, she tore a piece out of her too. It was a hell of a scene, especially for a small town like Eckhart where naming a section of highway is a major unveiling. Tongues wagged for weeks over that."

Sebastian's brows drew together tighter as I relayed the story. He reached out and took my hand. I hadn't mentioned it had been my left wrist that had been injured. I didn't know if it was intentional on his part or not, but his thumb gently stroked over the wrist I had sprained.

"I'm not sure I understand," Sebastian murmured.

"I learned to laugh and deflect to cover my hurts. If I didn't, my big sister would have torn the world apart to protect me."

"You're right," a soft female voice said from the doorway. "And she still would."

"Shit," I winced theatrically to Sebastian. "Does she look angry?"

His lips twitched. "No more so than usual."

I snorted at the same time as Alys growled, "Could I please have a moment alone with my sister?"

Instead of answering, Sebastian looked directly into my eyes as though waiting for something.

"In case you haven't noticed, I already have one over-bearing protector." I chucked my thumb toward the door. Since I was already in hot water, why not stoke the fire a bit?

His expression turned wicked. "Then, I shall have to find another way to service you."

He brought the hand he was still holding to his lips and laid a gentle kiss on the knuckles.

"Holy hot flash, Batman," I muttered when he was safely out of hearing distance.

"Damn, Sibby." Alys sounded more like me than herself.

Maeve trailed her into the room. "I have no idea how

you're restraining yourself around him. The heat you two are throwing off could power the lunar module."

I took a minute to make sure that my knees wouldn't give out and then slid off the worktable so I could face them. "About what I said—"

Alys put her hands up. "Look, you don't have to."

"I was raped," I blurted. "In Peru."

Maeve gasped but Alys didn't move a muscle. Their shocked silence filled the small greenhouse.

"Technically gang-raped, by a guy I knew and his buddy who thought they needed to bring the arrogant *gringa* down a peg or two. They died right after. That was the last time I had sex."

"Oh, Sibby," Maeve put her hand on my arm.

My gaze was fixed on Alys as well as the night sky behind her. No lightning striking down. Yet.

"That was the memory I was reliving," I explained. "The one Sebastian pulled me from."

Alys swallowed once. "And you didn't say anything? Not to Maeve even?"

"Like Maeve can keep a secret from you for long" Damn it, there I went again. Deflection was a hard habit to break. I shut my eyes and murmured, "I'm sorry."

Alys didn't say a word. She didn't ask if I had gone to the police or seen a doctor or talked to a therapist. She didn't harp on the fact that I had kept what had happened to myself for so long or tell me what to do. She just held me.

On her stool, Maeve was wiping at her face. "How? How did you get through it?"

I shrugged. Alys held me tighter and I felt the damp trickle of tears that rolled down her cheek as well.

I didn't cry. I'd shed all the tears I ever would over what happened in Peru. I'd sobbed myself to sleep for the better part of a decade and jumped at every noise. Those men had hurt me, had brutalized me, and stolen my feeling of security along with my belief that deep down people were good. My curse had stolen their lives. It had taken a long time for me to make peace with that.

They were evil men and I had killed them. Not by choice. But I was still responsible for their deaths.

But this two-decade-old bulletin was breaking news for my sisters. I held Alys and squeezed Maeve's hand and murmured things like, "I'm okay. Really."

"I'm sorry," Alys whispered.

"What could you have to be sorry about?" I asked her.

"That I made you hide how you really felt. That you couldn't talk to me. That I didn't believe you about Kyle hitting on you before our wedding. That I made you feel unwelcome. That I wasn't there for you when—" She broke off on a choked sob.

And it was my turn to embrace her and I found out that I did have a few tears left to shed.

***

Sebastian sat beside the werewolf on the front steps of the cottage. Neither of them wanted to venture too far from the sisters in case their witches needed them. He had no idea what to say to the werewolf and Brock made no overtures so they waited in uncomfortable silence.

Headlights appeared around the bend and then the sound of a car maneuvering around the deeper potholes in the rutted road. Sebastian stiffened but Brock remained at ease so he didn't get up.

"It's Kal," Brock said as though reading his mind.

"How do you know?"

"Would you want to be away from Siobhan right now?"

The wolf had a point.

A moment later a battered sedan appeared and Maeve's human mate got out. A scraping sound from the direction of the greenhouse and then Maeve's voice. "Kal? What are you doing here? Where are the kids? Are they all right?"

"The kids are fine. They're at Lora's." Kal moved up the path to the greenhouse and took his wife in his arms.

"You have much knowledge," Sebastian murmured.

Brock grinned at him. "Stick around and I shall teach you the way."

Sebastian fully intended to stick around.

Maeve and Kal were still embracing and blocking the door but Alys squeezed out past them. Brock stood and she walked right into his waiting arms.

"You've been crying," Brock murmured as he stroked the side of Aly's face. "Is everything all right?"

"Fine," Siobhan said brightly. Too brightly. He hadn't intended to join the party congregating on the lawn but the sound of her voice, strained and tight, drew him like a magnet.

His true north.

Siobhan moved to the chairs around the fire pit. Before she could sit, he scooped her up and then placed her on his lap. She startled and made a sound of surprise but then settled against him.

"I told them. About what happened in Peru."

He kissed the top of her head and remembered how she had come to him in the shower. "You're the bravest person I have ever met."

He could feel her smile against him.

The others joined them and Kal started the fire. They sat together in silence but it no longer felt uncomfortable or strained.

"Is there anything anyone wants from anywhere that's not

here?" Siobhan asked. "We have less than an hour until midnight."

"What happens at midnight?" Kal asked.

"The Beltane reprieve ends," Sebastian told the mortal. "The magic hunters will be free to go after the sisters any time they leave the convergence."

"It feels like we're battening down the hatches for a natural disaster," Maeve murmured. "Or getting ready for a siege."

"We can't spend the rest of our lives here," Alys grumbled.

"What choice do we have though?" Siobhan asked.

"I don't know." Alys leaned back in her chair, clearly frustrated.

Siobhan placed her small hand over his heart. As far as prisons went, he couldn't ask for better. Everything he desired was within reach.

But Sebastian understood the sisters' frustration as well. As a magic hunter, he had been part of a community. And his choices had lost him those connections. He would not have called his fellow hunters friends, but they were inextricably linked. At least until he had severed himself from the collective.

"Stupid Cedric," Siobhan muttered. "Who died and made him king of everything anyway?"

Sebastian stiffened. Her words echoed in his head. *Who died.*

"The queen," he murmured, looking at her.

Her face glowed in the firelight. "What?"

"The fae queen died. That's what allowed Cedric the spot on the council of elders. Only it shouldn't be his spot. It belongs to the one who dethroned her."

The image of the woman at the festival. The small, pale human. Robin Goodfellow's mortal mate.

He rose and caught Siobhan to him so she didn't end up on the ground in a heap. "You are a genius," he told his witch.

"Tell me something I don't know," she quipped.

"What is it?" Alys was on her feet too. "Where are you going?"

"To find the rightful ruler of the fae."

SIOBHAN

"So, explain to me again exactly how this will help us?" I turned to face Sebastian's profile that flickered as we passed cars on the highway.

We had all piled into Maeve's minivan. Kal sat behind the wheel and Alys directed us to the address she had found for Robin Goodfellow on an internet search. It had shocked all of us to discover that the fae prince had settled down in a town less than thirty miles from Eckhart.

Help up for grabs right here in the high country. Sure, we couldn't get decent Chinese takeout, but the place was crawling with magic folk.

Sebastian turned so that he was facing me and made sure his words would reach Maeve and Brock who sat back in the third row. "Robin Goodfellow's mortal mate did the impossible. She tricked the most powerful fae queen who ever ruled and won the queen's magic. But Robin told me his mate didn't desire the magic and didn't want to live in the fae realm. So, she allowed it to dissipate. That left a power vacuum in the fae courts."

"Allowing Cedric to take control," Alys inserted.

Sebastian nodded. "Precisely."

"We have to convince this woman that she has to step up and be a queen?" Maeve asked. "That shouldn't be too difficult. What woman wouldn't want to be a queen?"

"One who doesn't want to live in the fae realm or make bargains to stay here?" I suggested. "She already said no once. What makes you think we can convince her to change her mind?" I was eyeballing the clock in the dash. 11:37. At 11:50 I was going to jump all six of us back into the convergence, no matter if we had found this mysterious woman who had the guts to go up against a fae queen and the smarts to win.

She was kind of my hero. I was trying hard not to get too excited about our little potential coup.

"Up ahead on the left," Alys called out.

I peered through the window at a stately Victorian. Lights were on and figures moved about within. At least we wouldn't be yanking them out of bed to hear our hare-brained scheme.

We unloaded from the van and headed single file up the walkway beneath budding magnolia branches. With the full moon behind us, I could see the hodgepodge of flowers in the neat beds. Since Sebastian was somehow related to Robin, it had been decided that he would be the one to knock.

A gust of wind made him shiver and he knocked brusquely. Poor guy had redressed in the damp clothing that had come out of our little lake. He didn't want to wear someone else's duds for this visit and since there was no washer or dryer at the cottage, he wore his soggy garments. He didn't complain though. All his attention was focused on his task as he knocked on the door.

It swung in. A middle-aged brunette stood there, a chubby toddler perched on her hip.

"It is you," Sebastian breathed.

I stepped forward. "You two know each other?"

Behind her, a very handsome blond guy sauntered down the hall holding a baby bottle. "Lamb, who's there?"

I caught sight of his brilliant blue eyes, the color of polished sapphires. I'd seen him before. Not in the flesh, but a shade version of himself in the Amazon. He'd helped Sebastian then. "Your brother," the woman called back, not taking her eyes off Sebastian. "The one with the price on his head."

She didn't look afraid exactly. Wary and she clutched the baby closer. Sebastian's focus shifted from the woman to the child and he cringed slightly.

The baby had the same unearthly blue eyes as Robin.

The two men stared at one another. Robin had gone out of his way to help Sebastian before, Why was he throwing up a roadblock now?

Then I caught sight of the slight movement as Robin placed himself between Sebastian and his family. Ah, so that was it. Brother or not, Robin didn't like the former magic hunter on his home turf.

Sebastian lifted his chin and waited with an arrogant expression on his face. My guy was not rocking the people skills. Good thing he had me.

I surged forward, sticking out my hand. "Hey there, I'm Siobhan Silver and these are my sisters, Maeve and Alys. And their baggage," I chucked my thumb at Brock and Kal.

The woman let out a little laugh but stifled it when Robin turned to stare at her.

"What?" she asked. "It's funny."

"You never laugh at my jokes, lamb." The man's brilliant gaze turned affectionate.

"That's because you only think you're funny." She poked him in the chest.

I decided that she was my people and continued. "We're

so sorry to bother you so late but we're in a bit of a jam and could use your help. Mind if we come in?"

Robin opened his mouth to protest but the brunette handed him the baby and gestured us in. "Of course. I'm Joey, by the way. Joey Whitmore."

I followed her into an ornate front parlor that was covered in baby paraphernalia. A portable crib was set up in the corner along with a baby swing and a basket full of stuffed blocks. The remains of a partially eaten meal sat on the sideboard, steam still rising from it.

A teenager sat in the corner with a set of headphones on while she made a series of quick lines across a sketchpad.

Joey tapped her on the foot. "Dragon, we've got company. Would you mind clearing out?"

The girl had crimson streaks in her hair and the back of her head was shaved. She wore a black muscle shirt paired with a leather miniskirt over intentionally ripped black stockings and combat boots. Another outcast. She looked up and started at the sight of so many strangers in the house. She removed her headphones and then stood up. "Who are all these people? More freaks?"

It was my turn to laugh. "You got that right, kid. Are we in the right place then?"

The corner of Dragon's mouth hiked up. "Most definitely."

"Would you put Josh down, please?" Joey asked. She had the same strained but contented look on her face that I recalled Maeve having when the twins were young. A baby who didn't sleep plus four decades of life took its toll.

Still, a pang went through me as I looked at the baby.

"Yeah, okay." Dragon got up, flipped her pad closed, and then reached for the infant and the bottle Robin still held. "Come on, nugget. Time to let the weirdos do their thing."

"Nugget?" Sebastian's gaze was fixed on the baby. "I thought you said his name was Josh?"

"It's a nickname. Actually, a nickname of a nickname." Robin told him.

"Nugget is short for butt-nugget." Joey rolled her eyes.

"Kid poops bricks," Dragon added helpfully. "Probably because Joey's milk has curdled by now."

"Good night, smartass." Joey sighed and then gestured for us to sit on the antique fainting couch. "And that was probably way more than you wanted to know about me or my son. Can I get you anything?"

My gaze went to the grandfather clock at the foot of the stairs. Eleven forty-three. "No, and we need to make this quick. We need you to take over as queen of the fae."

Joey sat down across from me. "I'm sorry, but no."

"They respect you," Sebastian said. "You called off those magic hunters."

Joey wrung her hands. "I know they do, though I'm not really sure why and other than today, I try not to abuse it. I promise, I'll do anything else to help you that I can. But I don't want to live with the fae. Especially not with Josh. From what Robin's told me changelings aren't treated any better than thralls."

Sebastian flinched and Joey picked up on it.

"I–I'm sorry," she stuttered. "I didn't mean—"

"It's all right," Sebastian said though I could tell by the drawn look on his face that it wasn't. Of course not. If Joey had heard about the changeling abuse from Robin, it didn't take a genius to figure out who the star of those horror stories had been.

I thread my fingers through his and squeezed. He glanced over at me and his shoulders relaxed a bit.

"Besides, the thought of using magic freaks me out," Joey

added. "I'm sorry, I wish I could help you, but it took me a long time to get my life on track. I won't give it up."

"Joey has made her choice." Robin sat beside her and put an arm around her shoulders.

Alys let out a long breath. "Then I guess we're out of options as long as Cedric sits on the council."

"He shouldn't be," Robin said. "Andreas is the rightful heir."

●

Sebastian stared at Robin. "Andreas? What does he have to do with this?"

Andreas was yet another of the queen's children. He was not one of the ones Sebastian knew well as he tended to keep mostly to himself. Andreas had never abused Sebastian, had never even seemed to notice him on the rare occasion he was present in the fae realm.

There had been rumors about him having a mate and a child. Murmurs that sounded like court gossip. But perhaps there had been more to it.

Robin nodded. "Andreas was there the night Joey tricked mother. It was he who dealt her the death blow."

Shock reverberated through Sebastian. Andreas had killed the queen? "Do you think he would help us?"

Siobhan leaned forward, an eager expression on her face. "We're running out of time. The magic hunters will be coming after us as soon as Beltane is over."

After her. Because Cedric would use his influence with the guild to capture Siobhan alive and use her for his purposes, even as Maeve and Alys powers' were divvied up as a juicy reward for the faithful hounds.

For the first time in his life, Sebastian was beginning to understand how easily the system that had been designed to keep the whole community safe could be corrupted. Considering his part in it made him ill.

"I don't know," Joey hesitated a moment and exchanged a glance with Robin. "We're not even sure where he is. He's been…reclusive since it happened."

"Do you have something of his?" Maeve asked. "Something we could use to scry for him?"

"We don't have time," Alys began.

"We do if we split up," Siobhan murmured as though speaking to herself.

"Split up?" Maeve and Alys said in unison as though the idea horrified them.

But Siobhan's gaze fixed on him. "Cedric wants me the most and Sebastian probably just as bad, since you're his anchor, right?"

He nodded.

"So, we'll lead them away from you. You two can scry for Andreas and convince him to stage a coup and we can take care of Cedric once and for all."

"But—" Alys began.

"There's no time," Siobhan insisted.

"Time," Joey muttered and then glanced at Robin. "Where is it?"

"Where's what?" Sebastian asked but the fae was heading out of the room.

"It's the enchanted object I used to trick the fae queen with. A pocket watch that can rewind time. It's a valuable part of Robin's fae hoard and might come in handy."

Robin returned and dropped the watch into his hands. He also held a blue t-shirt splattered in blood. His eyes were apologetic as he gave it to Alys, who wrinkled her nose and took it between two fingers. "This is the only object I have of Andreas's. It's his blood, so you can use it to track him."

"Thank you," Alys grumbled.

"We appreciate your help," Sebastian said stiffly.

"I'll see you out." Robin leaned down and murmured something to his female. She put her hand over his and squeezed. The expression on her face was so tender and Robin looked as though if there were beasts to slay he would happily battle them just for the chance to lay them at her feet.

Sebastian knew the feeling. He could see why neither of them would be eager to give up the life they had built.

Siobhan stood by the vehicle, bouncing on her toes, but Robin caught his arm. "You are without magic?"

Sebastian stiffened. Robin released him and put his hands up to show that he wasn't going to take advantage of his powerless state.

"Forgive me, brother. I wish I could do more to help but my powers have dissipated as well. And I am glad for it."

"Words I never thought I would hear you speak."

"Some things in life are more important than others." He glanced back over his shoulder with a soft smile. "When all this is done, perhaps we can get together with our females as is the mortal tradition. For a holiday, perhaps."

Sebastian's brow furrowed. "You would want that? To bring your wife and child near me?" It was a show of trust he could hardly fathom.

"Joey has a great deal of family and they are always near. It has made me realize how important it is to cling to those who knew you when you were young and foolish." His grin turned rueful. "To have those you could count on when you are in distress. I would like very much to be that for you as well as for Andreas."

A lump formed in Sebastian's throat but before he could decide what to say, Siobhan called his name. "I must go."

"Safe travels, brother," Robin called.

The others were clustered around Siobhan, who had one

hand on the van. Her gaze fixed on him and Sebastian put both hands on her shoulders.

"This is a lot of weight," Maeve muttered. "Maybe you should leave the van."

"You might need it." Desire glowed in Siobhan's blue eyes as she stared up at him. "I have what I need."

Sebastian wasn't so sure. There were limits to even a Silver sister's power. If she overtaxed herself she would leave herself weak and vulnerable for days. Magic was a wellspring that needed time to refill. Before he could voice his protests however, they traveled. To the lawn before the cottage. Siobhan staggered and went down to her hands and knees. Fear for her gripped Sebastian's heart.

"Sibby," Alys was by her side in an instant. "What's wrong?"

"I'm okay," Siobhan said. "Just a headache."

"You drew too deeply," Sebastian chastised. "Are you going to vomit?"

When Siobhan shook her head, he scooped her up. She made a surprised-sounding squeak. "Where are we going?"

"You need rest." And he needed to get out of his wet clothing and hold her.

"But the plan—,"

"The plan can wait until you've slept and eaten. Besides, it will take time to prepare the scrying potion, will it not? No one has anywhere to go until it is ready." He knew it would. Scrying was a useful skill but it would take time. She'd volunteered to be bait. To leave her sisters behind and run with him. He had no magic, nothing to protect her any longer. But he could still care for her. Make sure all of her needs were met.

They were a team. The partner he never knew he wanted.

He passed the ghost on the stairs but Ethan said nothing as he carried Siobhan into the room where he'd been staying.

He kicked the door shut with his foot and then laid her upon the bed before he began stripping off his wet clothes.

"What are you doing?" Siobhan groaned.

"Giving you what you need." Naked he crawled on top of her.

19

SIOBHAN

"I have a headache," I grumped even as panic warred with lust in my veins.

Sebastian smoothed his hand over my face in a caress that was both comforting and arousing. "I know you do. It's because I haven't been giving you enough raw desire to fuel your power. I mean to make up for that."

His voice was low and husky and sent a spike of want through me.

"My curse," I whispered.

"We won't have sex," he assured me. "But let me stoke your fire, Siobhan. Let me help you the only way I can."

And okay, it was a cheesy freaking line but the thing about lines is, when both parties are interested, they work. Like really effing well.

And I was most definitely interested. Even though it felt like a herd of woodpeckers had taken up residence in my skull.

"Is this all right?" Sebastian asked as he stroked my temples lightly.

"Mmm-hmmm." I'd never thought of that as a particularly

erogenous zone before. But when he touched me there it sent a gentle wave of pleasure rippling through my body.

His lips followed his fingers, brushing so softly against me. "Tell me no at any point, *Annwyl*, and I will stop, all right?"

My eyes had been shut to block out the pain. It was beginning to ebb as he touched me and since I was pretty sure my head wasn't going to split open like an overripe melon, I dared to crack an eyelid.

Sebastian was watching me very carefully even as his hands glided up and down my arms in soothing strokes. As though waiting for something. Reassurance maybe?

"I'm not going to freak out," I said and hoped fervently that it was true.

Honestly, I didn't know. Lima had been my last sexual encounter before Sebastian and memories from that night still made me wake in a cold sweat. Just the thought of sex made me feel panicked.

He took my hand and brought it to his lips. "We both have scars." He placed my hand over his chest so I could feel the steady beat of his heart. "The worst ones are trapped in here. But I'm tired of letting my past dictate my present. I'm tired of running. Of hiding and pretending that I am okay when I'm not."

He had that same air of vulnerability about him that he'd had in the shower. Like then, my instinct told me exactly what he needed. It was time for me to heed the moon card. Follow my intuition.

"I love you," I told him. "And I trust you."

I wasn't sure which statement affected him more. His whole body shuddered and his amethyst eyes lit up the darkened room.

"Siobhan," he murmured softly and I knew that no matter what he had promised, our relationship was about to change.

Because the truth was? I was tired of being afraid, too.

Warning! Warning! Danger, Will Robinson! We're gonna get busy in a big way. And it might last a while because I'm pretty much sex-starved and Sebastian is really freaking hawt. And naked. If you're not into all the gory details, close your eyes and think of England and then head on over to the next chapter. My happy ass will meet you there.

But if you stay, you randy little perv? You're totally my tribe.

The headache was barely noticeable. His touch did wonders. Each gentle caress made me aware of how much I wanted to be touched. He had promised we wouldn't have sex. But there were other things we could do.

More. He needed to give me more. I pulled him down on top of me. Directed his lips to meet mine. It felt like ages since we'd kissed, even longer since we'd done so without the intent to stoke desire so I could travel.

This wasn't for magic's sake. It was for ours.

My lips parted and my tongue twined with his even as his hand crept under my shirt. It skimmed over my ribs. I arched into him. Could feel his erection pressing into my hip. I'd seen him naked before but this was the first time I felt free to touch him. To explore all the planes and angles that I had been lusting over since the first moment I'd seen him.

His skin was clammy from the damp clothing. I stroked his naked flesh, trying to share my heat with him while exploring his hard body.

I wanted his hands on my boobs already, or between my legs where I was wet and needy. Too much fabric in the way, though.

He groaned when my teeth sank into his bottom lip, not hard enough to break the skin, but enough to let him know I needed to come up for air.

"Let me up," I gasped.

He scrambled off of me in a moment. "Are you all right? Did I hurt you?"

I shook my head and then whipped my t-shirt over my head. Unfastened my bra let it fall to the floor and then started working on my jeans.

Sebastian's gaze turned molten as he watched me wriggle out of the denim, then hop on one foot to remove my boot so I could be totally naked.

Silence stretched out where all I could hear was my pulse pounding in my ears.

"You're incredible," he murmured. His hand actually shook as he reached for me again. I didn't know how well he could see in the dark but that amethyst gaze devoured me from uneven purple hair to bare feet. He took his time, just looking as though my four-decade-old body was some sort of priceless work of art.

"Jeez," I said because I couldn't take another second of his silent scrutiny. "If I knew this was your kink, I totally would have been sexting you dirty photos for months."

"I prefer the live version," he said and then was on his feet beside me. I didn't know what to expect but he picked me up and laid me down on the mattress. He drew my fingertip up to his mouth and sucked the pads of the first two between his lips.

"I've been imagining this every night," he said. "Show me how you pleasure yourself, Siobhan. I want to know what you need so I can give it to you."

Hot dawn. His filthy words made my heart beat faster. My hand trailed down to the shaved mound between my legs. I parted them wide. He hissed in a breath when I parted them wider and began to stroke the piercing on my most sensitive bundle of nerves. Wetness had seeped from my core and the contact made me arch as though electrical current was running through my system.

"Wider," he commanded. "Spread your legs wider."

I moaned and my eyes slid shut and moved my feet further apart. My finger dipped down to my core, capturing the wetness there and using it to heighten my pleasure.

"Inside," he instructed. "Let me see you put your fingers inside."

I did and arched off the bed. Not enough. It's not enough. I returned to working the piercing on my clit.

"What are you thinking about?" Sebastian's fingers traced along my cheeks. "What is it that brings you pleasure?"

"You," I breathed the word.

"Look at me while you do this. Tell me what it is I do in your fantasies?"

"Touch me," I moaned and my fingers sped up as he rolled a nipple between two fingers.

"Like this?" He pinched lightly.

My teeth sink into my lower lip and I nod. So close.

Then, a second before climax ripped through me, he caught my wrist and dragged it away from my saturated sex.

"What?" My eyes flew open just in time to see him lick my juices off my fingers. The protest died on my lips as he groaned. His tongue twirled over the digits as though he didn't want to miss a drop of my taste.

Hot. As. Fuck.

I shivered with need, my legs trembled. My body ached for release. "Why—?"

"Because," Sebastian murmured. "You were right. I am the wicked one. And I never want you to doubt it again."

Before I could lodge a protest, his lips captured one nipple. I arched into him as that clever tongue swirled over the tight peak. My fingers roved over his head, feeling the scar from his injury.

I could have lost him.

But there was no time to think about that. Desire blotted

out every other emotion. My thighs pressed together to ease the ache that masturbating my sex left me with. The unsatisfied urge made my blood pound between my legs.

He suckled my nipple hard. The hand holding my wrists let go to cup and play with the other breast. His thigh wedged between my splayed legs. I rubbed against it like a cat in heat, needing the friction.

He switched to the other breast, tongued the stiff peak until pleasure arrowed into my core.

My headache is a thing of the past and in a moment of clarity, I realized why desire is my magical trigger, the feeling that enhanced my traveler gift.

Like anger, like fear, there is no measuring it, no stopping it, no controlling the emotions once they are set loose. Like magic, feelings can't be contained. A body can ignore them for a time but in the end, they will claw their way free and devour you.

"I want to taste you," he rasped. "I want to bury my tongue inside your body and lick you until you come."

"Yes," I panted and part my legs wider. "Do it."

Once he secured my permission, he lunged. No slow kisses down my stomach. He dove in face first and I cry out at the contact. His tongue speared me deeply. I arched off the bed, crying out his name.

His tongue moved inside me and lapped its way up. His teeth closed gently over my clit, holding it steady as his tongue lashed the piercing.

"Sebastian," I panted. "I'm so close."

I could have traveled. Felt the magic around me, in me, thrumming in my veins. But he held onto me so tightly that there was nowhere I would rather be.

"Come for me," he growled. His fingers finding my entrance and pushing into my body. So much deeper than I can touch myself. He finds a spot inside and rubs it in slow circles. Withdraws and then pushes in again. And again. Tightening, coiling, and then….

I'm lost. My body bowed as pleasure rushed to every digit, through every cell I possessed. It went on and on as I rode wave after wave of hot, wet release. I forgot everything and everyone, forgot the world. Nothing existed outside of my physical body and the lover worshiping it so skillfully.

And then it was over. I slumped back on the bed. Spent and boneless.

His arms wrapped around my thighs and his head rested on my stomach. He was utterly still.

And a jolt of fear goes through me. My body stiffened. Did we trigger the curse?

Then he looked up at me. His amethyst eyes full of satisfaction and male pride. The icy tendrils of fear release my heart and I take a deep, shuddering breath.

"Are you all right?" I whispered.

"I have never been better a day in my life."

"Don't you need to…you know?" I gesture down his body.

He lays a soft kiss on my stomach. "Rest, Siobhan. I am fine."

Maybe a better woman would have worried about his not having a release. I closed my eyes and with a deep contented sigh, drifted into dreams.

●

"*Annwyl*," Sebastian brushed a lock of her purple hair away from her eyes. Her even breathing told him that she slept and slept deeply. It was near dawn and soon, they would need to leave to execute her plan.

But first, he could have another taste of her.

His hands glided over the smooth softness of her belly and through the bare mound of her sex. A jolt of lust speared him as he recalled the first sight of her most delicate flesh, pierced and proud.

No fae woman had anything like that. It had worried him that the memories would overtake him and he wouldn't remember where he was or who he was with. Or worse, that he would lash out violently as he had after being used. But that tiny bit of metal combined with her warm vanilla scent had kept him grounded. He had reveled in the moment with his Siobhan.

He'd come against the sheet at the taste of her release. The experience had been better than any sex he had ever had.

He was a greedy bastard. He craved more.

So he moved down the bed and curled his arms under her pale thighs to splay them open. She glistened as though ready, her female flesh pink and perfect in the morning light. With a pleasured groan, he set to work.

She moaned in her sleep at the first soft sweep of his tongue on her pink folds. The metal was cooler than her hot core, so he dipped low to drag the wet heat up and over it, to coat her properly.

Her fingers found his scalp and her soft sigh filled the quiet morning air. "Sebastian?"

He laved her again, needing more. Needing all of her sweetness, craving her cries of pleasure. His cock ached but he ignored it as he feasted on her feminine core.

Then, "Wait."

He stopped, looked up, his heart in his throat. Maybe she hadn't wanted this. Had he pushed her too hard?

But her smile was mischievous as she wriggled up. "I have an idea. Roll onto your back."

He did and then groaned when he realized her intent. She straddled his face and he almost lost it when he felt her soft breath against his shaft. The sight of her open and wet for him made his mouth water.

"As you were," she murmured, and then gripped him hard. He held his breath as her tongue traced over him. His hold on her hips tightened as she laved the head. And then he remembered he was supposed to be giving her pleasure as well.

His bold, beautiful witch. He would never get enough of her.

It became a contest. To see which of them could hold out the longest. And Sebastian was fairly sure he wasn't going to win. Not when her small hands cupped his sac and he forgot what he was doing. Not when she took him deep into her mouth and he cried out her name. He dug his heels into the mattress, determined not to give in before she did.

It was a close thing. He set to work and let his body move in time with hers. Her own gasps told him she lost her rhythm as well. And they traded power back and forth until she shattered. Satisfaction filled him as she released again. As the final shudders wracked her body, her lips drew him in once more and he let it all go, coming in her mouth.

She rolled off him onto her side, her body trembling but there was a small smile on her face.

"That," she said, "Is how I want to start every day."

His chest swelled and he made himself a silent promise that he would do everything in his power to grant her wish.

20

SIOBHAN

"Feeling better?" Alys asked with a raised eyebrow. There was a spring in my step and a huge grin on my face as I headed toward the French press coffee pot. "Worlds better. Galaxies better. Universes better."

Alys let out a little laugh. "Yeah, I can relate. I'm surprised it took you two so long. The chemistry alone could solve the energy crisis."

"The curse, remember?" I took a sip of the coffee then made a face. When would I learn to set the stupid pot up the night before so I didn't have to endure this vile brew?

"It's still there? I thought—" Alys hesitated. "Then how…?"

"We worked around it." I wasn't the sort to blush but damn, how we had worked around it!

She shook her head. "Well, okay. As long as you're happy."

I narrowed my eyes at her. "Who are you and what have you done with Alys?"

My sister sighed. "Sibby, we're under a death sentence. Even my uber cautious self is going to tell you to grab whatever joy you can while you can."

"Oh, I grabbed it all right, I grabbed it right by the—"

"Stop," Maeve called from the stairs. She was dressed but looked rumpled as though her outfit had spent the night on the bedroom floor. "Do not finish that sentence before I've had coffee."

"Short and curlies," I said just to see if she would flip me off. She did. I grinned. All was right with the world.

Well, other than Cedric and his agenda.

"So, what's the plan?" Alys asked. "Where are you two headed?"

"East," I said. "Sebastian says there's another huge convergence on the coast. We're going to go that way and maybe set off a few spells to draw the magic hunters after us. That should leave you plenty of time to track down Andreas and convince him he needs to step up to the plate."

"What if we can't convince him?" Maeve worried her lower lip. "What if he is as dead set against ruling the fae realm as Joey was?"

"Let's not borrow trouble," Alys said. "Sibby and I will get started on the potion if you want to spend a few minutes with Kal before he leaves."

"Leaves?" I asked.

Maeve twisted her hair up and put a clip through it. "He needs to be with Bella and Philip. I don't want any of them to be a target."

"Smart thinking." Sebastian moved into the room behind me and put his hands on my shoulders.

I scooted out from under his touch even as I wanted to sink back into him. The things we'd done together had been mind-blowing. Better than even my dirtiest fantasies. I wanted more. But I was still cursed. Didn't dare undo it, not with Cedric. I pulled away slightly.

His hands fell to his sides but he picked up the thread of the conversation as though nothing had happened. "That's the exact kind of tactic a villain like Cedric would use. Gain leverage by capturing a loved one and using them as bait. Not the magic hunters, it's forbidden," he added when Maeve sucked in a sharp breath.

Maeve still looked unsteady as she pushed away from the counter and headed for the stairs. "I think I'll just go talk to Kal."

"Sex him up good for me," I called and Maeve flipped me off but I saw her shoulders shaking with silent laughter.

"Breakfast first or potion?" I asked Alys and Sebastian when she was gone.

"I already ate with Brock. He was up at first light so he could check in with the pack at shift change."

I blushed and shot a look at Sebastian who smirking behind his coffee mug. No doubt thinking about what we were up to at first light. The memories were seared into my brain. His clothes were rumpled but at least they had dried out overnight. I wanted to make a comment about how wet things were but suddenly, felt too awkward with the two of them just staring at me like I was a trained monkey about to perform for their amusement.

Hot damn, that man was sex on a stick. I didn't miss the way Alys was glancing between the two of us either. Breakfast was going to be awkward as hell.

"Potion then." I pushed back from the table. "I think I remember which book the enchantment was in."

Alys followed me into the greenhouse, deliberately shutting the door to the kitchen. "So... I see Sebastian is still alive and well."

"Mmmmm." I knew from all the times I'd tried to listen at the door when Aunt Jess was in the greenhouse that it was soundproof. "Do you think Aunt Jess magically soundproofed this room?"

"Do not even try to change the subject. Why didn't the two of you have sex last night?"

I glanced over her shoulder but saw that Sebastian was no longer at the dining room table. "Because I don't want to kill him, okay?"

"You're the one who laid out the curse. So, you can, unravel it, right?"

"Like I even know how." I cleared my throat. "Besides, it's a good fallback in the even that Cedric does manage to snatch me."

"Do not even joke about that." Alys's perfectly sculpted eyebrows drew together. "I hate that you're striking off on your own. I feel like we should stick together."

I knew how she felt. "There's no way, not with Cedric and the magic hunters looking for us. We have to divide and conquer."

I found the spell for enchanting personal objects and skimmed the list of ingredients. "I'm pretty sure we have everything here that we need."

"Sibby," Alys put a hand on my arm.

I looked up. "What?"

"Look, I don't want you to take this the wrong way but I'm wondering if maybe you're using this whole thing with Cedric as an excuse."

I blinked. "Come again?"

She shook her head. "You get so wrapped up in the witchy stuff and it makes me wonder if maybe you aren't doing this to avoid dealing with other things."

"I told you, Sebastian and I fooled around. We went as far as I could without risking him."

"Without risking him? Or yourself?"'

I moved to the cupboard where the jars of dried herbs were stored. "What's that supposed to mean?"

"Remember when you came back to town and we went

out and got pizza? You asked me if I wanted what Maeve and Kal had."

I did recall the conversation, vividly. "You said no."

"Right but you didn't. And it got me to thinking, that it was the sort of question that someone would ask because it's what she wants to be asked in return."

"What's your point?"

"Only that Maeve and Kal did not get to be Maeve and Kal by accident. Brock and I will never be as close as the two of them because we are different people. I could spend all day every day with him and never get tired of him, but I don't *need* him the way Maeve needs Kal. I just want him. Do you see the difference?"

I didn't say anything as I broke out the big cauldron and set it on the camping stove we used to heat and combine ingredients. I did see the difference, now that she pointed it out. I had been looking at them as two happy couples who had everything I didn't. But they were different. Very different. Alys might love Brock but she would always need to keep a part of herself separate. Brock understood and appreciated that. She didn't want to meld into another person. Maeve was different because she had Kal, she became something new, something stronger because of him. Alys and Brock were happy together but what Maeve and Kal had was...beautiful.

Alys settled on a stool next to me. "The thing is, you can keep Sebastian at arm's length. And I think he loves you enough to give you whatever it is you'll accept. But if you want what they've got, you need to take bigger risks."

"No risk, no reward?" I quirked an eyebrow at her. "That doesn't sound like your motto."

She shrugged. "Hey, I am plenty rewarded. I just know what my limits are. And I know what I want. Can you say the same?"

Maeve

"*H*ow are you feeling?" Kal asked as he pushed more disheveled hair off my face.

We were naked together, our bodies damp with sweat from our recent activities. I knew he had to leave but I wasn't ready to let him go.

"Evie?" Kal whispered.

I knew he was asking about my MS, but honestly, my emotions took center stage. "Like I'm going to miss you. And the kids. And even those damn dogs."

He placed a kiss on top of my forehead. "I wish I could stay with you."

"You need to look out for the kids. And yourself. I mean it, Kal. If you get one whiff of trouble, you better come right back here and take shelter."

"I will."

I closed my eyes and clung to him.

"I've decided about the wedding," Kal said.

I straightened and looked up at him. "Oh yeah?"

He nodded. "I want to go. Just you and me and the kids. I want them to see Alaska at least once. To have a chance to get to know their cousins."

And maybe even their grandfather. He didn't say it but I knew he meant it. I hugged him fiercely. "Okay then, it's a date."

"That means you need to wrap all this magical stuff up," Kal murmured. "The sooner the better."

I folded my arms on his chest, leaned forward until I could press my lips to his. "How much of this decision has to do with you wanting me to have something to look forward to?"

"Most of it," he admitted. "I'm not magical, but I still want to protect you as much as the werewolf wants to protect Alys or the guy with the creepy eyes wants to look out for Sibby."

For Kal, that was a long speech. "I know you do."

He caressed my cheek tenderly. "I never wanted to be the hero, Evie. That's your job."

Tears filled my eyes. "I wouldn't trade you for anything, you know that, right?"

"I know," Kal said and kissed me again, before rolling out of bed and picking up his discarded clothes. "I should get going. The kids will be waiting."

We got dressed in silence and then, hand in hand, walked down the stairs and out to the minivan.

My heart was in my throat. "Text me when you get home and let me know you are all safe."

"I will," Kal murmured. He held me against him in the chill morning air, not saying anything about the tears that spilled from my eyes. Then he brushed his lips gently over mine, got behind the wheel of the minivan, and drove away.

"Shit," I snuffled as Sibby and Alys came out of the greenhouse. "I really want to kill that fae bastard for doing this to us."

"It won't be for long," Alys promised. "The potion is ready. We just need the Enchantress to baste the t-shirt so we can find our rogue fae prince."

I wiped my eyes and then we headed into the greenhouse. The bloody t-shirt made all the hairs on my arms rise, but I took up the silicone basting brush and began to slather Sibby's magical concoction over it.

Alys had a map of the high country out and was dangling our mother's scrying crystal over the top of it.

"I figured we would look closely at first," Alys murmured as the light caught the pendant. "With Robin Goodfellow and Joey Whitmore being so close, maybe we will luck out."

The chain on the pendant tugged and the crystal zoomed down.

We all stared at the location. At first glance, it was the middle of nowhere, halfway between Eckhart and Ashville. The map listed no roads, which meant private property. But trespassing was the least of our current concerns.

"Shit," Alys said. "Shit shit shit."

"What?" Sibby asked, confused.

She had been too young. She wouldn't have remembered the significance of the place. But I did.

"That's the gorge where Mom died."

21

"You're sure it's the same place?" Sebastian asked as he studied the map.

"I'll never forget it," Maeve murmured. Alys appeared even more, pinch-faced than usual and his Siobhan looked as though all the color had been leached from her skin.

"There was an abandoned mine somewhere in the gorge," Alys spoke slowly as though the words had been stored in a buried vault in her chest. "Knowing what we know now, I think perhaps mom was looking for crystals or stones to help with her magic when the accident happened."

"An abandoned mine would be an excellent place for a fae to hide his hoard," Sebastian said. "All the energies from his magic would be dispersed into the gemstones and minerals and eventually reabsorbed into the ley lines. Unless someone had a personal belonging of his, like that shirt, he couldn't be tracked."

"You sound as though you've considered this," Siobhan murmured.

"I have."

She glanced up at him and there was sympathy in her eyes but she didn't say anything more.

Sebastian wanted to pull her back against him but refrained. She had withdrawn from him earlier. Perhaps she did not wish him to demonstrate his affection for her in front of her sisters. He was new to the concept of being in a relationship. He didn't know all the rules and the last thing he wanted was to upset her.

He craved her touch. The urge to comfort her, to ease her worries in whatever way he could, overwhelmed him. But he didn't want to push. She had given so freely of herself the night before. And earlier in the morning.

Was she having regrets about their intimacies? Or perhaps it was her declaration of love that was causing her strain. Did she want to retract the sentiment?

The thought made him ache.

"This doesn't change anything," Siobhan's attention returned to the map. "We'll stick with the plan. Head east, toward the coastal convergence, while you two go southwest."

"I'll go get our things," Sebastian murmured and left the sisters to say their farewells.

Siobhan had packed a backpack full of food and another with her spare clothing and a few magical bits and bobs as well as a handheld scrying mirror. They had cash as well as her cell phone so she had both a magical and a modern way to keep in touch with her sisters.

Sebastian felt wholly inadequate. He had no magic, and his bag had been abandoned at the Beltane festival. The clothes on his back were badly wrinkled and smelled none too fresh. He held no magic.

How could he protect her?

The sisters stood by Alys's vehicle when he exited the

house. Siobhan took the keys from her sister and said with a ghost of her usual sass, "I'll try not to wreck it."

"Fuck the car," Alys said. "Just come back safe."

Siobhan hugged her sister fiercely. When Alys let go, Siobhan clung to Maeve, leaving him and Alys standing awkwardly side by side.

"Oh, the hell with it," Alys grumbled and then embraced him.

He was so startled he dropped both the packs. Slowly, his arms went around her. He felt as though he was holding a bomb.

"You come back safe too, you bastard changeling," Alys murmured. "And watch out for my baby sister."

"I will." Emotion clogged his throat. That she would willingly entrust Siobhan to him, or that she would worry over his own wellbeing and wish for his safe return had never been something he considered. It was nice, though. As though Alys was indicating he belonged in their group.

Sebastian had never belonged anywhere before.

She released him and then Maeve hugged him and whispered, "Don't let her push you away again. She needs you." The middle sister, the one he had always thought of as the weak link, offered her advice and then let him go.

Siobhan tossed him the keys and then donned a baseball cap over her purple hair. "Give us an hour's head start. I'll set off a few minor spells as bait to get them to follow. And we'll check-in at noon and midnight."

"Noon and midnight," Alys nodded and then stepped back.

Sebastian reversed the vehicle, turned the wheel, shifted into drive, and then they headed toward Eckhart. They passed through town and he saw Siobhan press her hand to the window as they passed *Silver Demo and Design*.

"I was starting to think of that place as a home away from

home," she murmured. "I don't even technically work there. Just help out with my sisters but I thought…."

She didn't finish and he wanted to hear her words. "What did you think?"

She did a quick up and down with her shoulders. "It's not important."

He picked her hand up from where it lay atop her denim-clad thigh and brought it to his lips. "It is to me."

She laced her fingers through his and turned to face him. "It was just really nice, working with my sisters. Like I belonged somewhere and had a purpose."

Hadn't he felt the same way when her sisters offered him luck? "You'll see them again," Sebastian reassured her.

"I hope so." Her hand fell back to her lap and she stared down.

Both of them were on high alert for the first dozen miles. He stopped at an outlet store and bought himself sunglasses to shield his eyes along with several changes of clothing, not bothering to try anything on.

Siobhan was fiddling with the radio when he returned. "Is everything well?"

"Fine." She wouldn't meet his gaze.

"Siobhan. I grew up with the fae. I know a lie when I hear one."

She said nothing.

"Talk to me, *Annwyl*. Tell me what I can do to lessen your hurt."

She looked at him out of the corner of her eye. "I'm not sure now's the right time."

"It is the right time if you wish to speak." He brought her hand to his lips.

She pulled away and his heart sank.

"Are you regretting last night?"

"What? No. Of course not." She sounded genuinely surprised. "What would make you think that?"

"You withdraw whenever I try to touch you. Have I done something wrong?"

"It's not you. It's me."

He waited.

"I want to have a baby," she blurted.

Sebastian forgot how to breathe.

"It's ridiculous, I know. I keep hearing Alys's voice in my head screeching the question, *at your age*? Until a few days ago I didn't know I could remove the curse any old time and it just wasn't a possibility. I can remove it though. But it's my ace in the hole against Cedric—which is a really bad turn of phrase considering the subject matter—and since Alys was the one who encouraged me to be honest about what it is I want I'm sitting here trying to convince myself that it doesn't matter if it's the worst idea in the history of ideas because the clock is running out and—"

Sebastian couldn't take another and. He put his hand over her lips. His head spun as he imagined the possibility.

Cedric wanted to impregnate her. Because of that, Siobhan was reluctant to lift her curse. Yet there was another way, wasn't there? Cedric couldn't have a child with her if she was already carrying Sebastian's child.

Their child. That was what she was saying, wasn't she?

To be sure he asked, "You want me to give you a baby?"

She huffed out a breath and pushed his hand to the side. "Well, I don't mean you should go steal one or anything. I just thought that since we're together and my biological clock sounds more like a metronome these days, we should at least discuss it. See if we're on the same page."

A child. Their child, his and hers. Another changeling. The idea had always terrified him. A witch-born changeling. Yet he recalled the way Robin Goodfellow and his mortal cradled the infant. The way they had removed themselves from the magical community to keep him safe. To protect him.

Siobhan was fiddling with her uneven hair. "Say something?"

Sebastian was a dark fae. He could lie whenever the mood struck him. But he couldn't now. Not when the subject was so important to her.

And there were things she didn't know. About him. What he'd been before he was a magic hunter.

He couldn't agree. She had hated him for months when he had kept his identity from her. If she knew what he truly was though….

She wouldn't ask him to give her a child.

"Sebastian?" Her tone was full of hope. And a trace of fear.

"The idea…overwhelms me."

"Oh," Siobhan swallowed and then shifted in her seat to stare out the window. "Okay then. Forget I said anything. We should get going anyhow."

He hated how quickly she'd shut down. As though his needing time to mull over all the angles was some sort of rejection of her and her wish. "*Annwyl—*,"

"Let's just go, okay?" She closed her eyes. "We have magic bombs to set off."

He swallowed and then turned the key. Started the vehicle and then pulled out into traffic.

A baby. Their baby. Sebastian had nothing to offer her. No home, no magic, no people. A price on his head. And he was a changeling. The taint of it still sullied him.

Then he thought of Robin's offer. He wasn't completely alone.

Siobhan deserved the world. Sebastian wanted to give it to her.

If only he could figure out how.

Alys

*D*espite the cool breeze off the lake, sweat pooled under my arms. I shouldn't have worn a white t-shirt. The pit stains were going to be a beast to get out. My knuckles were clenched white against the steering wheel of the minivan as Maeve climbed into the passenger's side.

She looked from my death grip to my face and her brows went up. "Everything okay?"

I nodded and then turned the engine over. "We should go."

She blinked. "Brock's not coming?"

I shook my head. "He wanted to but I told him I would rather he and the pack keep an eye on Kal and the kids." Especially after what Sebastian said about Cedric using mortal loved ones as bargaining chips."

"Thanks for that." Maeve exhaled and then picked at a loose string on her cargo shorts. "I know he would rather be here with you. You probably would rather he be here, too, so you have someone you can count on."

"Are you saying I can't count on you?"

She looked me square in the eye. "I'm saying that you look about two seconds away from having a full-blown panic attack because you're terrified of taking your spoonie sister to the place where our mother died."

I flinched.

"Yeah, so there's that big ass elephant in the room," Maeve said. "If it makes you feel any better, I promise I will wait in the van if anything seems even remotely hinky or I feel tired or numb or any of that, okay?"

"It's not you, I'm worried about." I turned to look out at the rutted drive that our mother had long ago designated Witch Way.

"No?" Maeve asked.

"Well not until you put that shit in my head," I grumped.

"Then what's wrong?"

"It just feels like a really bad sign. That this guy we need to find is hiding out in the same place where mom died. What if we can't get him to agree to our plan? What if he's batshit crazy and attacks us? What if the magic hunters show up and we're trapped without Sibby to jump us to safety? What if they've already got Sibby, or Cedric has her or—"

Maeve grabbed hold of my wrists and clutched them tight. "Breathe, Alys. Take a deep, slow breath. That a girl. In through the nose. Hold it for the count of three. One…two… three. Now exhale."

I followed Maeve's instructions, letting her soft voice wash over me a little at a time. Gradually, my shoulders relaxed.

"Good." My sister said at last and released my wrists. "Okay, now we're going to switch places."

"Huh?"

"You need to chill out and stop borrowing trouble. Whatever happens, we'll deal with it then."

She sounded so sure and I didn't have the strength to argue with her. Something about seeing Sibby and Sebastian drive off had gutted all of my resolve. The terror over losing one of my family members was lurking right over my shoulder. I didn't dare look back and acknowledge it.

We both got out of the car and swapped seats. Maeve adjusted the seat, checked her review mirror, and then pulled down the road.

I glanced back at the cottage. A flicker of movement from the upstairs window, like a curtain fluttering in the breeze. For a moment I thought perhaps Siobhan had left a window open. Then it dawned on me. Ethan. The ghost who had loved our mother, trapped in the convergence. He was seeing us off. Maybe wishing us luck on our journey.

Tension returned as we turned off the dirt road. Instead of heading into town, Maeve pointed the vehicle toward the county highway. As the crow flew, the trip to the gorge was about twelve miles, but it would take us almost an hour, sticking to back roads so as not to draw attention to ourselves.

I loved that Maeve seemed to be all Zen master of her emotions. It made sure that her magic wouldn't slip. If we didn't use magic, the magic hunters couldn't track us. The werewolf patrol kept them physically away from our property and Sibby's magical trail of breadcrumbs would surely lead them in the opposite direction.

So why was I so uneasy?

"I was overconfident," I mumbled to Maeve.

"What?" She glanced at me out of the corner of her eye. "When?"

"Yesterday, with the council of elders. I thought we were a shoo-in, that it was just a formality. I should have realized that people who are so serious over magical slip-ups that they have a whole subset of magic hunters to suck out their souls wouldn't just welcome us to the tribe."

"But they let Becca's coven in," Maeve said. "We saw it ourselves. Barely any questions were asked. It was a formality for them."

"We're different." I shook my head. "Aunt Jess kept all this magical stuff from us for a reason. Do you think...she knew? That they would reject us? Like the way you know things sometimes?"

Maeve cast me a dubious look. I didn't blame her. In the past, I'd ignored her clairvoyance, ESP, whatever she called it. It made me uncomfortable that she would have a sixth sense and make decisions based on that instead of cold, hard facts.

The problem with cold hard facts was that sometimes, they let you down in a big way.

Maeve sighed. "I doubt we'll ever know why Aunt Jess didn't give us the empowerment brew or tell us about any of this. But does it matter? We are where we are and we need to deal with the here and now?"

She was right. We were where we were. On the road, heading into the sunset to the place where our mother died under mysterious circumstances.

Some days just sucked canal water backward.

Siobhan

"*P*ull over here," I said to Sebastian when we reached a narrow stretch of road with nary a car in sight. We'd left the mountains behind hours ago and it was time to set off the first of our magical breadcrumbs.

He did as I asked, then turned to me. "Are you sure?" If anyone arrives via ley line, they'll see us."

I couldn't see Sebastian's eyes behind the cheap lenses of his sunglasses but the tightness around his mouth told me he was anxious.

"Stay here." I popped the door on the Yukon and slid to the ground.

The bag with the magical supplies was stowed on the

floorboard behind me. I rummaged in the bag until I found what I was after. The little blue bottle was half full of a clear liquid that would erupt into a light show that the untrained eye would mistake for fireworks.

Someone who knew that magic was real, however….

I moved a safe distance from the back end of the Yukon, just to make sure that the vehicle's electronics didn't shit the bed when I uncorked the potion.

I reached out with my mind in the way Sebastian had explained to me, searching for the nearest ley line. It was several miles to the east, away from the road. I could feel the thrum of the magical pull in my chest like a second heartbeat.

I pulled on it, feeling the earth ground and center me. Magic, I was learning was about a lot more than my innate traveler gifts or even the politics from the various factions. It was about our world and getting in touch with nature and her rhythms. Relishing her abundance of gifts. The cool breeze that dried the sweat on the back of my neck, the cry of a seagull overhead. A fresh snowfall that blanketed the earth in the winter, or the crisp taste of an apple hanging from a heavily laden branch at summer's end. Everyday miracles. Abundance was all around if a witch knew where to look.

And I was learning to pay attention.

I cast my circle by pulling on the line and called the winds in turn. North, east, south, and finally west, I asked that they do my bidding and sent my signal out.

Then, plucking the clear quartz crystal, I infused the amplifying stone with my aura and dropped it into the bottle.

The reaction was immediate. The bottle lit up with a brilliant blue light. It was so bright that I had to turn away. It flashed in a set of three. Paused. Flashed again.

I set it down in the middle of the circle and then let the protection drop. My feet hit the heated asphalt and I ran for the Yukon and flung myself into the passenger's side.

Sebastian had left the engine running and the moment my seatbelt was fastened, he took off down the highway, heading toward the convergence.

"You sure that will work?" I asked him.

"You charged the crystal with your energy?"

At my nod, he said, "Then it ought to work. Even if the magic hunters are too new to recognize your energy signature, Cedric definitely will."

"How long until we reach the convergence?" I asked.

"Another two hours, perhaps. There's a place there, a bed and breakfast that's run by a retired coven. We'll stay there the night."

I nodded because we had already been over the plan. Every twelve hours we would leave the convergence and set off another "Sibby beacon," in a new direction then retreat within. I had enough materials to keep us going for several days, but was really hoping Alys and Maeve would have good news for us long before we ran out.

Not only did I worry for my sisters, but I was also seriously regretting my confession to Sebastian. He had been very quiet since I'd blurted out my desire to have a baby. While confession might be good for the soul, it was the special hell before a road trip with your new lover.

Of course, he wasn't exactly new, was he? We'd been sharing intimacies for months. Kisses and a little heavy petting last fall. Then I was sleep traveling to him every night because my body craved his. And last night had been…

Magic.

Then I had to open my big, fat mouth and ruin it. Was there anything as off-putting to a guy as a woman who burped up the fact that she wanted a child and her biological clock was on countdown to auto destruct? *Hey, no pressure while we're on the run for our lives or anything but still, the window is kinda closing and my eggs are shriveling as we speak so we better get cracking. Let me just lift this pesky curse that means you'll die if we do have sex and then I'm good to go.*

Do I know how to woo a guy or what?

I could kill Alys for telling me I needed to invest more of myself in the relationship. Like she would know.

Me and my toxic hoo-ha and baby craze were too much for any guy to handle.

"Siobhan," Sebastian began. "I've been thinking."

"Yeah, me too. I should just go hate-fuck Cedric. That would solve all our problems." The bitter words were burped up without thought.

The Yukon swerved. *"What?"*

And me being me, once I got a reaction from someone I had to keep going. "Yup, go and take him out. Hey, they might even make me the new queen for offing him. Then I can rule on the council and my sisters will be safe to go back to their lives."

The light was fading so it was hard to tell if Sebastian was really pale or the color was leaching from the world around us. "You're not serious."

"I'll just "negotiate" with him." I glared out at the flat expanse of the coastal plains around us. "That way everybody wins."

Sebastian slammed on the brakes. Hard. The ass-end of the Yukon slid sideways across the road.

"What are you doing?" I spun to face him and swallowed hard when I caught sight of Sebastian's face.

I'd finally pushed him past his breaking point.

22

"*W*hy did you stop?" Siobhan dared to ask him.

"Why bother running since you now wish to be caught?" He growled the words like an animal. His hands shook. His entire body quaked with the tumult of emotion that ripped through him because of her statement. Hand herself over to Cedric. He wanted to throttle her. Did she not understand?

"And why not?" She pulled that silly hat off and ran a hand through her purple locks. "Why shouldn't I use what I've got to protect my sisters, to protect you?"

"*Why not?*" The thought made him sick. "How about because you are worth more than either a breeder or a weapon? How about because you deserve to think about what makes you happy instead of what will benefit everyone else? You keep risking yourself because you don't see your own worth."

"That's not true."

"How did your sisters react when they found out about what happened to you? Now imagine their reaction if they heard this."

She flinched.

He wanted to touch her, but she looked so fragile, as though one caress might shatter her. "If a sacrifice needs to be made, *Annwyl*, then I'll be the one to make it. Sleep with me with your curse intact. If I die, Cedric must return to the fae realm."

Her blue eyes went wide. "You're not serious."

How could he make her understand? "I would do anything to see you safe and happy."

She lifted her chin. "And what do you know about what makes me happy?"

"Nothing," he admitted. "I know nothing of happiness or joy or love. But I do know the other range of feelings. I know what it is like to be used, Siobhan, and I would die before I see someone use you that way."

Her brows pulled together. "What are you saying?"

Was he really about to tell her of his shame? He had to, he realized. It was the only way he could make her see.

Sebastian hung his head and stared down at his lap. "I am not a fit sire for your child."

Her hand brushed his arm. "Sebastian, talk to me."

"I was a pet. Kept by the fae queen for her amusement. And later for her pleasure. Or that of...others."

Siobhan's hand tightened on his arm. "No—"

"Yes. You do not understand the jaded cruelty of the fae, Siobhan. You speak of giving yourself to Cedric as though you are disposable and that is precisely how he would treat you. He learned it from the queen. She would feed me poisons because watching me sick amused her. She would cut my skin and force me to write her missives in my own blood. They have drugs, aphrodisiacs, that bring forth lust and turn a male of reason into nothing more than a rutting animal. She would beat me until I passed out and then dose me and have me tied to her bed. Use me and leave me there in pain and filth for endless days because it amused her. This is the treatment that awaits you with Cedric. This is the disgraced remains of a slave that you would have father your child."

She made a choked sort of sound and he regretted his harsh words, his temper. He had no magic, had no way to protect her. But he had knowledge and if sharing it with her changed her attitude, then he would offer his pain and humiliation and consider it a bargain well struck.

Everything he had Sebastian would give to keep her safe.

He shut his eyes and took a breath. "Forgive me. I should have told you all of this earlier. Long before I touched you. I have wanted you from the beginning and knew that you would never desire me, not after you knew what I am."

"What you are?" Her tone sounded confused. "Sebastian, I'm...sorry that this happened. That you were treated so horribly. But this doesn't change the way I feel for you."

He stared at her. How could it not?

"Can we go, please?" Siobhan gestured to the car. "It's getting dark and I don't feel safe out here."

He nodded and then righted the car and headed east once more.

Siobhan didn't speak and he didn't either. But he hoped.

Maybe he hadn't killed her feelings for him after all.

●

Siobhan

*W*ell, aren't I the world's biggest bitch?

Crap, I'd known that Sebastian had a rocky past and that things for a changeling child weren't good. But the things he had told me.... Remembering them made me want to upchuck in a big way.

Tortured, raped. All because he was different. Powerless in a world filled with powerful creatures. And because that evil fae queen could do it.

I was almost sorry she was dead. I wanted to kill her myself.

Those things I'd said to him made me cringe. Lashing out at Sebastian all because he hadn't hopped on board the let's have a baby train with me the second I'd suggested it.

He probably thought I wanted to use him, too.

I was about to ask him to pull over so I could vomit when the Yukon slowed to a stop. I glanced up and spotted stilts and a staircase leading up to the main floor of a blue cottage style house. "Is this the place?"

He nodded. "I'll get us a room."

I wanted to say two but the urge to puke hadn't left me. I slid out of the car and kept sliding until I was flat on my face on the crushed shell drive. My gorge rose but I forced it down.

"Siobhan?" Sebastian's alarmed voice. "*Annwyl*, are you hurt?"

Was I hurt? I wanted to laugh. To weep. How could he still cherish me after everything I'd said?

Get your shit together, Sibby. Now is not the time to have a total meltdown.

There would either be time for that later...or not. Either way, I had to keep trudging forward.

"I'm fine," I said and let Sebastian haul me to my feet. "Let's go get a room."

"You're sure?" he asked.

The air smelled of saltwater and sea air. I breathed it in and stiffened my spine so I didn't collapse again. I swallowed and offered him a tight smile that I hope at least passed for reassurance. Looking him in the eye was tough. Damn it, he would think that was because of what he told me. I'd been sending the man mixed signals all day. Wake up for a little 69 action, then I avoided him, then demanding he impregnate me while on the run, followed by me mouthing off about hate-fucking his fae counterpart. And that was just today.

Poor guy wouldn't know which way was up by the time he was done with me.

"Let's get that room," I said. One room. Because damn it, I still wanted to be with him. To hold him and comfort him. Or maybe have him comfort me.

Sebastian held my elbow as we walked up the stairs and crossed the white porch to the door. He put his hand on the knob and turned.

The floors were dark stained. The place smelled musty and felt damp. The room was crammed full of furniture, none of it particularly beachy. No light colors or wicker. A woman sat behind a desk in a battered recliner covered with orange and green checked fabric. It looked like it belonged in a 1970's rumpus room, not a B&B on the beach.

"Can I help you?" The woman stood, though it didn't make much difference from her seated position. She came up to my shoulder, her gray hair was permed in neat rows. She wore a white cardigan over a maroon dress and leaned heavily on a cane. She wore glasses, the lenses thick as old-fashioned coke bottles.

"We need a room for a few days," Sebastian was back to his charming self. The polished façade he put on to fool people into thinking he was in complete control. When had he developed that?

The woman bobbed her head and then shuffled over to the wall behind her where a row of brass hooks held keys on burgundy cords. "You'll have your pick. A little early for the beach crowd. How about number three? That's the turret with the ocean view. There's a small kitchen and a private bath."

"Perfect," I said and Sebastian put a hand on my back.

"We serve breakfast bright and early at six AM and afternoon tea at four. Do you have any bags?" She came around the desk as though ready to carry our luggage herself.

I shot Sebastian a panicked glance. I didn't want her to even attempt the stairs, which looked overcrowded with even more stuff. The place was clearly neglected. This lady had her hands full.

Maybe if we stuck around a few days we could help her out. Sort through a few things and get rid of some crap.

Where was Marie Kondo when you needed her?

"I've got the bags," Sebastian said. "Just point me in the right direction."

She nodded and then gestured to the stairs. "Two flights up, door's on your right."

I waited while Sebastian headed out to get our things from the Yukon. I poked around the space. It seemed familiar somehow, though I couldn't put my finger on why.

"I'm sorry, dear, I forgot to get your name for our log." The small woman said.

"Oh, it's Siobhan. Siobhan Silver."

"My name's Alba Moss and I'm the caretaker of this here place." She moved her dentures around before offering me a smile. "Much like me, the old gal ain't what she used to be." She cackled as though that was the greatest joke in the world.

I couldn't help smiling along with her. "I'm looking forward to seeing her in the daylight. My sisters renovate homes up in the mountains so I know a thing or two about design."

"Really?" Alba said. "Well, ain't that a pip. Here comes your young man. I'm sure you two are wanting a little privacy. Gawd knows I would with a man who looked like that one."

She winked at me and I couldn't help but grin even though the thought of being alone with Sebastian terrified me at the moment.

What could I say to him to undo that awful moment in the car? I'd been a brat, lashing out because I was scared and couldn't get my way. Because I wanted more. More for him and more for me.

Sebastian was doing his best though. He hadn't left me by the side of the road. He hadn't attacked another unsanctioned witch to drain her for magic so he could protect himself or me. I'd dropped a huge bomb on him right when we were stuck together, never mind that my lady parts were still cursed and I hadn't discussed undoing the spell. Nope I just said *here I am, please impregnate!* He probably thought I'd devour him after like a Black Widow.

He deserved so much better from me.

As we bypassed the second floor and moved on to the third, I considered the spell itself. I'd riffed the curse, a sort of spur-of-the-moment thing. Should I just go with the flow to undo it? How would I know if it had worked?

Distracted, I tripped on an old accordion, of all things, that seemed to materialize out of nowhere and fell up the last few steps and onto the stained third-floor hall runner.

"Siobhan." Sebastian dropped the bags and crouched beside me. "Are you all right?"

"I'm fine," I said, waving off his proffered hand and getting to my feet. "Just had a spaz attack. What is going on with all this crap everywhere?"

"It's not crap. It's storage from a faery hoard."

I frowned. "Come again?"

"When a fae dies, the contents of his or her magic vault travels to the nearest convergence. My best guess is that the queen's vault was nearest to this place. When she was killed, her stuff started coming here."

I didn't know what to say to that so I asked, "Where's our room?"

He was silent for a moment, assessing me.

"What?" I searched his face, but his expression was stoic.

He shook his head and then moved past me to the first door on the right and inserted the brass key.

I didn't know what I'd been expecting—more clutter, perhaps—but the room was pristine. Very beachy, with off-white and pale blue bedding and curtains and whitewashed furniture. A jar, half full of seashells sat on a nightstand that seemed to be constructed from driftwood. There was a small gas log fireplace in one corner and a mat of woven seagrass before it. A glass-top table sat before the wall of windows that overlooked the sound.

"Wow," I said. "I wasn't expecting this."

"This is the room where I stayed several weeks ago," Sebastian muttered.

"Why did you leave?" It looked like a perfect hideout to me. "The magic hunters can't trace you in a convergence."

He frowned and rubbed his forehead. "I'm not really sure."

My teeth sank into my lower lip. "Did I come to you when you were here?"

"You came to me every night." He was still frowning though as if he wasn't quite sure of his answer.

There was a knock on the door. I moved to open it and Alba poked her head up. "Package for you."

"What?" I frowned. "What do you mean, a package? I didn't hear a delivery truck."

"Oh, it was left here." Alba handed me the small box wrapped in butcher paper along with a sealed envelope. "I'm sorry, I should have given it to you at check-in, but I forgot."

"Left here?" I looked down at the envelope and all the small hairs rose on my arms.

"Who gave it to you?" Sebastian demanded.

"Why, you did, dear." Alba chuckled and then moved away.

Sebastian lunged forward as though to go after her, but I caught his arm. "Close the door."

"This might be some sort of trick." His tone was full of caution.

"It's my handwriting," I held it out to him. There, in my spidery scrawl were our names.

Setting the box aside, I opened the letter and began to read. Halfway through the first paragraph, I stopped and then shook my head. "This can't be."

"What? Siobhan? What is it?"

"It's from us," I said. "From you and me. To you and me. I was with you last time you were here. And according to this, I was *very* much awake."

Sebastian took the letter. "I don't understand."

I reached for the package. My hands shook. I didn't have Maeve's highly developed intuition, but the moment felt heavy, important. Something major was about to happen.

Sebastian looked down just as I revealed the contents of the gift we'd sent ourselves.

Two pregnancy tests.

MAEVE

"*A*re you sure this spell is working?" Alys asked as we huffed our way uphill in the dark.

I glanced down at the blood-spattered t-shirt that glowed a slight green color. "It's definitely doing something. Either that or I'm seeing trails."

A coyote yipped and we both froze. A moment later another scavenger took up the eerie cry. Then another.

There were no lights, other than the flashlight in Alys's phone, and that had gone out as soon as we recited the incantation to activate the spell. Technology and magic just didn't play nice together.

"Come on, I see the entrance to a cave." Alys huffed. "Maybe that's our guy's hiding spot."

Oh goodie, another stinking cave. We'd wandered through half a dozen of them since we'd arrived and there was still no sign of one rogue fae prince.

The good news was that we hadn't used magic and there were no signs of any magic hunters. The bad news was I was sure it was after midnight but because of the whole magic and tech issue, we had missed checking in with Sibby.

I hoped she wouldn't freak out. Hell, I hoped I wouldn't freak out.

"Are we sure that isn't the coyote den?" It would be just our luck.

"At this point, I'm not sure I care," Alys huffed and then wrapped her arm around my waist.

It had been slow going, especially with me leaning heavily on my walking stick. Hard to not feel like my MS was slowing my healthy sister down. Equally frustrating that the glowing shirt didn't actually take off to find its owner. It just shone brighter the closer we got. Or maybe it was the darker it got.

We made it up the hill and into the mouth of the cave. Alys set down her backpack and pulled out the makeshift torch she had assembled when we realized just how freaking dark it was inside these things sans a flashlight.

My sister was more diligent than the Boy Scouts and always prepared. She had a book of matches sealed in a plastic sandwich bag as well as a small Bic lighter in her pocket.

She'd used a hair elastic to bind a bunch of fallen dry leaves and twigs to a long branch and used her lighter to ignite it. I never would have been so clever, which was why I was glad I wasn't out here on my own. The torch smoked like crazy when she lit it and she stuck it outside as the leaves burned away. The kindling helped catch the dried twigs and Alys nodded the way she always did when she was satisfied with her work.

Had our mother tried to fashion a way to see? I hated thinking about her final moments, caught in a storm, lost, and completely unprepared. Had she stumbled into a wild animal's den? There were worse things than coyotes in this area. Bears, as well as mountain lions, were scattered throughout the high country. Most of the time they left people alone. But not when a meal walked into their territory.

"Do you hear that?" Alys asked, pulling me out of my morose thoughts.

I listened and frowned. "It sounds like water. Moving water."

We exchanged a glance. Fresh drinking water was something somebody would need if they were living rough. I glanced down at the shirt and maybe it was my imagination but it seemed to glow brighter.

We moved deeper into the cave. I saw Alys shiver. "You cold?"

"No, just thinking about the last time I was in a cave."

When she had nearly died. Yeah, our family and caves weren't the best combination.

The space narrowed like a funnel and then turned sharply. I leaned heavily on my walking stick. Tomorrow was going to hit me like a freight train because I was pillaging my energy reserves just to keep going. There was only so long I could do that before I had to pay the piper.

At this point, my only hope was that I wouldn't run out at a critical moment when Alys needed me.

The shirt blazed to brilliant emerald light and began tugging me forward. "I think it's working."

Suddenly, the cave opened onto a spacious cavern. There wasn't just an underground river but a waterfall, which accounted for the sound. Little floating orbs drifted above our heads and I gasped as I caught the sparkle in the rocks. "Alys, this looks like a gem mine."

"That's because it is," a lilting male voice said from behind us.

We turned and I stumbled back from the filthy figure. His dark hair was down to his shoulders and a scraggly dark beard covered the lower half of his face. His clothes were dirty and torn and he didn't smell too great either.

His eyes were the color of new spring leaves. But there was no light in them, no life.

"Andreas?" Alys asked.

"Who sent you?" The question was flat as though he didn't really care one way or the other.

We exchanged a glance. "No one sent us. We scried for you."

"Why?" He sounded genuinely puzzled.

I swallowed and stepped forward. "My name is Maeve Silver and this is my sister, Alys. We need your help."

"With what?"

He didn't speak much but I detected the same sort of accent that Sebastian had. Welsh, I thought Sibby had said.

Alys cut right to the chase, as was her way. "We need you to rule the fae and take Cedric's spot on the council."

He let out a bark of laughter and all the hairs rose along my arm. *He's insane,* I thought.

Had we leaped from the frying pan only to land in the fire?

"I can't rule anyone," Andreas said.

"You killed the queen," I said. "Your brother Robin told us."

He leaned in close to me and it took every ounce of willpower for me not to hold my nose. "And I would do it again in a heartbeat. That bitch took everything from me."

"I...I don't understand," I whispered.

Andreas plucked the torch from my shaking hand. "Then follow me and I'll show you what can happen when you go up against the fae and lose."

●

"*R*ead it again," Sebastian said as he paced the confines of the bedroom. His mind was whirling, trying to make sense of the puzzling letter.

"*Siobhan, Sebastian. Yeah, it's really me, your smartass future self.*" Siobhan read. "*I know this is going to be difficult for the two of you to accept, but then so is that some people put ketchup on eggs. Here goes nothing. Sibby, babe, you are going to get pregnant tonight in the most convoluted way possible. And before you ask, it's totally legal in most states.*"

"If there is any doubt that you wrote this, that would put it to rest," Sebastian grunted.

Siobhan snorted and then continued. "*Listen, babes, I know this is crazy but I want you to go take the first pregnancy test. It's going to come up negative. That shouldn't be news to either of you. We decided to include that because Sebastian is probably right now insisting this is some sort of fae trick and he is half a heartbeat away from interrogating the nice old lady who delivered the letter.*"

Sebastian paused. "I see nothing wrong with questioning her about how she came to receive this note."

"Ssshhh," Siobhan said and then read on. "*Poor Alba doesn't know anything, okay so tell him to chill. Look, I know things have been really rough on you two. Sibby, I know you are all baby crazy and I also know what Sebastian revealed to you in the car and that you feel bad about it.*"

She paused, cleared her throat.

"*This is where Sebastian, my Sebastian, wants me to tell you that he isn't angry, he's ashamed about his past and thinks you're pulling away from him because it disgusts you. See the irony here, kids? Go ahead and ask him. He won't lie to you, even though he can.*"

She paused again and looked up at him. "Is that how you feel?"

He thought of the way she'd flinched from him when he'd

tried to help her up. His throat was thick with emotion. "Yes."

Siobhan reached out took his hand and led him over to the bed. She plunked down and sat crossed-legged, still clutching his hand before refocusing on the letter.

"Sebastian, she's not repulsed by you. She hates hurting you and doesn't know how to fix it. Nothing you could do will make Siobhan stop loving you. The murdering innocent witches thing tripped her up for a while but you've proven yourself to her. And Sib, he's not hopping on board the baby train because he's currently homeless, jobless, and on the run and he feels like you deserve better. Sebastian always puts your well-being first. As long as you remember that, you'll be fine.

I know you have both been through more than your fair share of bad shit. Guess what? It doesn't matter. You can help each other. That's why you've been drawn together in every lifetime and now it's time for you to get it right. You two deserve each other. You deserve the world.

"I never realized this is what it felt like to be on the other end of one of my truth bombs," Siobhan sniffled.

He wrapped an arm around her. "You are an unstoppable force of nature when the mood strikes."

She gave him a watery smile. He rubbed her back and waited patiently for her to compose herself.

First thing's first. Sib, babe. This is going to seriously suck but you need to go back in time. By yourself. Use the watch Robin gave to Sebastian. Wind it back six weeks, to when Sebastian stayed in this room. It has to be just you because the Sebastian you are about to encounter is different from the one you're sitting next to. He hasn't been through all the craziness with you. He doesn't know about your curse or what happened to you in Lima. He will not trust anyone but you and space-time paradoxes aside, he will view anyone else as a threat and destroy them.

She considered a minute. "Has that changed?"

He thought about the way Alys had hugged him, how

Brock had teased him and how the sisters had included him in their plans. They'd extended their trust and he reciprocated. "Yes."

She squeezed his hand and continued reading. *"You need to go back and convince him that he needs to get you, the other you that sleep travels to him every night, on his side. Tell him what to say to get her to give up the goods. You need to lift the curse from her and leave before he wakes her up. And before you go, you need to cast a memory charm over the two of them. This is* vital. *They cannot remember anything after they leave the room. If you don't and one or both of them reveal what has happened, it could get back to Cedric. This has to stay between the two of you, past, present, and future. Good luck you crazy kids. -S."*

She set the letter aside and turned to face him. "What do you think?"

He had no idea. His whole body felt raw and exposed. The Siobhan in that letter didn't mince words. Not that Siobhan ever did.

"Is it all true? The things she said?"

Siobhan let out a big breath. "I do feel horrible about what happened in the car."

He shook his head. "That you love me."

Her scowl was adorable. "I told you that last night."

"But that was before you knew the truth," he murmured. "About what I was."

"What you are, Sebastian, is a survivor. Just like me. Do you think less of me because of what happened to me in Lima? Or because I cursed myself?"

"Of course not."

She raised a pierced eyebrow. "Then why would you believe my feelings are so fickle that they would switch off. Newsflash, I knew you had baggage. You're not exactly well-adjusted. Neither am I. But we made it this for. That's got to count for something, right?"

Hope swelled in his chest. Could it be possible that she still wanted him, even knowing his whole truth? That she would still choose him to father her child?

"Is everything she wrote about you true?"

Wordlessly, he nodded.

She rose and reached for the boxes, the pregnancy tests. "Pick one."

"Why?"

She rolled her eyes. "So, I can go pee on a stick. If you choose then you can't claim it was tampered with later on."

He tapped the one in her left hand and she shot him a nervous smile. "Okay then. I'll be back in a jiff."

She disappeared into the bathroom. Sebastian got to his feet and then turned to the window. The water over the inland waterway was still and calm, almost as though it were mocking his inner turmoil.

"Negatory," she said and then shrugged. "No surprise there. So now we need to decide. Do we trust this?" She held up the letter.

"Why back in time?" he asked. "Wouldn't it make more sense for us to remove your curse now?"

"Couple of things. One, my cycle is irregular, always has been. Six weeks ago, I was probably ovulating so the best shot for pregnancy. And two, mentioning the watch and what it does. More proof that she is who she claims to be and that this isn't some elaborate fae scheme."

He held his breath. "You have decided to go through with this then?"

"I haven't decided anything, Sebastian. We're going to decide this, together." She resettled on the bed and then patted the mattress. "Talk to me."

He settled beside her. "We could wait for your sisters. Stick to the plan and hope they can convince Andreas to step forward."

"We could," she said the words slowly. "Is that what you want?"

"I want you safe," he whispered and caressed her cheek. "I want you happy. Your joy is sunshine for my soul."

She turned her face and kissed his palm. "Do you want to have a baby with me?"

He did but he couldn't overcome the dread that twisted his insides. "The thought of bringing another changeling into the world...terrifies me."

She gripped his hands in hers. "Sebastian, listen to me. Do you think I would ever let anyone harm my baby? A baby I never thought I would get the chance to create?"

He shook his head. "You would tear any threat apart."

She nodded. "Right. This is hard. I'm not used to talking about serious stuff. Or being so open with my feelings. It makes me feel vulnerable, you know?"

He did and nodded his understanding.

"But Alys was right, damn her black soul. If we want true intimacy, we need to open up to each other. I want you and you want me and that's a great start. But it's only the beginning of the journey. I want us to be like Maeve and Kal, you know? They are best friends as well as husband and wife."

"You want to get married? To me?" Never in his wildest dreams would he have thought he could have her forever.

"Eventually, yeah." Her blue eyes were filled with hope. "I want to stay in Eckhart and be with my sisters. Raise my child with family around. Work with my sisters and get together for holidays as well as witchcraft. I want my body to be free so I can share it with you. So you tell me, is this a picture you want to be part of?"

A lump formed in his throat. "It's more than I ever would have dreamed."

Siobhan let out a sigh. "Okay then. I guess you need to teach me a memory charm."

24

SIOBHAN

"There are twenty-four hours in every day, twelve hours on the watch. Two turns back is one day. When exactly were you here?"

"Exactly six weeks prior," Sebastian said. "To the day."

"So that's forty-two days times two is..." I trailed off, needing a minute. Math was not my best subject.

"Eighty-four turns," Sebastian offered.

"Oh good," I murmured. "You can keep the checkbook."

He flashed me a grin and I absolutely loved seeing the glimmer of hope in his eyes. It wasn't until it appeared that I realized how he had kept his emotions on lockdown.

Sebastian had had nothing to look forward to. He'd been planning to turn himself over to the council and let them punish him. Maybe with one of those awful memory charms. And since he had told me a small bit of what had been done to him, I could truly appreciate what a sacrifice he'd been willing to make. He would have gone through with it too, as soon he was sure I would live.

"*Annwyl,* I wish..." He paused with his hand half raised to my cheek.

"What?" I leaned in to nuzzle his hand. "What do you wish?"

"That you didn't need to do this alone. That I could be by your side."

"You will be." Well, sort of. I was paying attention to the letter's warning. Who knew what kind of resistance Sebastian from six weeks ago would come up with?

He pressed his forehead to mine. "You won't be asking me to do anything I don't dream of doing."

I placed my palm over his heart. "Me either. Any last-minute advice?"

"Don't die."

"Good advice," I said and withdrew. "Okay then, I guess it's showtime."

I sat on the edge of the bed and began winding. One turn. Sebastian vanished and the sun peered in through the windows. Another. Night once more. Another. Another.

"Twenty-six. Twenty-seven." I spied Alba stripping the linens from the bed. "Twenty-eight." I blanched at the sight of two very large people doing some very kinky things with a can of Reddi-Wip and hurried the dial back another round. Good thing this room wasn't rented very often.

My fingers felt numb as I wound and wound the watch as day faded into night only to pop into day again. I kept careful count.

"Eighty-two," I muttered at the darkened bedroom. "Eighty-three." I gasped as I saw a naked purple-haired woman sprawled on a familiar chest, her hand covering the tattoo. The morning after. I wound again quickly.

And waited.

There was no sign of Sebastian. Was I here too soon?

The toilet flushed in the adjoining bathroom.

Quick as I could, I stowed the watch in my jeans pocket and then cast the first spell. The memory charm that would keep what happened in the room safely hidden from the occupants after they left. Stealing their memories felt like a crummy thing to do, but this was for the life of my child.

Our child.

My hand hovered over my empty womb. Not yet. First, I had to do a little fast-talking.

The bathroom door opened and Sebastian emerged. His hair was longer once more, his expression hard. He froze when he saw me.

"Hi," I said and then got up to approach him.

"*Annwyl?* You are awake?" His gaze darted to the window.

"Yeah, awake and I know I've been traveling to you at night."

"The convergence. I thought it would be safest here." He moved toward me and then paused.

So wary, so careful. A wounded animal ready to fight or flee.

"It is, for now. Listen, Sebastian, I don't have much time. The other me will be here soon and I need to explain a few things."

"Other you?"

I nodded. "I'm from six weeks in the future. After Beltane."

He released a long breath. "Then you are safe."

"I'm not. My sisters either. Our petition was denied. Cedric is going to take the place of the old fae queen on the council of elders."

Sebastian shook his head. "It cannot be."

"It will be," I insisted and took his hands. "Listen to me, love. The me that's coming here tonight? She loves you. You need to believe that, no matter what she says or how she acts. She's just scared. And I need for you to put the moves on her."

"The moves?"

"Sex, Sebastian. You need to consummate your relationship with me, the other me. Tonight." I blew out a breath. "After I lift the curse I put on myself?"

"What curse?"

I waved my hands. "Doesn't matter. What matters is you need to convince her to make love with you. Tonight."

"She, you…." He frowned as though considering. "Wish this?"

"More than anything. So does she. So when she gets here, I'm going to lift the curse. And I need you to be one hundred percent honest with her. Because believe me, I already know all about you. It doesn't change how I feel. Not at all." I held his gaze so he could see the truth there.

He looked sick at the thought but then swallowed and nodded.

"One more thing. After you leave this room, you'll forget. So will I. But this night will make everything right between us. If you trust me." I held out my hand.

"I trust you," he said.

A moment later I appeared on the bed beside him. His amethyst eyes flit from her to me and then back. Talk about stellar timing.

I stepped back into the shadows. "Don't wake her up until I'm gone, okay? We don't want the space-time continuum to blow its o ring."

His gaze is fixed on her—my—sleeping face and the expression he wore…

I look down at myself and see Siobhan Silver through his eyes.

Brave. Bold. Beautiful. All the things he wanted and never thought he would have.

The convergence was there, the mass of ley lines and power ready for me to tap into them. I reach for the power, cast my circle, and then turn to face the couple on the bed.

The words come to me, just as they had before. "You will know love. All the joy a human heart can hold will be yours. I release you from your past. I free you for your future. So mote it be."

I slip into the bathroom as he reached for her shoulder. Tears sting my eyes as I silently weep.

"I forgive you," I whispered and I wasn't talking to Sebastian.

And then I start winding the watch forward.

Time to go home.

⚫

Sebastian had just stepped out of the shower and was reaching for a towel when Siobhan appeared in the alcove across from the sink. "Did it work?"

Her shoulders lift and then droop. She looks tired, defeated. Too much magic use in too short a time. Her reserves were low.

Questions tore through his mind about what it was like, how his past self had responded. Had she lifted her curse? Had she convinced him?

Not that it would take a whole lot of convincing for his part. He knew what he wanted. But Siobhan had hated him then. What if he hadn't been able to convince her?

She was drooping like a wilted flower. Answers could wait. Instead, he guided her out of the bathroom, removed her shoes and then reached for her pants.

"What are you doing?" She halfheartedly batted at his hands.

"Preparing you to sleep."

"I can do it."

"I know that." The button sprang free and he tugged the denim fabric over her hips. "But I can do very little without magic, so please allow me to take care of my woman."

Her hands fell to her sides and she waited as he pulled the pants off her legs and then reached beneath her shirt to unfasten her bra.

When she was left in nothing but a t-shirt and underwear, he pulled back the covers. She slid between the cool, clean sheets and then sighed.

"May I hold you?" Something had changed. A week ago, he never would have asked. Would have waited for her to come to him.

But that letter, the utter forthrightness of Siobhan's confidence in herself and his love, had set him free.

"I would like that," she murmured.

He eased down beside her and then wrapped his arms around her. His Siobhan. The witch that had stolen his purpose and captured his heart.

His hand drifted to her belly. Had it happened then? Was she pregnant with his child?

She turned to face him. "I could have refused. I could have left."

"Do you think you did?"

She shook her head. "No. I saw us the morning after. Still in bed together. Whatever you said, it worked."

"Wish I knew what that was." He sighed. "Wish I could remember it."

"Me too." She swallowed audibly. "I know I should go take the other test, but I'm scared."

He held her tightly. "It can wait a few more hours. Go to sleep, *Annwyl*."

With a deep exhale, she did. And as he held her Sebastian realized that for the first time, he knew peace.

Alys

$\mathcal{M}$aeve and I followed the dirty wretch with the emerald eyes out of the cavern with the waterfall and into a small chamber. It was set up like a shrine around the statue of a woman.

The detail was remarkable. A woman's soft expression as she stared down at her pregnant belly. I wondered if Andreas had carved it himself.

"My Gwendolyn," Andreas murmured as he caressed the statue's face.

"What happened to her?" Maeve whispered.

Andreas looked over at the two of us. "The queen did not like the idea that I was to have a changeling child to act as my anchor. I released my former one but hadn't settled on another. But then Gwendolyn became pregnant with my child. The babe was a threat to her rule. All changelings are. They can hold magic without the restrictions of the fae. It is why the courts treat them so poorly. Why their spirits are so often broken."

Maeve was holding my hand tightly and I could see in her eyes that she was thinking what I was.

Sebastian.

"What did the queen do to her?" I asked and braced for the worst.

He held the torch closer, drinking in the statue's every expression. "She tricked Gwendolyn into eating a stone fruit. This was the result."

My heart stopped. "This is actually her? Is she still alive?"

"I do not know." Andreas touched the frozen face again. "My magic cannot reach her. The queen was a witch before she became fae. It was what made her so powerful. And so treacherous."

"What if…we helped you?" Maeve moved forward. "We're

witches, very powerful ones. And we know a few of the fae. Perhaps together there is a way we could restore her."

If I'd been expecting Andreas to fall to his knees in gratitude, I would have been disappointed. He didn't even look in our direction. "There is nothing to be done."

"I call bullshit," I said.

"Alys," Maeve hissed. "What are you doing?"

I didn't know but I wasn't going to just stand around while the sad-sack fae flushed our futures down the crapper. "Listen, buddy. I get that you've had a raw deal. We all have. But would she really want you to spend your life skulking around this cave mooning over her? Or would she want you to do something to stop all the injustice in the magical world?"

He frowned at me. "You don't understand."

"No? My mother died in this place when we were kids. We didn't know anything about magic until we stumbled into the belly of the beast. No one to show us the ropes or let us know what was at stake so you better be glad that your little changeling in there isn't here to see you fiddlefucking around instead of fighting to bring her and her mother back."

"They might not be alive," Andreas whispered.

"You said the kid was your anchor. If the baby wasn't alive wouldn't you be back in the fae realm instead of skulking around Appalachia like Mothman's unwashed cousin?"

"Nix the tough, love, Alys," Maeve's tone was exasperated.

But I was getting to him. Andreas had been left alone for far too long to sulk. There was so much wrong with the world that I couldn't do a damn thing about. But this... guy moping around? Him, I could fix.

"So what's it gonna be, Andreas? Take charge of your destiny or curl up and die? Because you have three of the most powerful witches of all time willing to help you."

"Three?" He frowned.

"Yes, our youngest sister, Siobhan. She's out there risking her neck to keep Cedric and the magic hunters off our backs so we can convince you to step up."

"Three witches." He nodded. "Perhaps a full coven of thirteen could lift this."

"Oh, Becca and her girls," Maeve said. "The ones from the gathering. I bet they would help us."

"They will help us. Once we are sanctioned." I said to Andreas. "See, we want to help you, but we can't without risking our souls. You see the problem."

He looked back at the statue and then nodded. "All right."

I blinked. Had he just agreed?

"All right as in you'll do it?"

Andreas cupped the cheek on the statue. "It's what my Gwendolyn would want me to do."

He reached out a hand. "It is a bargain well struck,"

I put my hand in his and repeated the phrase. "A bargain well struck."

Maeve patted him on the shoulder and cringed as dust flew off him along with a musty stank. "Pretty sure she would also want you to take a bath. Just saying."

Siobhan

*T*opened my eyes and stared out at the pink and gold dawn. Sebastian's arm was curled protectively around me, his hand splayed over my midsection.

Had it worked? Future me seemed to think it had, but I had my doubts. The curse was gone. I could tell. It felt as though I'd shed a two-ton invisible parasite. But had we conceived? Or was I more at risk than ever?

Carefully as I could, I crept out of bed and snagged the remaining box then tip-toed into the bathroom. The tile was cold on my bare feet and I hopped a little as I tore open the box. The instructions were pretty much dummy-proof but I went over them again, just in case.

Open wrapper. Pee on stick. Wait five minutes. Pray.

I was onto step three when there was a knock on the door. "*Annwyl?*"

I opened the door and gestured him inside.

Amethyst eyes scoured my face.

"Just waiting," I said. "Anxiously."

He held out his arms and I went into them. The intensity was like that night in the shower, the relief I had felt that he had come back, that he hadn't abandoned me.

"I'm glad you're here," I whispered.

"As am I." He placed a kiss on top of my head.

The timer on my phone went off and as one we turned.

Two pink lines.

My hands flew to my lips. "Oh, dear sweet dark chocolate. I'm pregnant."

Sebastian pulled me close against him and kissed me.

"I'm so proud of you, *Annwyl.*"

"For getting knocked up?" I laughed up at him. Suddenly all the shit I had been stressing over, all the things that had been eating at me, didn't matter. I was going to be a mother.

"For that. And for being brave enough to forgive yourself. I know how hard it is to let go of hate and blame."

He did too. No one else would ever understand me the way Sebastian could. He had seen me at my worst. And he was still here. Tears welled in my eyes. Sebastian scooped me up and whirled me around. I held him close, my arms around his neck, my nose buried in the spot just above his magic hunter tattoo. Joy flooded my whole system.

Him and me. And soon our child.

His lips pressed against mine as he carried me into the bedroom and laid me on the mattress.

I reached out to caress his face and then realized I was still holding on to the pregnancy test. I made a face and rolled over intending to toss it.

"Where are you going?" He gripped me by the hips and dragged me back toward him.

"To toss this. Yanno, since I peed on it."

He plucked it from my hand. "I want to save it. It's a symbol of our trust and capacity to forgive."

"Dude, I *peed* on it."

"You say that like it will affect my decision." His eyes turned to amethyst slits.

"Okay, weirdo. Whatever springs your trap. Though I'm pretty sure we didn't pack any rubber sheets so if you're looking for a golden shower you can just—"

"Siobhan." He gripped me by the back of my hair and murmured in my ear. "Shut up."

I squawked in mock outrage and struggled to get up. "Why don't you make me?"

His smile was pure wickedness as he murmured, "I thought you would never ask."

Fair warning: it's going to turn into another one of *those* scenes. Skip ahead to the next chapter or do what I'm gonna do which is to make up for lost orgasms.

His lips pressed against my neck as his fingers hooked inside my underwear and dragged them down my legs. He flung them aside and his fingers moved between my legs, petting me until I squirmed and moaned.

"You drive me mad, *Annwyl*," he murmured in my ear as he thrust two fingers into me.

My eyes are closed as I breathed, "Ditto."

"I want to know what happened." His thumb stroked over my clit in slow, lazy circles. "What I said to you. How I convinced you to trust me. To touch you."

"It wouldn't have taken much," I gasped. "You always have tripped my trigger."

"I'm weak when it comes to you as well," he breathed. The fingers leave me and I whimper at the loss. The sound of a zipper being slid down fills the space. Sebastian pressed against me and I went almost dizzy with lust. I rocked back on my knees, trying to entice him to come closer. But his hands stilled on my hips.

"Tell me you want this, Siobhan. I need to hear you say it."

"I want you, Sebastian. Please." I was not above begging when it came to him and me. But I knew Sebastian. He wasn't playing some sort of game. He was making sure that we were on the same page.

"We deserve this," I whispered. "We deserve each other."

That snapped his control. He surged into me in one swift thrust and I cried out in sensation of him filling me, stretching me.

It feels right. Familiar even. Idly I wondered if we had done it this way before.

And then Sebastian moved and I was lost in the feeling of him and me, our union. Our baby.

"More," I pant.

He shifted his weight and then pulled me upright, yanking the t-shirt free. Still, inside me, he settled me against his body. His left hand cupped my breast, the right went between my legs to circle and stroke my hidden piercing

I writhed on his lap as he shoved me closer and closer to orgasm.

"Sebastian," I panted his name.

He nipped my earlobe and then thrust up hard. Once twice.

And I exploded. The release rocketed through my body and stole my breath, my strength. Distantly I can hear his strangled cry, the sound of his pleasure spiking my lust even higher.

We collapsed in a tangle of satisfied flesh, him covering me with his heat and weight.

Maybe I didn't need to remember every detail of our baby's conception. Reenacting the possibilities is so much better.

"Siobhan," Sebastian murmured. In my blissed-out state, I didn't immediately pick up on the significance of his tone.

"What?" Forcing my eyelids up, I blinked and then blinked again.

The room in the B&B was gone. Instead, we laid on a mattress in a cold stone room

And we weren't alone.

"I've been waiting for you," Cedric said.

*I*n the throes of their lovemaking, Siobhan had traveled them.

Right into a jail cell. And on the other side of the bars....

"Cedric," Sebastian put himself between the fae and Siobhan.

Cedric tipped his head to the side. "I've been waiting for days for her to use her magic. I was beginning to think the boomerang spell I bought from the high warlock was worthless."

"Boomerang spell?" Siobhan's knuckles turned white where they gripped his arms.

"It's a tracking spell used by some of the witches. If the person uses a traveling spell or taps a ley line to move from place to place, the boomerang will redirect them back to where the owner wants. Very useful for one such as yourself. You try to escape and the spell brings you right back to me." Cedric smirked at her before turning back to Sebastian. "And thank you for taking the risk for me, dear anchor. I guess we'll have to wait and see if you keel over before I can get what I want from the little witch. Her curse must be potent.

Those mortals I hired to test drive her several years ago never reported back."

Sebastian saw red and he lunged for the bars. "You paid humans to attack her?"

"Just an experiment. To see if she was safe to breed."

"You won't lay one of your filthy hands on her," Sebastian snarled.

Cedric laughed. "And who will stop me? You, changeling?"

"The council—"

"I own the council of elders. At least, enough of it to get them to bend to my every whim. You are a wanted man, Sebastian. The punishment for your desertion has already been set. You get to spend the next two centuries trapped in your memories of my dear mother. If there's anything left of you by the time your sentence is over, your little witch will be long gone."

Siobhan had been silent. She approached him and squeezed his arm as though trying to silently communicate something to him.

"What is it you want with me?" Siobhan asked calmly. Too calmly as she faced down the male that had orchestrated her attack. Did she not understand that Cedric had trapped them? That even now the web of spells that isolated this room from the outside world would hold them like insects caught in a spider's web?

"I want what I deserve. Permanent residency in this realm." Cedric did a slow up and down of her body and Sebastian felt a primitive growl growing in his throat. "I want to rule here. The mortals have made a mess of every-thing and the magical community has allowed it to happen. They've let these creatures think that they're in charge. It is time for a reckoning. Humanity will serve those with true power."

Quick as a flash, Siobhan disappeared from his side. Sebastian let out a brutal yell, worried that Cedric had taken her. But she had reappeared before Cedric, naked and vulnerable.

"Tell me more," Siobhan said. Her voice was…sultry. And wrong.

"*Annwyl*," he croaked. His fear for her made him dizzy.

She didn't even turn to look at him. Cedric smirked as though he had won.

"I will show you, darling witch." Cedric put a hand on her arm.

Would she attack? She had no weapons, not even the pocket watch to wind back time. She was reckless enough to do anything. Sebastian shifted his position ready to spring after her.

But she simply sauntered alongside the fae, hips swaying as though he didn't exist.

A hollowness filled Sebastian's chest. Had she decided to seduce Cedric after all? Her curse was lifted. Cedric wouldn't die from their mating. She carried Sebastian's child even now.

"Siobhan, please." He thought she had understood, that they were on the same page.

But she wouldn't even look at him as Cedric led her from the room.

When you look at me, all my masks fall away.

That was how she had described understanding the difference between him and Cedric. Perhaps she couldn't look at him…because she needed her masks to conceal her true feelings.

Hope stirred in his chest. His clever, beautiful Siobhan had a plan.

He gripped the bars tighter. Gods help them all.

Siobhan

*P*oor Sebastian sounded gutted. Idiot man. Didn't he realize I was doing my level best to keep this power-hungry psycho distracted?

I hadn't forgotten what Cedric did to Owen. How he'd buried him alive to get him out of the way. Never mind that he had confessed to orchestrating my rape.

Cedric was going down.

I wasn't going to abandon Sebastian again. Not ever. Note Sibby had called it right. This was our shot—mine and Sebastian's—to be together. Even if it meant strutting naked in front of this cheap knockoff who made my skin crawl and acting like I didn't have two braincells to rub together.

Good thing I wasn't shy like Maeve.

I didn't have any real plan other than to get Cedric away from Sebastian, ASAP. I was not the planning girl. I lived from moment to moment. Being a planner went hand in hand with being a fretter. And I didn't want to fret. Or to think about the six-week-old life in my womb. Or Sebastian being stuffed into one of those heinous memory charms where he would have to relive his abuse.

I had to focus on the megalomaniac in front of me.

Cedric brought me to a large room that looked a bit like the ruins in Cusco, Peru. No mortar and you couldn't fit a sheet of paper between the stacked stones. Candles were lining the walls and flickered over an odd assortment of everyday objects. Barber scissors, knives, a scarf, several mirrors. A shovel. Two stools. A box of printer paper and an old-fashioned typewriter. A sword with jewels encrusted in the hilt. A blender. A charcoal grill filled with what looked like rubies. Stacks of coils in colors ranging from copper to silver to yellow and rose gold. Baskets of fruit and bread were lined up against one wall. Blankets and pillows were spread on the floor. It was as big a hodgepodge as the B&B on the outer banks.

"Where are we?" I asked as I glanced around.

Cedric reclined on a bolster pillow and reached for a bunch of grapes. "My vault. It's where I keep all of my treasures. I hope you like it since it's going to be your new home."

Ugh, control freak hoarder much? To hide my grimace, I reached for a blanket and wrapped it around my naked body sarong style. "How did it all get here?"

"The ley lines of course. When I claim a magical object I send it through the ley lines, to my hoard. And when I need something, I simply call it to me. Like magic." He smirked at me. "You really are new to this."

"I really am." My brain was churning things over. I knew that we could travel by ley lines, which meant we could escape.

But as long as he had that boomerang spell on me I would end up right back here. Unless….

I reached for a baguette that stuck out of a wicker basket and broke off the end to nibble. "Tell me more about this boomerang spell. It sounds clever. Is it tied to you or to this place?"

"To me of course. I can't stay here, I have far too much to do." He ate a few grapes and grinned at me. "Including you."

Ick.

I thanked my lucky stars that Cedric was a total braggart as well as a condescending jackass. Why not just whisk the girl away from her family and friends, steal her right out of her lover's bed. Of course, she would take one look at your hoard and fall into your arms, happily abandoning her whole life after you sent men to rape her. Dumb shit.

Then again, my former self had given him no reason to think that his scheme wouldn't work. But I wasn't that spineless traveler witch anymore. I was Siobhan Silver, badass.

I grinned at Cedric and thought *Go ahead, underestimate me. That'll be fun.*

"So, I can leave, as long as I'm with you?" I made the question sound innocent as I offered him the bread.

He took it and frowned. "You'll never leave this place, Siobhan. It's too dangerous for you, with all the magic hunters. We wouldn't want them to destroy your soul now would we?"

"And what if something bad…happens to you?" I widened my eyes and did my best to sound terrified by the prospect. I couldn't bring myself to cling to him. If I laid hands on him, I'd be going for his throat.

"Relax. My current anchor is safe and will remain so until you give me a new one. Even if something were to happen to him, I would simply go back to the fae realm."

Meaning that the vault would disappear and all the objects within would be dispatched to the nearest convergence. Like Sebastian had told me.

"Sounds like you've got it all figured out," I muttered, just to keep him talking.

He talked to me the way some women talked to their purse dogs. I was half expecting him to produce a bow and a sweater along with a jeweled collar.

It didn't matter though. He'd told me exactly what I needed to know.

"Are you ready?" Cedric actually crooked a finger.

My smile was genuine as I crawled towards my King of Wands. I gripped him by the lapels of his expensive suit, cast a circle over the two of us, binding us together and then dragged him down into the ley line.

He hadn't expected it. I could feel him struggle and fight but I was a traveler and I followed the flow into the nearest convergence.

Sensations flowed through me. The rush of power, the absolute thrill of belonging to magic. My body was gone, as was Cedric's but he was there, still snared in my circle.

I held him with the force of my will. Not letting him escape. Letting the promise of power sing to him. To coax and tempt him to go deeper, to spread himself thinner in a futile effort to collect all the power. To become one with it.

It tempted me too, but I ignored it. I didn't want power anymore. I had only ever wanted the safety it provided. Like Sebastian. He was what I wanted. Him and our baby. I wanted to see my sisters, to buy a house and that big slobbery dog, and to spend long days in bed making up for lost time with my guy.

I held myself together even as Cedric reached and stretched, trying to take in more and more and more power. Greedy for it.

And I felt the moment that he joined with the convergence, spread too thin to hold form any longer. I felt his hoard release. And then I let the current take me to where I belonged.

●

Alys

I was lying on the couch with my head in Brock's lap when I heard a *thunk*.

"Did you hear that?" I sat up and looked around.

Another distinct *thud*. And another.

In the bedroom, Maeve shrieked.

"Stay here," my mate urged me.

I ignored him and charged for the bedroom door. And tripped over a… radio flyer wagon?

"Where the hell did that come from?" I grumped.

Brock helped me up and then led the way into my bedroom where Maeve had been taking a nap.

Maeve stood, cellphone in one hand brandished in front of her like a weapon. "He came out of nowhere!" she cried.

I looked down at the naked guy in my bed and tapped one bare butt cheek. "Hey, guy? Who the hell are you?"

"Alys, look," Brock pointed to the shaved head, the scar where the hair wasn't growing back quite right.

"Shit, Sebastian?" I shook him. "Where's Sibby?"

Sebastian groaned and rolled over. "Siobhan?"

I leaned down and got in his face. "Where is my sister?"

He sat up, smacking his forehead into mine. "The vault. She must have dragged Cedric into the convergence."

My heart tripped at the thought of Sibby with Cedric. "Where are they?"

But my question landed on his naked back as he sprinted for the door. He hopped over a basket of fruit that thudded down in his path and then ran for the door.

I followed with Brock at my side and Maeve trailing behind.

Sebastian charged into the lake and I shrieked when I saw it, the purple hair floating face down in the water.

"Sibby." I cried and raised my hand to shove the lake back.

"He's got her already," Brock's hand encircled my wrist. "Damn, he can move fast."

We reached the edge of the water just as Sebastian hauled Sibby's unconscious form to the shore.

Terror gripped me.

Maeve dropped to her knees and felt Sibby's neck for a pulse. "She's alive."

I was focused on her pale face and could feel the water in her lungs. Maeve was moving as though intending to give Sibby mouth to mouth, but my way was quicker. I reached out with my fear for my sister and gathered the stray water droplets in her lungs, then yanked.

Sibby rolled over and vomited up what looked like half the lake. She choked and coughed, but then her blue eyes opened and she looked up at me.

"I am so damn mad at you," I snarled.

"Of course you are," she wheezed.

Sebastian wrapped himself around her. "You took such a terrible chance."

"I wasn't going anywhere." She patted his arm. "Too much mischief to make here."

"We need to get you to the hospital," Maeve said. "Have you both checked out."

"We can't leave," I grumped. Stupid Andreas. There had been no sign of the bastard since we dragged his unwashed carcass from his cave at dawn.

"You can." As though summoned, Andreas appeared behind Brock. "It is safe."

He looked cleaner than the last time I saw him, though he hadn't bothered to shave his scraggly beard and his green eyes held that hollow look.

"We can leave?" Maeve asked.

He nodded. "Your application has been reevaluated and approved, retroactively. There will be no magic hunters coming for you. You are fully sanctioned witches."

I sagged and Brock reached over to steady me. "That was fast."

"I had very little to do with it." Caution crept into Andreas's tone. "Some of the council of elders grew suspicious since Cedric didn't want the power of your small coven to be part of the community. It seems he was bribing a few of the other members with fae treasures."

There was a splash and a freaking pontoon boat landed in the lake.

"Speaking of which," Sibby wheezed.

"Where is all this stuff coming from?" Maeve asked.

"Cedric's vault," Sebastian said. "This must be the nearest convergence. His entire hoard will show up here over the next several hours."

Andreas leveled his emerald eyes at the other man. "He is dead then?"

"Yeah," Sibby gasped. "I made sure of it."

My head was spinning. We were free and totally street legal.

"I did not get a chance to fulfill my end of the bargain." Andreas looked defeated.

I shrugged. "We got what we wanted. We're fully sanctioned witches." I intended to keep my promise and ask Becca and her coven to help us find a way to free Gwendolyn. For her sake and that of her unborn baby.

"What about Sebastian?" Sibby's knuckles turned white as she gripped him. "He's still got a price on his head."

"Is there something you can do about that?" I asked the fae.

Andreas nodded and vanished.

I eyed the sky dubiously. "Okay, so since we can leave, maybe we should just go over to Brock's place until stuff stops raining down from the sky?"

"Sebastian can't leave. And I'm not going anywhere without him." Sibby clutched his hand in hers.

He nuzzled her hair. "Nor will I be separated from you and our child any longer."

"Child?" Maeve and I said at the same time.

Sibby grinned. "Right. I haven't told you guys the good news. I'm six weeks pregnant!"

"Ohmigod!" Maeve shrieked. And reached for her. "Congratulations."

"Wait, did you say six weeks?" I was busy trying to figure out how that was possible when they had just left yesterday. Six weeks ago she had been cursed and hated Sebastian's guts. Six weeks ago—

"Just go with it, Alys." Sibby beamed up at me, looking happier than she ever had.

A baby cradle landed right next to me. A sign from the universe perhaps?

I picked it up and brought it over to her, then hugged them both. "You're going to be a mom," I whispered.

"Yeah, I am." She grinned up at Sebastian who was staring at her with total adoration and love. "Just what I always wanted."

EPILOGUE

Siobhan

"*D*o you think it's finally done?" I asked Sebastian when it had been over an hour since the last fae treasure appeared.

"It appears to be so." Sebastian sighed and squeezed me tighter. He hadn't let me go since he'd pulled me from the lake. Not in the shower where he'd soaped me up until we were both hot and panting. Not upstairs in the room that had been my mom's but I was beginning to think of it as ours. And not as I made dinner in the kitchen, dodging around the magical appliances that seemed to perform their tasks with only a thought.

An enchanted kitchen. How freaking cool was that?

We were cuddled together in front of the fire. Alys and Brock had left to drive Maeve home and then were going to celebrate with the werewolf pack.

I picked at a thread on his shirt. "I suppose I should go

261

and get Alys's Yukon at some point. It's still parked in front of the B&B."

"Not without me." He squeezed me tightly. "Besides, you still need to pen that letter and since I was the one to deliver it, I will have to be there."

"We don't know how long Andreas will take to get you a pardon," I warned.

"He's determined. His woman and child hang in the balance." Those amethyst eyes gleamed as he stared at me. "In his position, I would move mountains."

"Alys and Maeve and I will help him anyway." I shivered to think of what had been done to Andreas's baby mama.

"I know this but he wouldn't understand. It is not the fae custom to give without getting something in return."

I ran a hand over his whiskered cheek. "I love you. You know that, right?"

He brushed a gentle kiss over my knuckles. "I would give you anything and everything, my Siobhan. I have no desire to leave this place where I have first discovered the meaning of happiness. But to be by my traveler's side always, I need freedom."

I sighed and looked up at the stars and thought about my bizarre tarot reading and the final card. My future. My hand crept over my stomach and a smile stole over my face. "Silly man. Don't you know you've already given me the world?"

*K*eep reading for a sample of *Midlife Bed and Broomstick*, Coming in September.

AUTHOR NOTE

Thank you so much for coming on this journey with me. I know there are tons of books you could have picked up and I am honored that you chose mine. When I first started the Silver Sister's series with *Witch Way After Forty*, I had intended for each of the sister witches to have her own book. But Sibby—impatient little troublemaker that she is—didn't want to wait. Alys, being the angry sister might be a little tough for some readers to connect with so I thought why not let Sibby have her say now? Then there was Maeve, our witch equivalent of Jan Brady, who was dealing with chronic illness. Shouldn't we get to look inside her head and see how she's coping with all these magical shenanigans?

And then Sebastian, the villain piped up. I knew right away that he was going to be Sibby's hero and she was going to be his because he was just so bad and she felt so damn drawn to him right from the beginning, even when she thought he was a little creepy. No, I didn't tie it all up with a neat little bow and get Sebastian his magical get-out-of-memory-charm-jail-free pass. I thought about it, but then I realized this guy has been bad for a really *really* long time and it goes against my nature to let him off scot-free.

So instead, he is sequestered in an enchanted cabin with his pregnant witch for the foreseeable future.

Am I a meanie or what?

Maybe you are wondering about Andreas and Gwendolyn. Yeah, me too. I've got a pregnant midlife heroine encased in the magical equivalent of carbonite. I can't just leave her there while poor Andreas suffers. (To see how these two met, join my newsletter and get Faery Wine, their short story free)

Plus, there's Ethan the ghost and the magical B&B on the outer banks, the enchanted things showing up all over the place, the council that's been running this sideshow is in shambles, Maeve and Kal's trip to Alaska, Becca and the coven.

So is there more midlife magic to be had? You betcha. You keep reading, I'll keep writing.

It's a bargain well struck.

Jennifer L. Hart

PS. Cant wait for more? Become a Patron of the Hart and read along as I write my next midlife story, get behind the scenes info, Advanced Reader Copies, cover reveals, book and author updates and more.

PPS. Please consider leaving a review for this book. They really help authors as well as other readers.

MIDLIFE BED AND BROOMSTICK

COMING IN JUNE

I hate it when he drinks.

I could hear Robert rummaging in the garage, crashing into various items and cursing. Something hit the concrete floor with a thud. He'd be black and blue in the morning with no recollection of how he'd gotten into such a state. It was too late for him. It was my job to make sure he was the only one who woke up that way.

The thought echoed in my mind as I ushered my two corgis, Wally and Wilma, into the bathroom. It was the only door in our small house that had a decent lock. The dogs must have picked up on my anxiety because they weren't their usual yappy selves. When I'd gotten the mutts from the animal rescue three years before, I thought I was bringing them home to a better life.

Then Robert started drinking. Not enough that he couldn't do his job. No, he showed up at the bank every day with his game face on and no sign of the havoc he'd wrought. It was like he was two totally different people. Dr. Jekyll by day and Mr. Hyde after knocking a few back at the corner bar.

Wilma sidled up next to me, her small body shaking. Wally stood between where I sat on the closed toilet lid and the door, his brown eyes watchful. How messed up was it that I felt more guilt and worry over my mutts than myself? After all, I had chosen Robert. They were along for the ride on the crazy train. John was away at school so at least I didn't need to worry about him seeing his father in such a state.

There was enough to fret over.

Another crash, this time closer. Heartbeat. Heartbeat. Heartbeat. And then he slurred my name. "Sam?"

I should leave.

It wasn't the first time I'd had that thought. My fight or flight instinct was screaming at me to run. Hiding wasn't good enough. The door was hollow. If he was really determined to pick a fight, he could get in. Do damage.

A shudder went through me.

I eyeballed the window. Our house was a ranch with a full basement. Robert's mancave was downstairs. My car was outside. No keys though. They were nestled up against my cell phone in my shoulder bag that was perched on the coat tree by the front door. Should have grabbed that. Too late now. So stupid.

"Sam!" he bellowed again.

I hugged Wilma to me and shut my eyes. Wally pressed up against my legs, his ears laid back flat, gaze trained on the door. He was a natural protector. Too bad the mixed breed was only twenty-seven pounds. Not exactly Cujo.

Where could I go? We'd only lived in the New York suburb for a few months. I had no friends, no family to lean on. No support network. I'd been looking for work but no one wanted to hire a middle-aged woman with Multiple Sclerosis. Part of what kept me with Robert was the need for his healthcare benefits. Without them, my meds, my doctor, the monitoring MRI's and other tests, the whole house of cards fell apart. He was the lesser of two evils.

But oh, what a choice.

"Sam!"

Sleep it off, I silently implored my husband. *Just go to bed and sleep it off.*

He didn't. Instead, the crystal doorknob rattled. Every cell in my body froze. "Sam? You in there?"

Even in his inebriated state, he knew it. Hastily, I put Wilma on the floor then lunged for the tub, pulling the lever to turn on the shower.

The door crashed open and there he stood. Two hundred and forty-pounds of angry husband.

"Hi," I chirped, trying my best to pretend everything was fine when it clearly wasn't. "I was just about to take a shower—"

He stalked into the bathroom, his suit pants rumpled, his tie hanging undone around his collar. Wally lunged forward but he lashed out with a foot and punted the dog halfway across the floor.

"Robert, please," I began, hating him and myself.

He didn't answer, instead, he grabbed me by the hair and yanked. His face was mottled red, his eyes bloodshot. "Where is it?"

"Where's what?" There was a quaver in my voice and not just from the stinging pain in my scalp. "Please. I don't know what you're looking for."

"The money, you stupid cow," he snarled.

Terror filled me. "What money?"

He tossed me out of the bathroom. I slammed into the wall hard enough that the sheetrock dented.

My legs felt weak and the strain of my impact caused my knees to buckle beneath my weight. I wanted nothing more than to curl into a fetal position and just ride out whatever came next. But if the dogs got between the two of us, he might kill them. I didn't think he would kill me. No matter how drunk and angry he seemed.

Robert stalked toward me. "Don't play dumb. You're the only one who knew about it."

I shook my head. "I have no idea what you're talking about."

Another grip on my hair and he yanked me to my feet. Shook me so hard I had to clench my molars together to keep them from rattling.

"Tell me where it is!" he roared and then backhanded me. My lip split on impact and I fell to the ground again.

Another angry bellow and something charged past me. I blinked up just in time to see John with his forearm pressed against his father's throat.

"If you ever put a hand on her again, I'll kill you. Do you hear me?"

Robert gurgled something.

John leaned back and before I knew what he was doing, he threw all his strength into a punch. His fist connected with Robert's cheekbone, the force turning Robert one-hundred and eighty degrees before he collapsed into the middle of the floor.

John shook out his hand as he stared down at his father's inert form. Then he turned to me and reached out a hand. "Are you okay?"

"I'm fine." I rasped, even though I wasn't. "You shouldn't—"

He held up a hand. "Do not tell me I shouldn't have hit him. I've wanted to hit him since the first time I saw a bruise on your arm. Why didn't you leave?"

I hated how disappointed he sounded. Hated that I felt the same sort of disappointment. But how could I explain to my big, strong son that I was terrified. That the world wasn't kind to women my age or with my health restrictions. That running into that great gaping void of possibility was just as terrifying as anything I'd faced in my marriage.

I wouldn't do my son the disservice of defending Robert. Who knew how much he had seen. So I said the only thing that came to mind. "He's going to be so angry when he wakes up."

John's blue eyes fixed on my face. "Then we better be long gone by the time he does."

Preorder Midlife Bed and Broomstick now!

Made in United States
North Haven, CT
02 May 2022

18804407R00153